BonBon Street

Debbie O'Brien

BonBon Street

ISBN: 978-0-645325-0-3

Printed and bound in Australia.

Publisher Deborah O'Brien Australia

www.facebook.com/debbieobrienaustralia
www.instagram.com/debbie_obrien_author

Also by Debbie O'Brien

a Million Stars

ISBN: 978-1-64999-644-2

www.debbieobrienaustralia.com

To my family,
For all the laughter we share,
And the adventures we have.

also

To my friend Louise Parmenter,
Who raised her hand to support me,
And never took it down.
Thankyou.

BonBon Street

As he turned into BonBon Street, it looked like every other outlying suburban street in Australia. Three ordinary brick houses on the left, numbers four, six, and eight, each with a roller door garage on the far side of them and a fenced yard with a gate and a path which led up to the front door. The third one had the addition of a small porch, and a short untrimmed hedge of shiny leaved bushes on which crimson buds looked poised, as if waiting for their moment to open. On closer inspection it appeared they would outnumber the leaves, yet most would probably fall, scattering the petals to leave a pretty pink stain on the grass below. Each house had good frontage and sturdy tall fences running between. The normality of it could almost be ticked off a list somewhere of requirements for a suburban lifestyle.

A few metres beyond number eight's boundary, the sealed street curved and continued on under two large metal gates. The gates swung in from either side, and were firmly held by a heavy chain and a large security lock. He had been on a job in the next street and decided to have another quick look at the possibilities for the abandoned development site. The plans had been approved though money had run short as the pandemic spread its invisible fingers across the country. Now would be the time to jump in and secure it before some other joker had wind of it. He could really make some good money on this site and felt this whole area was set to boom. He turned away jiggling the lock as he did, fingers crossed, he would have the key soon and hopefully be able to start when restrictions began to ease.

Turning back, he noted the houses on the other side. The one closest to him, number nine was surrounded by a tall hedge, and was set slightly back on the block, its gate looked overgrown, although he could glimpse a neat lawn inside. Continuing back towards the main road he crossed a grass pathway, then hurried slightly as dogs barked from behind the next house not wanting them to come rushing around to the front. His planning mind registered this was number seven and as he passed number five he thought it could use a bit of a tidy up, it was the one house in the street which looked a bit unkept. The corner house faced this street with its driveway and garage around the corner fronting onto the main road. It was a bit unusual, yet at the time when it was built, it would have made sense to face the quieter street. An older bloke looked out from his shed and he raised his hand to acknowledge him, calling out, *good day for it,* though not breaking his stride.

Pausing at the corner he turned and surveyed the quiet street one more time, I like it he thought, it's a good street and I will only make it better, funny name though, BonBon Street. He half shrugged. Oh well, as long as there are not too many surprises in this bonbon I should make a pretty penny or two, and with that he strode back towards his car whistling an old classic and dreaming of the future.

Number 4 BonBon Street

Maisie

Maisie pulled her cap brim lower over her face. The removalist liked to chat, when all Maisie wanted to do was get off the street. She could also see a man making his way toward her. Maisie had spotted him trimming the hedge outside the house on the corner, and also saw he had been keeping his eye on the movements at number four at the same time.

'All good then Luv, take care of yourself.'

The driver raised his hand and pulled himself up into the truck. Finally he was heading off.

Maisie knew he had meant well, they all did, but sympathy was not what she could handle right now. The new neighbour was bearing down, increasing his pace as the truck pulled away.

'G'day, I'm Harry, just moving in eh, well if you need a hand, give me a holla, happy to help.'

His face was flushed from hurrying, the sweat beading across his forehead as his tongue came out to run across his dry lips. At the same time he adjusted his shorts, pulling them up in a way which Maisie could see was a habit, whether they had slipped down or not. His skinny legs protruded from the bottom of the shorts and the top of them, which would never again see his waist were held in across his hips by an old fashioned ring belt.

'Thanks so much, it's all good. I'm fine. Well, I better get to it. Thanks again.' Maisie moved to walk away then realised Harry was not easily deterred.

'So have you moved far? It's a nice quiet street, no trouble here, if there is though, you let me know, I'll sort it out for you. Lived here the longest you know, mine was the first house built in this street.'

He puffed his chest out seemingly proud of this achievement. Maisie nodded, and knew if she didn't set her boundaries now, old mate Harry might become a tiresome visitor, well-meaning but unwanted.

Maisie could see he looked confused and sort of knew he was being fobbed off as she tried again to cut him short. Maisie's background had made her wary of people, although Harry seemed genuine and his intentions were probably pure and coming from a kind, helpful nature. Maisie turned back feeling a bit guilty at her attitude, and softened.

'Truly, thanks again Harry, I will let you know, thank you. I must go, I really want to get settled in, it's been a long day.' Maisie smiled weakly and put out her hand.

'I appreciate the welcome.' Maisie rested her hand briefly on his arm then turned and walked inside, closing the door firmly behind her.

Harry felt relieved. The girl had understood he meant to be welcoming, his wife told him he came across as a busy body, he thought of it as helpful. Harry liked to keep an eye on everyone, some more than others he thought as he turned to walk back up the street. Funny, didn't seem to have much furniture, and I didn't catch her name. Might put her on the keep extra check list, she seemed a bit lost somehow and he hadn't seen a fella, bit of a mystery there he mused as he started the hedge trimmer and lost all thoughts into the job at hand.

Number 6 BonBon Street

Claire

Claire let the curtain drop back into place. She had seen Harry rush up the street and speak to the girl. He was such a sticky beak! Mark banned her from talking to him, yet then again, Mark banned her from almost everything these days.

The girl had kept her head down, a baseball cap pulled low shadowing her eyes. Claire felt her stomach twist, she wore her cap the same way, to hide the bruises. Claire was not outside much, if they were in the front yard and someone walked by, she would dip her head and pull the brim in the same way. She hadn't seen a man, though she had thought she heard a baby cry, only once, before the truck pulled away, then again, it could have been a kitten. Maybe the girl was a lucky one, who had escaped, or maybe Claire was thinking of her own dream, to get away. Maybe the girl's man was coming later. Claire hoped Mark would like the new girl. Fingers crossed he would let her make one friend, if she promised not to tell.

Claire didn't go out much, Mark knew everyone in the street better than she did. He talked to them occasionally, although with the pandemic and the restrictions the world seemed to have closed in to the perimeters of their yard. Claire had been introduced initially when they moved in, then as the months went on, between the pandemic and fear, she withdrew into herself, partly scared they would find out, yet secretly hoping they would, silently praying someone could help her.

Things had been happy in the beginning, newly married, new job, new home, new state even, and the world at their feet. The pandemic which had swept the world changed everything, and the smiling congenial man the outside world still saw was not the man Claire now knew behind closed doors. Closeted in every day, his job no longer there, the old, *last in, first out, sorry mate* had left Mark feeling worthless and unhappy. Claire knew it was a phase, it would pass, he loved her after all and once all the borders opened and he could see his family, and his mates, it would all come good. He didn't mean it, she knew he didn't, it was the frustration, and being closed in. Added to this they hardly knew anyone more than a passing hello. Mark had no outlet, nowhere to let off some steam. If he could go out to the pub for a drink or to a game of footy it might be easier for him. It was hard for both of them, and although restrictions had eased, it was still a long way from the normal they had known before they moved here.

The baby stirred and Claire rushed over to hush her. Don't cry baby girl she pleaded in her head, not today, stay quiet and I can keep you safe. A tear rolled down her cheek. It would get better, he hadn't meant it, he'd said so the first time, he was so sorry, he loved her, and they were a team. She wiped the tear away and winced as the bruise on her cheek stung from the slight pressure, and those other times, well, he'd had a bit too much to drink, let himself get a bit out of control. Anyone would understand, with what was going on in the world. Mark had to let his frustrations out and stupidly I was in the way. If I could be a bit more understanding, after all it was Mark who had lost so much in all of this.

Claire took a deep breath. I'll try to be a better wife, I'll try to keep the house tidy, I'll try to be what he wants, she pledged to herself, not for the first time.

Claire was so tired, the baby woke hourly demanding to be fed, and night after night Claire wondered if she would ever sleep again. Mark snored through it all and then criticised her red eyes and clumsiness each day as she struggled to get things done. If only he would help. The only time he showed the baby attention was if someone else was around, then he was all over her.

One day when Claire laid down for a nap, barely able to keep her eyes open, he had snapped, called her lazy and incompetent, a bad wife and mother. His raised voice had set a neighbour's dog barking and realising someone else may have heard, he shut up. The anger boiled within him for the rest of the day and exploded when she set the overcooked dinner in front of him. The plate had gone flying and he had jumped up grabbing her beneath her chin, squeezing her face so tight with his fingers she couldn't open her mouth and the corners of her lips almost met in the middle. Her only sound of protest had come out like a tiny peep.

'What's this shit? What do you think I am? A dog, it's no better than dog food on a plate, a man deserves better than this crap at the end of the day. You lazy blah, blah, blah.'

Claire's ears were ringing by then and his voice faded in her brain as shock settled in and she struggled to release herself. The hard punch to the stomach shocked her even more and her body had tried to double up in a defensive move. He had held her up, her jaw feeling like it was crushing beneath his grip. The baby had cried out and he had thrust her away. Unbalanced she had fallen back against the wall before sliding to the floor. The baby's cry became a wail and he had given one short sharp kick into Claire's ribs before growling at her to, *shut that thing up*, before stalking out to the shed, slamming the door as he went. It had been the first time and unfortunately not the last.

Claire knew it was wrong deep down inside. Although she was scared, the unknown at the moment seemed far worse than where she was now. At least here there was a roof over the baby's head, and what if he took her, would he hurt Sophie too. Claire had to be careful, try to soothe him over, get him back on track to the man she used to know, then it would be ok, she was sure it would.

There had been a few tiffs while they were engaged, none of them violent, although now looking back realised she had seen a glimpse of the rage inside of him at times. They were young and partying, excuses could be found, and he always accepted her apology, holding her close, making her feel secure with him, telling her he would teach her how to be a better person. He was the centre of their friend's group and she had almost felt privileged he had chosen her. In any case, domestic violence couldn't happen to her, she was an intelligent woman, and a diploma in economics was right there on the wall, hung with pride the first day they moved in. It was the timing, all these outside influences coming together, struggling with a new baby and family support so far away, once things settled a bit, it would be fine.

Another tear rolled down as Claire lifted her baby to her breast for the second time in an hour, running her finger over her tiny brow and gently lifting the thin soft hair on her head.

'It will be ok my sweet, we'll be fine. Daddy's going through a hard time right now. This world I've brought you into is a bit crazy at the moment, but we'll be ok.'

Claire could barely raise a smile as her little one raised one eye up to look at her face before she slowly dropped it, as if it was too heavy to hold open any longer. The baby's sucking slowed and her little mouth fell open dropping away from her mother's nipple, her mouth still doing the motion.

'Hush my baby, I'll keep you safe.'

The tear rolled off Claire's chin and she caught it gently so it wouldn't splash on tiny Sophie's face.

Number 8 BonBon Street

Pat

Patricia worked at the doctor's surgery in the next town and was coming up to retirement at the end of the month. They were reluctant to let her go as her knowledge of the locals was sometimes invaluable, both medically and socially, especially in an emergency. Apart from being good at her job, Pat knew who was married to whom, and where their parents came from, all those little things which could point someone in the right direction if they needed to contact relatives or a quiet understanding was needed. Pat also had the biggest laugh and often people stopped in the street to listen, as it was a huge and joyful sound. As if to match it, her friendly face made her liked by all who met her.

Pat liked her street. Most people minded their own business, and because they could go north or south to see a doctor, not having one in their own little suburb, they weren't all clients so she felt more relaxed. She was sworn, of course, by patient confidentiality, however her work mask did not have to be on twenty four-seven in this street.

Pat had seen the truck pull away and Harry scurry down the street as quick as those skinny little legs could go, rushing so he didn't miss the chance to get all the gossip from the young woman in the cap. Harry meant well and had really been a god send when Pat's husband Keith had passed away unexpectedly two years ago.

Like herself at the surgery, Harry kept his eye on things. He brought peoples bins in if they were away, and even if they weren't, he popped them in the gate keeping the street clean and clear. Pat was grateful, however there were some days when Harry had to be told firmly to butt out. Pat knew she was certainly capable of telling him to do so, as Harry had trouble keeping his sneaky nose out of people's homes and lives sometimes. If only Harry would look inside his own house, he might see things needed attention at home.

Pat held onto the arms of the chair and pushed herself up. You're getting old, she thought, as the bones were starting to freeze up if she sat too long. Stopping to admire her flowering camellias, Pat glanced up again. Mm, now that was short and sweet, although she looks friendly at least, as she saw the girl reach out and touch Harry's arm. Pat knew the small gesture would put a smile on his face.

Pat headed indoors, the afternoons came in quicker and cooler each day it seemed. Pat was waiting for the solstice to come and go and hoped the winter would then pack its bags early and at least give some joy in this, what seemed to be, the longest year ever.

The pandemic was paying its price and luckily so far their little district had no fatalities and only a couple of active cases. Thank goodness everyone was doing the right thing and they could soon be out of it all. The added strain from the last few months had added to her decision to retire as well as the fact she was now in the vulnerable age group for the virus. Today she felt like it too, maybe it was her age which was the problem, some days she felt like she was twenty again and it was only when the mirror rudely showed her the truth, did Pat realise she should probably take some things a bit easy, then there may be less of these more awkward days.

The house was warm as Pat had closed all the internal doors and drawn the curtains before deciding to take in the last bit of warmth of the day out on the porch. The reverse cycle was doing its job and she stripped off her jeans and top, folding them neatly for another day, the bra was next and she let out a sigh as her ample bosoms fell free from their prison. It was always a moment in the day when Keith's absence was deeply felt, there's nothing quite like getting a man to do that job for you. Pat smiled sadly remembering his touch and missing him with what seemed like every cell of her body.

Finding Keith slumped in the car was a sight which still over shadowed her happier memories. Lucky, people had said, his heart failed him as he returned home, not on the road where others may have been injured. Keith had even shut the garage door with the remote, turned off the motor yet never made it out of the car.

Pat missed him every day in so many ways. He had been out to buy groceries but she never ate them. By the time she found them in the boot of the car weeks later, the fresh food was rank, and the packaged food tainted by them. She hadn't wanted it anyway, he had bought the food for them both to share and now they never would. Lying across the top of the bags was a dried up bunch of flowers he had obviously bought as an impromptu purchase, and a surprise for her. Pat had cried when she found them, clutching them to her chest, the sobs had been as hard and as fast as the day it happened.

Harry had taken care of it for her. He had cleaned out the car, found a buyer and also helped her choose a little run-about, second hand, yet in immaculate condition. Pat had been grateful. The day she picked up the car and came home, Harry had been in and packed up all of Keith's garage tools, only leaving out a few things he thought she may need and everything else was neatly boxed and the garage hosed out. Pat had been grateful, truly she had, yet as the roller door had closed behind her, tears had welled up and spilled over as the garage now was hers, stripped of Keith, never to return.

Pat had tried to ask Harry for her spare house keys back but he made excuses each time. She wanted to tell him she needed them for a friend, although if none turned up he would ask questions and her kind heart could not really offend him on purpose. Maybe he had lost them, he was getting forgetful. Damn her feeling guilty for wanting her privacy. Pat slipped off her panties, relaxing onto the towel which covered the lounge.

Pat was happy in her own skin, as she and Keith had been socially nude many times and enjoyed the company of other like-minded people. It was nothing to do with sex, far from it, just a need to feel free of all restraints. Pat belonged to a club up in the hills, and was looking forward to the time she could go back to her cabin there, to catch up with all her friends. Harry would be shocked if he knew her little secret, her comfortable larger size was not what people imagined a nudist to be.

The television blared a trumpet like call to announce the early national news and she settled in, adjusting her hips and drawing her knitting on to her lap. The club's craft group were making blankets for a women's refuge centre and Pat smiled as she thought of them all, as normally they sat in their circle, all ages, all sizes chatting and gossiping, totally oblivious to the fact they were all naked. It's what I like the most, they like me for my personality and again she smiled, and not my looks or what I do, only for being myself. Pat, for one, never judged a book by its cover.

The daily reports of the pandemic were too much tonight, too depressing, would it never end she wondered. Pat flicked channels over to watch some sitcom re-runs. She had the need of some brainless comedy to ease away reality. *I'll be right, a few more weeks and my days will be my own.* Different thoughts rattled through her head, *I must take a piece of cake up to welcome the new girl, and warn her to keep Harry at arm's length. I wish Harry would give my keys back as I certainly don't want him walking in on me like this. Ahh my Keith, I wish you were here.*

Pat rolled her head back and dozed lightly. Another day down, another day I managed through without you, she thought as sleep over came her and a slight snore escaped her lips.

Number 9 BonBon Street

Lisa and Brodie

Lisa saw Pat head inside and poked her head out through the gap above her gate to see what she had been looking at. Ahh, of course, Harry, what's he up to now the dirty little creep, she wondered, as she saw him pick up the hedge trimmer and pretend to shape the hedge. He was always trimming the hedge one leaf at a time, he must hate it when it rains, no excuse to be out spying in the street.

Sighing she turned back, catching the arch of foliage above the gate with her hair. Harry had been down several times with an offer to trim it. Lisa didn't care if she had to crawl out the gate as it gave her the privacy she liked, especially from him and especially after his antics this afternoon!

Lisa's house was set at the back of the block so the front yard was where she spent most of her time. The cream brick and terracotta coloured roof stood out against the rich green of the high hedges. It looked like the gate hole had been cut out after the hedge grew, the rough looking arch a contrast with the extreme neatness of the rest of the garden. Inside Lisa kept the lawn carefully manicured and clear of garden beds, the only other feature a twisted crepe myrtle tree on one side, its empty branches holding on to the last few dried leaves of autumn, reluctant to let them go and admit winter was here.

Lisa was lonely of late. Brodie was out early each day teaching his boot camps followed by his private lessons with clients which sometimes went late into the night. Social distancing outside numbers had increased and his business had picked up again with surprising speed, especially his one on one classes. Brodie had already been exploring social media lessons before the whole pandemic started and so was one of the first to implement online fitness classes, with live face to face teaching. Lisa had to give it to him, he worked hard and the media had picked up the story anxious for any good news in these troubled times. Brodie now complained about copy cats, although Lisa knew how chuffed he was to be recognised. It made him feel like a celebrity. Lisa thought it was more his fifteen minutes of fame in this life, though she kept this to herself.

Lisa was fit too, Brodie nagged her about doing more but she was content with her body. She hated the hard routine of cardio, happy with her self-taught yoga and tai chi, the gentle approach.

On this lovely winter's day, Lisa had put her mat out in the sun and this afternoon extended her routine as the hedge seemed to capture the sun's warmth and hold it inside the garden. She had slowed each movement flexing then stretching her muscles slowly enjoying the peace. As she lay on her side holding one leg by the inner thigh and stretching it up towards the sky, a tiny rustle in the base of the hedge caught her eye. Holding the pose she had squinted to see what it was. It was Harry, and this wasn't the first time either. Her body had tensed and whereas before she had run inside, this time she had made a plan. Lowering her leg, pretending not to see him, Lisa had risen slowly and tried to make it look like it was a part of her routine by doing slow lunges toward him.

Nearly there, she had thought when she saw a small flash. It was as if something was reflecting off a lens. Shocked, and now angrier than ever before, she had grabbed the hose, swivelled the nozzle and pushed it hard through the hedge. With her other hand she had reached and grabbed the object. It was a camera and she pulled it through on to her side of the hedge. He'd squealed and started to protest so she had thrust the hose further into the hedge while hissing at him.

'Stay away from me or I'll call the police. There won't be a next time Harry!'

Lisa had heard him coughing and snuffling as he tried to back away and clear his face at the same time. Muttering and mumbling he had called her name through the leaves. Lisa had turned away and to block him out, his excuses were something she did not want to hear.

Gotcha, she had thought, now go home and look after your wife you fool, keep your mind on your own business. The words had tumbled in her head though never escaped her lips.

Lisa laughed, although she had not been able to see him, she could imagine the water dripping off his face. She now had the evidence to show Brodie, he hadn't believed her, telling her to leave poor old Harry alone. To him, Harry was harmless. Lisa had argued, although the truth be known, Brodie probably didn't want to lose his three days a week, one on one, in the house at the end of the street with Harry's wife. Lisa thought Brodie should stand up for her and demand for Harry to stop spying on his wife.

Lisa had roughly gathered her things and gone inside when she heard Brodie's voice calling out and for some reason slid the camera under the cushion on the sofa.

Brodie had come in laughing.

'Did you see Harry? Our sprinkler wet him as he was going past, blew the glasses off his face. You must have not long turned it off, because he was still dripping.'

Lisa had let fly, although it seemed to fall on deaf ears.

'He had a camera this time, I told you he was a peeping tom! I hit him with the hose, the dirty old creep, I'm glad he's wet. It will be the police who get him the next time. I've had enough Brodie. I want to feel safe in my own home.'

Brodie had stood with his mouth open.

'You what! How could you, you're imagining all this, he didn't have a camera, I would have seen it. I need the income from them if I'm going to keep this ball rolling. How could you, he's our bread and butter! It's not like you're bringing in an income.'

Lisa, frozen in shock, realised he was blaming her, and he hadn't even given her time to explain before he stalked out of the house, slamming the door behind him.

Lisa sank onto the couch, the bulk of the camera sticking into her back. No tears came, just a silent rage at a mythical boys club which had once again reared its ugly head. Lisa was tired of it, it seemed Brodie never took her side, or lately even listened to her side, it was wearing her down and she was not sure how much more she could take. Every time Lisa heard rustling in the bushes and had gone to look, Harry was the only one in the street. Brodie had seen Harry wet, so was this not proof enough? Brodie seemed over affectionate as well, and in her current state of mind she wondered if he was trying to distract her from other things.

Lisa pondered on what Brodie had said for the third time, trying to see his point of view. Each time she came to the same conclusion, Brodie had to listen to her because she now had some evidence. Lisa glanced at the clock, I really should be doing something. The time had ticked away faster than her thoughts.

Still not ready to break her mood, Lisa slid out the camera and flicked it on. Selecting slide show her horror grew as the photos slid by, one after the other, it wasn't only Lisa, there were others. Lisa's head was reeling as she reached towards the phone, clutching it tightly as the anger rose up inside her. Her mother had often used the word livid, and finally Lisa knew what it meant. Touching the screen her finger hovered over the green phone icon as a variety of thoughts purged through her brain.

Damn it! Lisa threw the phone onto the soft cushions and stormed into her room, dragging open a drawer she roughly pushed her t-shirts to one side and shoved the camera to the back, dragging the clothes over again to cover it. Lisa knew the right thing to do was to call the police. Oh yes, they would come and get him, and maybe lock him up for a time or worse, he would get a good behaviour bond and be back in the street in no time. You couldn't trust the court system at all. The other residents deserved to be told, and if their partners were anything like her own, they may have to band together and do something about it themselves. Harry had to be stopped.

Lisa patted her head searching for her glasses and realised they must still be outside. Looking in each direction around the garden as she passed through the door, Lisa hesitated and felt angry. I shouldn't feel this way, this is my home, and I won't let one silly old peeping tom frighten me, not now, not ever.

Her glasses lay bent on the grass, droplets of water still clinging to the lens. Hearing a noise she hurried to the gate and peeked out. Pat, the neighbour across the street was seated on her porch, craning her neck to look past the house at number six. Lisa too leaned forward, putting one foot on the bottom of the gate so she could pull herself up and bend over it to see further. Harry, his back to her, was bending to pick up his clippers. I wonder what he's been up to now she thought. Glancing back, she heard the click as Pat firmly closed her front door. She would leave it for today, Pat didn't need this. Tomorrow would be soon enough.

Lisa retraced her steps inside. Another day on BonBon Street, they were starting to look the same, she may be about to make them change.

Brodie had stormed out, Lisa was becoming unbearable. He knew Harry was a bit of a busybody however he certainly didn't want Lisa stirring up trouble and spoiling his arrangement with Harry's wife Monique. Brodie was more than happy with the little arrangement he had going on there, after all what did it matter if Harry wanted to look? She should take it as a compliment, she had a nice body. Grabbing his bike, Brodie decided a quick ride would clear his head and maybe sort a few things rolling around inside it. Deep down he knew he had said all the wrong things to his beautiful girl, to him, Harry was a good bloke and he felt certain Lisa had a bee in her bonnet about something or other, and poor old Harry was getting the blame. This pandemic was affecting everyone differently.

Brodie pushed through the gate, cursing the overhanging boughs as they caught on his shirt. He threw his leg over the bike and pedalled away up the street. A light was on at number four, someone must have moved in. I'll put my card in the letterbox tomorrow, you never know, I might pick up another client.

Brodie grinned. Maybe he could service the whole street.

Number 7 BonBon Street

Jason

Jason was getting out of his ute when the bicycle went past. He could see who it was and deliberately turned slightly so Brodie would think he hadn't seen him. Brodie was not his favourite person of late. Jason reached in the back and pulled out his lunch esky, shaking his head he ambled around the back and was immediately welcomed by a chorus of barks as the dogs spotted him and strained against the wire he had strung across the yard to keep them in. Jason loved these dogs more than just about anything in the world.

'Hang on, hang on you two, give me a chance to get in the door, you know the routine.'

Some days he thought their tails would wag off as their fat little bodies wobbled so hard and their tails spun like helicopter blades. The dogs turned, not taking their eyes off him for a moment, scrambling over each other in their excitement to get to the roughly built gate. This happened every day, as the joy of a labrador holds no bounds. Each day is full of wonder and excitement for them.

Jason slid his esky through the door and grabbed the two leads which were hanging on a brass hook attached to the back of it. The dogs went crazy, twirling around and around, chasing their own tails then pushing each other, each wanting to be the first.

'Sit.' Jason spoke sternly and they both immediately did. Their tails were still going crazy sweeping the dirt beneath them and their faces, one yellow, one chocolate, seemed to shine, so full of love for their human. Jason swung the gate towards him and clipped a lead on each collar.

'Let's go' He braced himself as the leads pulled tight and they strained forward, like huskies pulling a sled. It wouldn't last, they were still young and he knew one day he would be pulling them along.

The dogs automatically turned right out of the yard, and right again to follow the path which ran between his house and

Brodie's, their noses on the ground anxious now to pick up a new scent, and occasionally stopping to leave their own. Lisa and Brodie's tall hedge ended neatly in a precise corner before continuing along the rear of their property. Jason and the dogs went straight ahead winding down the hill and into the bush reserve. At first the trees gathered close to the path, their branches reaching out to touch each other overhead and their gnarly roots pushing up through the earth, trying to reclaim some of the well-trodden path. On the last turn they thinned out and the path widened as it continued over a cleared flat, which sloped gently down to a bubbling creek.

Jason scanned the area and saw the last of the roo's bounding across the creek before disappearing into the scrub on the other side. Good, they had heard them coming. The dogs, so busy chasing their noses, had not seen them and Jason knew from experience it would be a long night if they did and gave chase. It wasn't really the kangaroos he worried about, because they would win the fight, nevertheless he didn't want the pups to think it was ok or a game to chase other living creatures. Having two dogs was good, they were company for each other while he was at work, yet it could also mean double trouble when they led each other astray, like children, to do naughty things and sometimes disobey him.

He let the dogs free and they raced each other to the creek, splashing and playing in the shallow water seemingly unaware of its temperature. Jason, arms crossed, watched on and felt the tensions of the day start to recede.

Jason liked his job and even this virus thing had not slowed his work too much. Being a tiler he mainly worked on his own anyway, though some of the building sites were shut down for a while and he was catching up, so he might have to take a break soon if they couldn't start back again in safety. On the other hand there were a lot of home renovations going on, people, stuck at home for extended periods, had decided their homes could do with a spruce up so he had picked up a few extra jobs here and there, most of it was fixing up their blunders.

Jason only had himself to look after and of course Pippa and Clyde, his cheeky companions. He had been married for a short time, although they had both known in the end their hearts weren't in it. Kylie was still his best friend and knew all his dirty little secrets, but living together hadn't made either of them happy.

Jason whistled loudly and the dogs' heads shot up. 'Come on you two, time for home.'

Pippa reached him first, shaking the last drops of water from her coat before sitting patiently to wait for her small treat after the lead was hooked on. Clyde liked to do a bit of a dance around before the treat won him over and he sat obediently, his adoring eyes trying to convince Jason what a good boy he had been.

Turning to trudge back up the hill, the setting sun fanning her final rays across the sky like a halo over the houses on BonBon Street, the dogs slowed as they reached the top, their tongues hanging out and the leashes not strained quite as tight as they were on the way down.

The lights from Brodie's house flickered through the hedge and he could hear faint strains of a piano as he passed by. Jason liked Lisa and certainly thought she could do better than her big headed, arrogant husband. Jason tended to pop over while Brodie was out now, it saved him having to pretend a friendship, which he only did for Lisa's sake.

In spite of his manly, tradesman appearance Jason liked many things which anyone looking at him would never guess. Yoga was a favourite and Lisa was teaching him tai-chi. He enjoyed the slow graceful movements. The scornful look on Brodie's face when he caught them one day practicing yoga said it all, if you weren't doing boot camp, well, his look seemed to say, this was sissy stuff. Since his interview on a morning news show he thought he was some kind of celebrity, puffing his chest out, he would be asking for autographs next.

It wasn't only Brodie's attitude though. Brodie had caught him one day when Jason had left the door unlocked for once by mistake. Distracted by the dogs as he had pushed them outside the back door, he'd heard a noise. Brodie had knocked and walked straight in before Jason had time to move. Looking at each other from each end of the hallway, the look on Brodie's face had said it all. Jason had seen the emotions race across Brodie's face, shock, disgust, and finally laughter. Brodie had backed out blabbering, his tongue not forming proper words to make any sense, and pulling the door firmly, shut it behind him.

Jason shook his head, he could still feel the embarrassment he had felt plus he had been scared. Would Brodie tell anyone? Jason had thought of confronting him to try and explain. The problem was, it wasn't as if Jason really knew why himself, it was the shame he felt which held him back, he felt guilty because of it every day. When nothing seemed to have been said, Jason at first thought Brodie was being a good friend by not telling, until the sly innuendos and snide remarks now made their way into conversations whenever he was around. Jason realised Brodie must not have told anyone for some other sadistic reason, almost like an unseen threat for the future if Brodie wanted something to go his way.

Maybe a few weeks off would be good, he could get the fence done properly and make the backyard a bit more private. They were all lucky on this side of the street no neighbours behind because of the hill sloping away and the reserve. If they ever finished extending the end of BonBon Street there might be more noise or traffic. Jason would not have to worry as it would wind around behind the houses across the road, but for now some mesh gates stopped people from even walking through past Lisa's. If the receivers ever found a buyer the whole development might start up again, though in a way, Jason was glad the developer had gone broke, it made it a nice peaceful area.

Pippa and Clyde had overdosed on water and flopped down patiently waiting for their dinner. Tails still wagged, yet at a much slower pace, the daily walk wore them out. Jason filled their bowls, straightened the bedding in their kennels and gave them the last pat of the day plus a gentle rub behind their ears.

'Goodnight you two.'

Inside he put the leftover casserole in the oven, pulled all the blinds closed then ducked in for a quick shower. Looking at himself in the bathroom mirror, he patted his face dry then carefully applied the eyeliner, mascara and lipstick. Opening the cupboard he withdrew the blonde wig and fitted it carefully on his head. Wrapping the towel around his waist he made his way to the bedroom and slipped the frilly night gown over his head.

Jason glanced in the dressing table mirror. Stuff you Brodie, I'm not hurting anyone so what does it matter, and it's none of your damn business anyway!

Jason, looked at his reflection and the conflict which seemed etched across his face stared back. Internally he argued this every day, he did not need someone else's judgement to burden his thoughts as well. Looking again he thought, I must ask Kylie if she could get me some of those slippers with the pompoms, like in the movies. He would really like them or even the ones with tiny kitten heels, if they make them big enough, he remembered his mother having some. He knew he was back in his safe zone, here he felt protected somehow, the thin line between how society thought he would be behind closed doors, and how he looked at this moment, had been stepped over, and Jason felt the shame on both sides.

The timer on the oven buzzed loudly and Jason slowly made his way to the kitchen for his solitary meal.

Number 5 BonBon Street

Alice

Alice let out a huge sigh. Some days, it seemed, there were never enough hours in the day. The washing was always done, only the folding and putting away of it seemed like the most strenuous job in the world. The more she neglected it, the higher the pile grew, and the more impossible the task seemed. Between the house, the yard, the whole virus thing, plus the boys, it all seemed to be insurmountable at times, and today, was one of those days.

Jay and Charlie were seventeen and between the home schooling, no weekend sport, thank goodness it would be starting again, and the double lots of driving lessons she wasn't sure how much more she could take. The minute one was out of the car, the other was in, and off she would go again. Alice's nerves were feeling the strain.

Jonathon usually worked fly in, fly out. With the border closures and restrictions, the last time he had flown out, and not back. Even though things had not been good between them when he left, it was now four months and Alice felt like she was a single parent. At least when Jonathon was here, he and the boys would be out throwing a ball around or messing about with the car they had bought and were fixing up. The weight of their care and education hung heavy around her shoulders and Alice felt she was losing herself somewhere in all of it.

If Jonathon decided not to come back and they called it quits, Alice felt it may be easier, as then she wouldn't be expecting his support. The boys called him occasionally and Alice enjoyed hearing them laughing and joking with their dad, she only wished Jon would realise he was not seventeen as well. Jon was their dad and he should be firm with them sometimes. Mostly she wished he would encourage them to give her a hand. Alice knew it was useless, a daydream she had, of a cooperative happy family helping each other without thought, not an overworked woman being slowly smothered by a pile of clean, but unfolded sweatshirts.

Well this isn't getting it done Alice thought, and started trying to sort the pile spread across the dining room table. Jay and Charlie were back at school, seniors were allowed now and there was talk other kids would return soon to the new normal routine. Kids were kids though and Alice wondered how they would keep them apart, especially these teenagers.

Through the window Alice saw Brodie on his bicycle. He was not her favourite neighbour. Brodie came in several times to ask her about a fitness class he was teaching and Alice clearly pointed out to him it was obvious he had no children, as getting two teenagers out of bed each day was all the exercise she needed. Brodie had a way of looking at her, and people in general, which seemed judgemental. Alice also suspected he was implying a very different sort of exercise. Brodie gave off a kind of vibe which made her at times, feel uncomfortable, and was insistent she would see the benefits of a regular routine. If he was genuine, well, you had to give him ten points for trying and another ten for enthusiasm.

Lisa was friendly and sometimes popped in for a cuppa, although Alice had avoided her a bit after the last time Brodie was here. Brodie had been a bit odd and in the end she didn't know why he had come in anyway.

Alice had seen him come up the street and knock on Jason's door. He had only been there a few seconds, before he was out and in her yard with an odd look on his face. Alice had asked him if he was ok.

'Wasn't Jason home?'

'Oh yes, he's home alright.'

Brodie had then mumbled a few things and left. Alice had felt glad she had been outside as it had made her feel uncomfortable in a strange way.

Alice liked Jason a great deal. Jason was kind and often lent a hand when he saw her struggling. She knew he would have liked to say something to the boys, give them a good kick up the bum would be his words, instead he held his tongue and gave Alice his friendship instead. Alice knew Jason was lonely and she couldn't quite put her finger on why. He kept to himself, loved his dogs and his ex-wife Kylie was lovely, there was something missing, as if he was holding back. No matter what it was, Alice was so glad he was her neighbour, and her friend, because it was what she needed the most.

The boys smashed their way in the door, it was the only way to describe it, shoulder to broad shoulder neither one of them liked to come second. They had always been like it, everything was a competition. Jon had encouraged it. Let them be, he would say as she picked up the smashed items the boys knocked over after some race to the kitchen, or bathroom, or to the backdoor. Two tall solid balls of muscle jostling down the hall with only the end winning goal in sight, never mind the pictures on the walls or her wedding day vase. In the end she had given up and the house seemed to constantly look dishevelled and the walls were bare except for the hooks where something used to hang.

'What's for tea?'

Alice sighed, glanced at the pile which still looked like she had not even touched it, and made her way into the kitchen before they opened every packet they could find. Boys! They could eat, their stomachs bottomless pits with hollow legs underneath. Jon didn't understand. When he complained about the state of the house or the dishes in the sink, he forgot it was Alice who had to shop three times a week to keep up with their appetites. It all took time and she wasn't sure what he would say when he came back this time, the yard was a mess. The boys never put anything away and she really didn't think they had ever mown the lawn or even knew what the whipper snipper was. It was a bit her fault, with Jon away she had always endeavoured to keep things up to date so when he was here, he could have some quality time, lately it seemed it was all too much. Alice had always thought, as the twins grew older, it would be easier, yet it seemed to get harder and she often wished they were still little, more in her control.

As the boys demolished the toasted ham and cheese sandwiches, Alice peeled the potatoes and marinated the steak for dinner. They ate early so the boys could once again scatter to a mates or girlfriend's house now mixing household groups was ok. The snacks disappeared, the dinner almost inhaled and with another jostle they were out the door, gone, leaving a sink full of dirty dishes and still a mountain of clothes to climb over.

Alice laid her head on the table, she was so tired. She wanted to wake up one day and the house to be clean, the boys to be adoring of her, and Jonathon to be here, or gone, whichever he chose. Alice needed him to at least have made the decision, and put his heart into it either way.

As Alice closed her eyes for a moment, and strands of her hair fell into the drops of gravy on the edge of her plate, she didn't notice the head rise slowly over the window sill to watch her as she slept, nor hear the door glide open and the man slip inside.

Number 3 BonBon Street

Monique and Harry

Monique heard the hedge clippers stop and a truck turn the corner. She eased the curtain back, and saw Harry talking with a girl outside the house across the street at number four. She should keep him occupied for a while, he didn't let them get away until he knew their whole lives. Harry thought he owned the street, and felt a, sometimes unwanted, responsibility to everyone in it.

Moni yawned and stretched, she was enjoying all the exercise she was doing and her body was toning up in places she thought would never be the same again. Brodie was an excellent instructor and talented in many ways. Convincing Harry she needed private lessons was the hard bit, and he didn't like it when she locked the door during workout times. Harry was a lot older than Monique and sometimes trying to temper his insecurities was tiring.

Harry and Monique had met at work not long after his first wife died. He was nearing retirement and she was finishing her university degree and was on an internship. As a mature aged student Monique, at thirty two, felt old in her class, although she had never really fitted in to any mould. Dancing had been her true love but a broken limb had put paid to it becoming a career, hence her late entry into university.

They had been the scandal of the office and she hadn't been invited back after she graduated. Harry's children were appalled as she was two years younger than his baby and they had not seen them since she moved in. Monique encouraged Harry to call them, but he ended up angry and upset for days afterwards.

After they came home one day and things were missing from the house, the children thinking they had the right to come and take their mother's things, he cut all ties with them. Monique would have gladly given them anything until she saw they had scrummaged through her drawers as well and taken some of her jewellery, later claiming it was their mothers, and even taken dishes and plates out of the kitchen which were of no sentimental value at all.

Harry had been furious, stomping around the house yelling.

'These things are mine, not theirs, I bought them and shared them with their mother, because they have lived in this house doesn't mean they owned anything.'

It went on and on for weeks and Monique didn't think she would ever ease his pain. Eventually they settled into a routine and except for shop assistants calling him her dad occasionally, they were happy enough. Monique had sneaked out and bought some more dinner plates so at least they had something to eat off.

Harry's friends were as bad, some crossed the street now to avoid them, somehow embarrassed their friend had been lucky enough to find love twice in his life and companionship in his senior years. Monique didn't really understand it, yet then again her friends were a bit the same though more honest.

It's a bit like hanging out with my Dad, Moni, they would say though at least they came around and invited them to a few barbeques occasionally. Both of them were paying the price for love.

Moni thought it would be easier, yet as the honeymoon stage of their relationship ended and reality struck, some days living in a house haunted by another woman could be lonely and a bit soul destroying. They both had to put a lot of faith in each other or this was never going to last.

Harry stowed the trimmer in the shed and locked the door. He felt tired, rubbing his eyes he glanced up and saw Brodie ride past. Harry raised a hand to acknowledge him, at the same time dropping his head in case Brodie could see the look in his eyes from way over there. Harry felt uncomfortable about the whole private lesson situation. It was what Monique wanted and it gave her some company around her own age, so he had given in. He hated hearing them giggle over the music which drifted out under the garage door and sometimes felt Monique was over compensating with affection afterwards. He wasn't sure, deep down if it was genuine.

Monique being so much younger had not concerned Harry at all, they had gotten along like a house on fire from the start and shared the same sense of humour. Harry had thought his friends and family would love her too. Selfishly, none of them could see past her age to get to know the warm genuine person underneath. It made him furious. A mate suggested to him to join bowls, then had sneered, turned to the others and laughed.

'Oh you're probably too worn out for that eh mate.'

The others had snickered and Harry had felt the fury building inside, he would never have said anything like it about their wives or partners. He could not understand the attitude, or the disrespect, and as for his children! Harry rubbed his eyes again, he missed them. He often wondered what they had expected. Did they want him to be alone, to be available to mind the grandchildren? Harry did not think they realised he was still a man, a human being who wanted love, yes, and sex, and most of all a companion, someone to share things with. Harry was not sure if he and Moni broke up, if he could go back to being friends with his so called mates, or a father to these people he had raised, he had seen a side of them he didn't like and he didn't know if he could forgive them for it.

Harry turned and stared up the street, he was reluctant to go inside just yet. He saw the boys next door leave their yard, not quite shutting the gate as they bumped and high fived each other, two separate beings who seemed joined together no matter when you saw them. Harry couldn't really recall ever seeing them apart, except for this afternoon.

Charlie waved as they passed, Jay turned away which didn't surprise Harry, he'd had to have words to those two on a number of occasions especially when their father was away. Charlie was the apologetic, so sorry we didn't think one, always joking and trying to deflect away from whatever it was they had done, whereas Jay was surly and rude, not in a verbal way, it was in his mannerisms, he never quite met your eyes and seemed to dismiss people with a turn of his shoulder, a jut of his chin and what looked like a sneer on his lips. Harry felt like they were two sides of a coin yet was sure, in spite of Charlie's friendly demeanour, they shared the same bad heart. He was keeping his eye on them.

Harry had taken their camera, it was not as if he was going to do anything with it. It had looked to him as if the boy was up to no good, and even though he had thrown it in the hedge, Harry had thought he would take it and have a word to Alice about their behaviour using it as evidence. Lisa had it now, and all he had was a still drying shirt and damp hair for his trouble. He had tried to explain through the hedge in between spluttering and heard her snap a reply then slam her door. Now he thought about it, Lisa was a bit odd with him lately. Harry arched his back and, glanced back up the street, doing his last check of the day. As the evening star winked at him in the darkening sky, the shadows lengthened then disappeared as the light slid over the horizon. Time to head in, he would deal with what to do about it tomorrow, there was always a tomorrow.

Number 4 BonBon Street

Maisie

Maisie opened the suitcase and laid it across the bed. Pulling out the tripod she expertly set up the surveillance equipment and fiddled with the curtains adjusting them so as to still have a good visual, and at the same time conceal the equipment she had erected. The sun was low in the sky as a bicycle went by, then two boys from the house, diagonally across, jostled their way up the street. Maisie followed them with the lens, checking its focus as they moved along. They almost looked like one person, the way they moved was like they were entwined around each other, it was odd to watch. A movement at the house on the corner caught her eye as the boys passed it, one raised his hand and Maisie saw the man who had spoken to her earlier, Harry that was it. He could be a problem if he gets too friendly. Seemed Harry was the cat of the street, the curious cat.

Maisie was pleased with the angles she could get as well as her curtain placement, she would unpack the other things tomorrow, her belly telling her to head to the kitchen and sort the groceries into some kind of meal. The fridge was still cooling down so she chose the Shiraz and put the white wine in for another day. Opening some crisps, Maisie made her way to the back door, glass in hand, to watch the last of the light slip over the horizon. Savannah stirred, rolled over and seemed to settle herself with a tiny sigh. Maisie was glad she had been able to pull straight into the garage earlier, as she wanted to keep Savvy a secret for a little bit longer, and she was no trouble at all, almost the ideal child.

When Maisie's boss gave her the address she had been stunned, it was like fate had stepped in and was forcing her down the path she wanted to go, though had been reluctant to take, no, probably nervous to take, was a better description. None of this assignment was dangerous, she couldn't do those now she had Savannah, some surveillance and fitting into the community was all they required. No one would ever know it was her who spilled the beans on them. Her keen observations and notes were permissible in court, her identity would be concealed from the public and once her initial file was completed it would be handed to someone higher up the ladder and they would do the full investigation, as well as take all the credit. Maisie was now a piece of a puzzle which would come together down the track, probably in a city office somewhere far from here.

She put a slightly defrosted packaged dinner into the microwave and set the timer to eight minutes, it hummed as the plate began to turn and the light flickered to its own tune. Maisie went to the cardboard box with *kitchen* written on it, she had opened it for the wine glass earlier. As she had done this many times before, Maisie always put a plate, knife, fork, glass and cup with a teabag in it, on the top, all resting on a towel with the kettle straight underneath, along with her bathroom bag she could therefore easily get through the first night without rummaging through half a dozen boxes. Now having Savannah with her, things may have to change. Savvy had her own little bag packed so they should be ok for tonight and tomorrow.

All things going well Maisie hoped she could stay here and never move again. Recently she had applied for another role in the force, and as the official wheels turned slowly, her boss requested if she could do this one last job for him, having a young child actually gave her the perfect disguise. When he gave her the address and she calmed down, she knew it was fate, maybe some good karma was coming her way at last.

Maisie sighed. All she wanted was to settle down and give Savannah a good home, which was something Maisie had never had.

The cool of the evening started to seep in around her feet, sliding unseen through the open door, so Maisie hurried to close the windows and draw the blinds then paused to tuck the rug a bit more firmly around the sleeping child, her sweet blonde curls falling over her face covering the scar across her forehead. The microwave dinged and the smell of roast lamb filled the room. Maisie stood at the bench to eat, she might take her time to settle in. In the next few days it would be so good to go for a walk and check out the reserve below the houses on the other side of the street, she had seen a map which showed a little creek. Savvy would love the freedom after being cramped up in a small flat. Only allowed out for short times during the lockdown, it was no way for a child to grow up, but then Savvy's life had been no way for a child to live. A ripple of excitement ran through her, yes this would be good, a new start, the two of them a little family which hopefully would expand in the time ahead, it was what Maisie wanted the most, a real family.

Maisie rolled out the swag next to the lounge where her sleeping sister lay.

'Goodnight my sweet baby girl.' Maisie searched the darkness for her promise and spoke it out aloud. 'Today we start a new life and I'll make sure no one ever hurts you again.'

Tomorrow would be soon enough to start making this their home.

Number 6 BonBon Street

Claire

Claire lifted her head and gazed out the window, the sun was higher in the sky than it should be, her eyes didn't feel as puffy as usual and Mark's side of the bed was empty and the sheets were cold. Panic seemed to grasp her throat and she sprang out of bed, fear gripping her. Sophie! Where was she, did he have her, oh my god I didn't hear her, I've overslept. Impulsively picking up her dressing gown she stumbled and the pocket caught on the door handle as she hurried to get to her baby. Claire heard the microwave ding and slowed, putting her back against the wall trying to slide down the hall to get to Sophie before Mark saw her. Her mind raced through all the things he would say about her neglecting their child. Claire slowly pushed the handle down on Sophie's room and slipped inside. The cot was empty. Oh dear god please let her be alright she pleaded in her mind. The mother in her fired up inside and she stormed towards the kitchen as Mark, baby Sophie in his arms, stepped out trying to slip a bottle into her mouth. She made no sound and had clamped her mouth closed shaking her head furiously. The look of exasperation on his face almost made Claire laugh.

'Here you are. You were out to it, so I picked her up.' Sophie turned as he spoke and seeing her mother let out a wail and stretched her little arms towards her. Claire gathered the baby to her and stepped back, running one hand over Sophie mentally checking she was unharmed.

Mark looked surprised, then sneered.

'What do you think, I'd hurt a baby? You're sick you know, as if I would.'

Claire edged back again, hugging Sophie tight.

'I don't know Mark, would you? Would you hurt your daughter?'

Claire saw the anger start to rise in his face. The adrenaline her fear had produced was surging through her body. It was time to say it out aloud, to tell him it was not to happen again, she felt like, for a moment, she had super powers and she could make this stop once and for all.

Mark took one step forward, raised his clenched fist and Claire sank to the carpet arching her back, crouching and tucking Sophie in underneath her as much as she could. The power she had felt drained away as quick as water running down a sink. Claire held her breath waiting for the blow. He walked away, slamming into the screen door then cursing as she heard him pull it off and throw it to the ground. Claire shivered, she could still feel his anger, like a fog, hanging in the room.

Sophie whimpered and Claire eased her hold slightly, this is not how a baby should react. A tear rolled down her face, I'm teaching my daughter to stay quiet and be afraid and she's not even a year old. Another tear followed the first and Claire stumbled to the nursery and collapsed on the chair opening her nightie so Sophie could find comfort at her breast.

Claire laid her head back as the baby tugged at her then settled into a regular rhythm. He was trying to help for once her brain argued, no you haven't looked in the mirror yet, he is feeling guilty, wakes up sober for once and has a good look at his handy work, he won't change now, and he was coming at you while you were holding her. Get out Claire, go anywhere, anywhere would be better than this. He is not the person you once thought he was, get out if not for you, then for Sophie.

Claire rubbed her temples, the war in her head should not be there, she knew the truth, yet it seemed so hard as she wondered if she had enough fight in her to do it. For Sophie, she had to. If Claire was looking for excuses there were so many she could use. She had no car, no money at hand, how would she survive and look after Sophie at the same time. It wouldn't be hard to spot her, especially at the moment when there were no people around, a woman with a baby and suitcases would be easy to see.

Stop it! Stop it! Claire's brain told her loud and clear. No excuses. Get out before it's too late. Get out before you can't.

Mark had the phone, he had cancelled hers, to save money he said, and they shared the same friends so why did they need two? He, of course, said he should carry it, in case a job offer came up.

Claire was slowly realising how he had been isolating her, and this pandemic had made it so much easier for him to do so.

Claire had to devise a plan, she had to completely disappear, she was never going to let him take Sophie away from her. It was her greatest fear because even if he killed her, the authorities would put him away and protect Sophie, if he took Sophie, he would know he was still torturing Claire no matter where he was. Even if he never harmed Sophie, he would kill Claire slowly in a different way, by breaking her heart. Claire tried to rally, she needed a plan, a good one, and I think I need someone to help me, she agonised, I just need to work out who.

Claire rose slowly and placed the baby in the cot, her little mouth open and her eyes closed. Claire briefly imagined her mother would come and save her, sadly she knew it was impossible to do so from the grave.

Work it out Claire and do it quick, one glance in the mirror told her to do it even quicker, if it were possible. Claire could hear Mark in the shed hammering at something in a slow and steady way. She hurriedly straightened the bed and dressed herself, tying her hair back without brushing it, as the bruises on her scalp could only take so much. Claire glanced around the room making sure it would meet Mark's approval and moved swiftly and quietly around the house straightening a cushion here, picking up a stray cup there. She slipped into the baby's room and taking a jumpsuit and a small cardigan from the drawer tucked it under her arm and went to the hall cupboard. Easing open the door she unzipped an overnight bag and thrust them in before throwing an old coat back over it and silently shutting the door.

Each day she had tried to take one thing which would not be noticed, a baby bottle, a light rug, even a small toy, enough so she could look after Sophie for a short time at least. Mark left his wallet out though Claire was too scared to take money, feeling if she did, and he noticed, he might wise up to her and those consequences would be severe.

After today she would try to be smarter, after today she would start digging the mental tunnel towards her escape.

Number 8 BonBon Street

Pat

Pat pulled in and waited while the roller door slowly rumbled its way open. It had been a good day, a mixture of tears and laughter as patients and staff wished her well in her retirement. The boot of the car was full of gifts and flowers, there were certificates for massages and facials, shopping vouchers and chocolates. The doctors had been generous giving her a sizeable bonus, in a card signed by them all. Although she would miss the daily routine and the company, one thing Keith's death had shown her, was, life is very short and Pat wanted to be available now for new opportunities, to meet people, and enjoy whatever time she had left. Pat knew Keith would have agreed.

As she pulled in and glanced in the rear vision mirror, Pat saw Lisa coming up the drive, a bottle in hand. Pat was pleased, it was exactly what she needed, she had felt a bit empty driving home and she wanted today to be a good one, a day to look forward not back.

'Hello Pat, I thought we should celebrate, are you up to it?'

Lisa was already at the garage door when Pat pulled herself out of the car.

'Just what I need, my lovely, it has been a big day and this will round it off beautifully.' Pat ushered her in. 'I've some goodies in the boot so pop in and I'll follow. A client gave me a hamper with different cheeses, dips and crackers. It looks delicious.'

By the time Pat had her arms full, Lisa was back.

'I've invited Alice as well, I hope you don't mind. I didn't ask anyone else though, I didn't think you would want a street party.'

Lisa was smiling broadly. 'Now we have a new person maybe we should have a get together, a breakout from lockdown, I'll check the outdoor gathering numbers and do a count up.'

Pat was glad of the chatter and soon they were both chinking their glasses and digging into the delicious pâté and cheese. The doorbell chimed and Alice called out she would let herself in. Pat told her to bring another glass and they all chatted happily, listening as Pat recalled her day and the women rubbed her hand as a few stray tears fell, a mixture of both joy and sadness. Not one to dwell, Pat enquired after each of them.

'I really need a girl's day, you know, so I can vent and say all the things in my head and not be judged for them. Also, actually there is an issue I want to discuss with you both, but, for tonight, can we celebrate with you Pat, and maybe drink a bit too much wine?' Lisa wiggled her glass as she asked.

The others agreed and glasses were refilled as Alice and Lisa competed with each other to see who could make Pat laugh more.

The sun fanned her last goodbye and the air chilled so the three women made their way inside to the comfort of the lounge. A rich smell filled the air and Pat realised Alice had put a quiche in the oven on her way in and there was a bowl of salad on the bench. She was so lucky to have such good neighbours, they didn't interfere and were always there if needed, maybe now Pat was not so busy, they could become true friends in spite of the age differences.

'What about the boys Alice, won't they be wanting their tea?'

'Oh they are staying with friends tonight so this was perfect timing Pat, it feels so good to talk to another adult.' Alice laughed. 'They are at an age where if it's not on their phone, it's not happening, so I usually only get one word answers. I'm thinking I might have to text them to get a better response.'

Pat turned on some music. As they sat drinking too much wine as instructed, and eating the delicious meal, Pat felt a small part of her uncoil inside, it would be ok. I have friends and good neighbours, a roof over my head and a new day tomorrow. Keith would always be with her but finally she felt a small part of her give permission to herself to have a life without him, and not feel guilty for it. A small step and a release as well. She would make it.

The conversation turned from one subject to another, it was what they all needed. All their lives had changed dramatically in the last few months, the world was the same, yet also different, and they all agreed they didn't think it would ever be what it used it be and hoped maybe some good would come out of it all as people reconnected, and changed their priorities.

'So what are your first plans Pat?' It was Alice who spoke up, as Lisa turned her eyes upon her, curious for the reply.

'Well, I'm going to spend some time in the garden and my club is opening up again soon, so I can see my friends there, and just relax really. If things tidy up I might do some travelling, I've even been researching camper vans. We always wanted to do the lap, and I can't see a reason for me not being able to do it on my own.'

They both jumped in. Alice was first.

'The lap what's that?'

'The lap of Australia silly.'

Pat felt herself slurring a bit, the words seeming to tumble around in her mouth a few times before she could get them out. The wine had gone straight to her head, and she didn't mind a bit, as long as she didn't dribble.

'Lots of people my age do it, camping on the side of the road together. I even found some single women's groups online where you can meet up with someone in the group, and you might travel with them for a bit and then move on. It's sort of knowing you have a companion waiting for you sometimes, and you can make new friends with the same interests.'

'Sounds fantastic, good on you. Jon travels so much with work he never wants to go anywhere, one day, you never know, I might be one of those people you meet.' Alice spoke like she was dreaming at the same time about her own future.

'You mentioned a club, is it Rotary or CWA? I wouldn't have picked you for either of them.' Lisa was surprised by the look on Pat's face, she seemed a bit lost for words for a second.

'Let's open another bottle ladies, I'm moving into the next phase of my life and I have nothing to hide, I do think though, what I'm about to say next, might shock you.'

Alice giggled as Lisa opened a new bottle and poured them each a glass. They sat, each of them swaying slightly and leaned in to hear what Pat had to say.

Pat took a deep breath and hoped she could trust them as it wasn't something she wanted everyone to know, though if she was going to be better friends with these women, she wanted to be honest with them too.

'It's like this, it's not a regular sort of club. Keith and I have belonged to it for years and we really enjoy the people we meet there, it is a bit like the travelling, you meet like-minded people, you know what I mean?'

They both nodded, Pat inclined her head indicating for them to take another sip.

'The club I belong to.' They both leaned in, more than curious now as their wine muddled brains tried to work out what Pat was going to say.

It's now or never Pat thought.

'The club I belong to, is a nudist club!'

Alice sprayed wine all over her, the shock of trying to gasp with a mouth full, did not work.

'What!' Alice started to laugh. 'Nooo, you're having us on. Oh my god, you mean it, wow, I would never have picked it, omg what's it like, oh dear. Is everyone naked?'

Alice had slid to the front of her chair. A fit of giggles she could not contain, burst out of her mouth, she tipped off the edge and rolled onto the carpet, flopping back spread eagled on the floor staring at the ceiling.

'Good on you Pat, you're a champion!'

Pat looked at Lisa, she didn't look surprised, more like relieved. Lisa looked her straight in the eye.

'Well, you have explained a lot. We must talk, not now, tomorrow maybe, yes tomorrow is soon enough.' She glanced down at Alice then started to giggle too, as images of naked people playing volleyball bounced into her head. Pat joined in.

The wine, the confession and a little bit of letting go, not of Keith, but of the grief which had been crippling her, all added up to make Pat feel a lightening of her soul. A new door was opening, the old one would never quite close and Pat knew it was alright to leave it ajar.

Pat led an unsteady Lisa and Alice to the front door, it had been a fun night and they had all agreed to do it again soon. Pat already felt some barriers had been knocked down and she looked at each woman with a new understanding and was eager to learn more about each of them. It had been fun too, and it was a long time since she had laughed so hard. It felt good. She watched them as they stumbled home, thinking it was lucky it wasn't far.

Pat closed the door gently and flicked off the patio light. The moon shone through the side panels causing a soft glow on the tiles. Pat leaned back against the door. I'll be good now Keith, don't worry, I'll be fine. She closed her eyes trying to force the message through the atmosphere to wherever he may be. Part of her wanted to hang on, yet part of her thought she had to let him move on as well. An image of his fingertips sliding off hers as he moved away filled her mind, small steps Keith she thought. Pat dropped her head then pushed herself away from the door and made her way to the bedroom. Slipping off her clothes she slid straight into bed as sleep wound around her. As it took its final hold, her last thought was, for once the tears had stayed away, and she hadn't cried herself to sleep. This was the first time since he had left her, she hadn't.

Goodnight my darling, she murmured as the moon rose higher and the breeze caught the curtain and blew it into the room, neither of which Pat saw as she drifted away.

Number 9 BonBon Street

Lisa and Brodie

Lisa's head had not felt like this in a long time. She could see the sun was high in the sky and raised one arm to shield the glare coming in the window. Rolling slightly to take in the empty space next to her, the crumpled sheet thrust back as Brodie would have sprung out of bed, eager for a morning run or a class.

A glass of water is what I need, and she literally dragged herself out to the kitchen, the cool water easing her throat and washing the headache tablet down to do its job. It had been such a fun night though, somehow she felt a sense of relief. Chatting with other women was such a comfort, not putting Brodie down, but he liked to fix things and always talked back about solutions, whereas girls, no matter what their age, wanted to talk about it over and over and over. It was the release they sought as deep down, they always knew the answer they were searching for.

Lisa smiled. There had been times during the pandemic when she had asked Brodie, could he be a girl for once and listen while she went over something repeatedly, and could he not solve it, could he... just be. He had tried hard, he was always eager to please her, although usually on the third telling he gave up or hugged her and said *I'll fix it Honey, no trouble leave it to me*. He didn't get it, but he tried and it was all she could ask for.

To have been out of the house to chat last night had been exactly what she needed. Losing her job with the downturn had isolated her even more than usual, she liked her own company but the part time café job had forced her out of the house and she had to admit she'd enjoyed the banter of the other staff and the customers. Lisa knew Brodie would like it if she took some classes for him and she had done a few online cameos for him, showing the clients different stretching techniques, only it wasn't her thing to be in front of an audience, even if it was virtual.

Lisa and Alice had always been quite friendly, although lately Lisa felt like Alice was avoiding her, even in a pandemic. She always waved, and Alice waved back, yet there was a distancing, something she couldn't quite put her finger on. Last night though, it all seemed to fade away, the wine had helped and Lisa felt the friendship slip back to normal and start to grow stronger, they had all been through troubled times, she really should not have judged.

When Keith was alive, he and Pat were always off somewhere. Although Lisa and Pat had been friendly, and more so since Keith died as Lisa kept a closer eye on Pat, last night a lot of barriers had been broken down and the warmth and kinship she now felt with Pat seemed to explode inside her. Pat had trusted them with her little secret, which told Lisa she had felt it too. It would be good to have some close friends nearby, the world was changing and Lisa was not sure what was to come. Now there was one thing she now knew in her heart, these women would be there to support her.

Dry toast was all she could stomach as flashes of the images she had seen on the camera bounced in her head, she would wait for her head to clear then pop over and see Pat. Pat declaring she was a nudist explained the photos of her sun baking in the backyard, as well as a few others, some at the clothes line or reading a book. The reason for the images was now clear, it was how Pat liked to live her life in her own space, although Lisa now realised in each one she had seen, Pat was preoccupied, not looking at the camera. Harry must have had a ladder to see over the high fence. How did he not get caught, she wondered, if not by Pat, then by someone else? Pat had no back neighbours, yet he would have been obvious, surely someone would have seen the bumbling old fool fiddling with a camera and a ladder. Lisa felt the anger rising, how dare he do this, violating someone's privacy, and to top it off, it was violation of women, a subject she was passionate about.

Lisa hated the term, violation of women. It put the emphasis on the women, where it should be on the men who committed the acts, the peeping toms should be in the same category as rapists and the wife bashers, trouble was there was no singular name for it which would brand someone for life. It was like the word paedophile, everyone felt abhorrent when they heard it, with peeping tom, some men laughed, *there's no harm in looking, well, if they put it out there, what do they expect*? It made Lisa's skin crawl, if the tables were turned it would be a whole different story. Society had come a long way, in her own experience, Lisa felt it still had a long way to go.

Lisa shook her head, as images of her sister filled it. Sally hadn't, *put it out there*, she was simply walking to school, it was two days before they found her battered body in bushland, and it was not something Lisa could ever forget or forgive.

Lisa stretched and rolled her neck, the tablets were doing their work and the pain in her head was now a dull ache. A shower then I'll go over and see Pat, with her help we can decide on a plan. I must remember to check her fence for holes as the angle of some of the photos were not taken from a height. I'll get you, you bastard, I'll slowly ruin your life one way or another. It will be worse than going to the police, they may do their job and some lousy judge may even let you get away with it, but I promise, and you can mark my words, I won't let the women in this street feel unsafe. Look out Harry, the red dot is on your chest and you can't even see it yet.

Brodie had woken early, Lisa was snoring lightly. He had chuckled to himself when she had stumbled in last night, giggling like a school girl then getting the hiccups and moaning at him to make them stop. He loved her so deeply and it hurt him to see her isolating herself from the world. Brodie thought she was one of the kindest and funniest people he had ever met though Lisa shied away from people, and often didn't let them in to see the side of her he loved the most. It was a trust thing, which he knew was a struggle.

When her sister went missing Lisa's whole world had dissolved before her eyes and even though he had been there for her, the walls she had built up to protect herself, was something he could not prevent, Brodie was only grateful she had let him stay inside it. The police had found photos of Sally, and Brodie knew she had been stalked. A young girl on her way to school, her perpetrator never found as DNA didn't work if you were not suspected and didn't have a previous record. If the police had no sample there was nothing to match to. Brodie wondered if any evidence would turn up one day, so much time had passed, it seemed almost impossible now.

Lisa was passionate about women's safety, as everyone should be, although there were times Brodie thought she took it a bit too far. In the past she would see a man taking a photo of a woman at the park and he would almost have to restrain her from grabbing his camera and flinging it away. It was an impulse, something would trigger her and she would pounce and not wait for the scenario to play out to see the man was trying to take an angled shot of his wife or children. The camera anger thing was her way of dealing with Sally, it seemed weird to others, especially at parties, and it didn't always happen, yet when it did, she had no control. Counselling had helped somewhat, though Lisa still shuddered when she saw them. Brodie hoped when they had kids of their own, Lisa would let him take photos and recognise the normality of the action, after all, it was not a camera which had killed her sister.

Lisa's parents had protected her from the publicity and many of the details, their lives had changed forever and they had fiercely protected the child they had left. It had killed them in the end, the grief. Knowing Lisa was safe with him had reassured them, sadly they had never been able to move forward and seemed to fade away dying within months of each other, another blow he had tried to cushion Lisa through.

Brodie was planning a big surprise for her 30th birthday, he had been working on it for months, it would make her laugh and hopefully bring her back to the girl he knew. Lisa wanting to take some wine and cheer up Pat across the road, was a sign to him she was ready to shake off the isolation of the last few months and take a small step forward. As he tied his laces he wondered if maybe they could start talking about a family soon. Brodie knew it would be a challenge for her, watching them grow and letting them find their own independence would be hard, very hard for her, he hoped together they would get through it, he knew they would, he couldn't wait.

Quietly opening the door, Brodie slipped out into the cool morning air, he shivered slightly although knew he would soon work up a sweat and it was always coolest in the hour before the dawn. Brodie stretched for a few minutes then set off up the street at a steady pace with visions of a child playing in his head, she had his sandy hair and Lisa's laughing eyes. Life was good.

Number 7 BonBon Street

Jason

Jason pulled his jumper over his head, work had almost ground to a halt now, the do-it yourself crowd were out in force, you could hardly get to the hardware store anymore it was so crowded, socially distanced and mask wearing individuals buying paint and grout and everything to do with renovating or gardening. It was one of the few places people had been allowed to go since the start of the pandemic and it also gave them something to do, this thing was going longer than anyone had predicted. Jason could see it was a social outing as well for them, even though no one chatted, it was visual human contact with others, a sense of community. Jason knew he would get a few calls in the weeks ahead from the inexperienced home tilers to fix up whatever mishap they had made, for now he was actually glad to have a break to get things done around the house and play with the dogs.

He hadn't seen Kylie in what seemed like forever, heavily pregnant now, she and her new partner did not want to risk going out until this was over and had kept in contact over the internet. Jason could see it was getting less and less as Tyler, Kylie's fiancé, accepted Jason for Kylie's sake, although did not understand their relationship at all Jason could feel the distance growing between them.

Jason knew it was confusing, he hadn't let many people in on his little secret, he still loved Kylie as a dear friend and he was totally into women, he wasn't gay or a transvestite, he was a cross dresser and his compulsion to do so was something he could not control.

Jason had been to counselling, his father had seen to it after catching him one day when he was young wearing his dead mother's clothes and lipstick. For a small child it would not have been anything except a game of dress-ups. Jason had been way past the age for make-believe. His father had been old school, and it probably would have been easier for his dad if he was gay, he may have been able to live with something which, in his dad's eyes, was more socially acceptable. To have a perfectly *normal* son who liked to wear women's clothes, was not something his father could fathom, nor ever would.

Jason's father had thrown out all his wife's clothes and sent Jason to one councillor after another. Although it helped Jason understand it a bit better, as they explained, it was his way of calming himself, relieving anxiety probably caused from his mother's early death, and a rigid controlling father. Going back to live in his childhood home after each session, and sharing the residence with his father, undid all the help he received. Jason had moved out as soon as he could. When a long term contract came up here working with a major builder, Jason had jumped at it. The steady income and the distance from his father being the two major factors in his decision.

Kylie had understood better, yet even though he had told her before they were married, she struggled with it when she realised it was a long term thing, it was not something she could fix, no matter how much she tried or how in love they were. Sitting opposite her husband each night as he wore a wig, or waiting for him while he applied his makeup, had been too much for her. As much as it hurt him, Jason understood and had called it quits before she did. He gave her an out with dignity, and she had been grateful. They told everyone Jason had an affair and they had not been able to work through it. It was the least Jason could do, to take the blame, and he was so grateful they had remained friends and was happy for her to have moved on to the happy place she was now at. It was lonely sometimes and he would like to have children as well, who knows, he might be lucky enough to find the right woman.

Jason was glad to have Alice so close over the fence, they could chat and have a laugh. She too, was a bit lonely, with Jon away so much. It must be hard and Jason could see she did everything for the boys, though they didn't appear to appreciate it. Alice had brought them up since they were nine, she was not their mother and he constantly heard them remind her of it when they couldn't get their own way. Jason thought Jon expected a bit too much from her, then again, it was not his business how other people ran their lives, and he certainly couldn't be the one to judge them.

Number 5 BonBon Street

Alice

Alice was enjoying the sunshine, having a few drinks last night had done her the world of good. She was still smiling about some of the things they had talked about and had to admit she was a bit shocked at Pat's confession, who would have thought!

The boys had returned from their sleepover and were changed and gone again for soccer in a matter of minutes. Even though she had a million things to do, today Alice wanted some time to herself, real time.

Alice could hear Jason over the fence moving in and out of his shed, talking to the dogs. He was building them a proper fence finally as they had escaped a few times, looking for human company while he was at work. They could be a bit mischievous, as Alice found out one day when her petunias were dug up. Never mind they were so loveable and when they looked at you with those eyes, who wouldn't melt?

Lisa had called earlier, the laughter in her voice made Alice feel good and she was glad of their deepening friendship, some days she felt more isolated here in BonBon Street, than Jon way up there in the Pilbara. The older the boys got, the ruder they seemed to be toward her, and Alice was sure it was more than a teenage thing. The time would come, and maybe not soon enough for her, when they would be mature enough to see what she had sacrificed for them. Their own mother had never cared enough to come back for them after she ran away to find herself. At times like this, when things were hard, Alice could see it might be easier to leave, she sort of understood it, at the end of the day though, they were her kids, and to Alice all else should become insignificant. Oh well, it was easy to sit in judgement from here, she knew Jon, and his career, weren't easy to live with either, and for the boys to be abandoned by their parents, Alice knew firsthand how it felt.

Alice shook her head to release the thoughts but they kept on pushing their way back in, it was probably the only thing holding her here if she admitted the truth. Alice had an inbuilt determination to do it right, be better than her mother, although she hated to feel better and have herself put another woman down. I shouldn't do it, she thought, though here I am sticking it out for no reward, with a failing marriage to a husband I don't see, and two ungrateful boys who constantly tell me I don't matter. I agreed to look after them so Jon could continue to live the life he wanted. These boys are somewhat like me, even though her mother abandoning her to strangers had been harsh, along with the endless foster homes which followed, at least Jon's wife had left them with their father.

Alice was coming to realise, Jon, lost in his job, had married her for this. In his mind he had found another mother for his children and could continue on with his life only ever being there for the good bits.

Alice sighed, maybe it was the wine, maybe it had loosened her mind, she did feel more relaxed today, usually she was so wound up trying to get through each day her own feelings were thrust aside, packed in a box in her brain for another day. Today she had opened the box, knew what was inside and knew she had to act, this was her life too. The boys, well, she wouldn't abandon them, though things would have to change. Once their exams were over and decisions made about their future, she too would move on, not literally she hoped, as she liked this street, more mentally. With Jon, she knew it was over, tonight she would start discussing with him the details of where they would go from here, if he would ever answer the phone.

The boys barrelled around the corner of the house, muttering to each other in their own kind of language and stopped short when they saw her. They probably have never seen me sitting, except at the table at meal times she thought, and to see her sunning herself in the backyard would be an unusual site.

'Hi boys, how was your game?'

They both were staring at her as if she was an alien or something.

'You'll have to make your own lunch today as I've taken the day off.'

Alice had to smile, their mouths had both dropped open as they waited, unsure of what to do or say. They probably think it's a joke.

'Oh, and while you are inside you each have a basket of clothes to put away, it would be nice if you folded them first, they fit in the cupboard better and are much easier to find if you do.'

Charlie spoke first, the outward jovial face he showed the rest of the world disappeared behind his sneer.

'Call yourself a mother do you, wait till we tell Dad you aren't looking after us.'

Alice glared at him then turned to Jay.
'So do you have something to say as well?'
Jay backed away, he looked confused.

'Ahh no, Alice, we only wanted our lunch.'

'Well there's bread in the cupboard and some ham in the fridge, you're big boys I'm sure you won't starve.' Alice adjusted her sunglasses and stretched out her legs a bit more, it was about time they grew up, they have been babied too long and if their father doesn't come back I'm not going to be a slave to them anymore.

Charlie slammed the screen door so loudly it made Jay jump back.

'Are you ok Alice?' Jay looked concerned.

Alice raised her sunglasses and held them there while she spoke.

'Yes thanks Jay, I've finally realised I no longer want to be a doormat, and you are both quite capable of making a sandwich or even doing some jobs around the house. I can tell you now I'm determined not to soften on this so get used to it or when school is finished you can both find a job and move out. I mean it!'

Jay looked startled and Alice was a bit sorry he was the one to cop it. Most people didn't like Jay yet Alice thought he really was the nicer of the two boys, much softer in his nature, and quieter, though sometimes she could see how his reserved nature came across as rudeness. Charlie was like a used car salesman, you could not always trust every word he said, not sly, it was more a controlled self-centredness. It was his protection barrier Alice often thought, when he popped into her mind. Their mother had left hidden scars and Alice was sure Jon didn't see them, yet she had to deal with them every day.

Charlie yelled from the kitchen.

'Jay get in here, I burnt me bloody finger on the toaster, ow!'

Jay turned to walk away then whispered.

'Good on you Alice.' Giving her a wink he opened the door and disappeared inside.

Alice felt a surge of pride, good work girl, now you have to stick to it, today is the first day of the rest of your life and you have to start living, not just existing.

Alice's phone vibrated and she glanced at it to check the message. Lisa had wanted a meeting with her and Pat this afternoon and she had sent through the time. They had laughed together on the phone though somehow Alice thought this might be serious, she hoped Lisa wasn't ill or anything. Alice suggested she could bring more wine and Lisa laughing had replied.

'No my head may not survive, but then again, yes we will probably need it.'

Alice was certainly feeling curious as to what it might be about, and glancing at her watch realised it wasn't long now and all would be revealed. She would find out soon enough.

A cool breeze whispered its way into the garden and Alice stood up, she might plant some roses in spring, it would be nice to have more than a worn out bit of grass and car parts as accessories for a backyard. A plate crashing to the floor made her sigh. Don't give in, be tough she admonished herself and stepped up through the door to a scene of chaos greeting her eyes and the thought that they were acting no better than two year olds dancing in her head. Be strong girl, be strong.

'The dust pan is in the laundry Charlie. I'm going to have a shower before I go out. I'm sure you two will be able to get your own dinner.'

Charlie's mouth dropped open and Jay gave her the thumbs up behind his back. Alice turned, it felt good, actually really good, only she was a tiny bit afraid she might take it too far. Considering the worst thing to happen would be Jon might finally come home, and at least then, they could try to sort something out.

Locking the door she let the shower steam up the room before stepping in. The warm water running down the rivets of her body, was washing away the anxiety and stress of the last few months, maybe even the last few years, and swirling them around her feet to disappear down the drain hopefully never to return. She had a plan, and it was all she needed, a direction in which to head. Alice knew she would be fine, she had faced worse things than this, she did hope, and crossed her fingers at the thought, Jon would walk away from the house and let her have it. This home was all she wanted and she had put up with a lot to be able to have the security of a permanent roof over her head, it was the one thing she wanted to keep.

The boys had made a half-hearted attempt to clean up after themselves, at least they now knew where the sink was she thought, and they had put the food away. Alice scribbled them a note saying she would be at Pat's house and left twenty dollars for the pizza van. Pizza would do them for their tea, in the end it would save her as she couldn't imagine the mess if they tried to cook something themselves. Alice grinned, when she had said she was taking the rest of the day off, she meant the whole day, which certainly didn't end at sunset.

Selecting two bottles of wine and grabbing a bag of crisps to put in the bag with them, Alice left through the front door, the lock clicking as she pulled it tight and made her way diagonally across the street.

Young Claire, though Alice thought she is probably older than she looks, was in the front yard, the baby on a rug taking in the last warm rays before the shadows from the trees started to lengthen their way across the lawn. Mark was washing his car in the driveway and raised his hand in a wave. Claire glanced up and adjusted her cap nodding slightly as a greeting.

'Baby's growing, isn't she?'

Alice didn't know Claire well, and Alice suddenly felt ashamed she hadn't reached out to the new mum in these lonely times. Claire only nodded not giving a verbal reply. Alice stopped and leaned over the fence, little Sophie, with eyes only for her mother, was gurgling and stretching her tiny legs, reaching out with her hands trying to touch invisible clouds with her fingers.

'We must get together for morning tea one day Claire, it must be hard for you with everything going on not to have a mother's group or family to visit.'

Alice saw Mark out of the corner of her eye, he was striding over and he hadn't even turned off the hose. Claire glanced up high enough and Alice caught sight of the bruise on her cheek, she almost gasped seeing the frightened look in Claire's eyes as she turned away.

Suddenly Mark was there and he firmly placed himself between herself and Claire. Alice hoped the horror she felt did not show on her face.

'When's Jon back? Oh sorry, Claire's not one for chatting, bit shy you know.'

He cleared his throat and there was a second of awkward silence before they both spoke at once.

'How are the boys?'

'I was asking Claire…'

'You go.' Mark laughed lightly, his handsome friendly face Alice now knew was trying to hide a terrible secret.

'I was starting to say to Claire, now we can have small gatherings outside I'm starting a ladies only book club. It will be in my front yard so you can keep an eye on them if Claire needs you to come and get Sophie. We can all bring a book and tell each other about it then can swap with each other as well.'

Alice felt herself rambling however she did not want to give him a chance to start making excuses.

'So what about tomorrow, at ten?' Alice looked directly at Claire who was staring up at her, the bruise quite visible and her mouth tense.

'It will do us all good to get out of the house even if it is only across the street. Thanks so much Claire you will be doing me a real favour and we can ask the new girl next door, you know, make her feel welcome. Don't be shy and bring a book ok.'

Alice glanced at Mark.

'And no excuses Mark or I'll be over here to have words, I need you to lend me your wife otherwise I'll go stir crazy the way this is going, be glad to see the end of it, well must go. Bye.'

Alice started to walk away before he could reply then turned.

'Oh and bring Sophie I can't wait to have a cuddle.'

Her hand was shaking as she opened Pat's gate and marched up to the door still trying to look confident. A mix of fear and rage was burning within and Alice was struggling to keep them both under control.

Glancing across she saw Claire had gathered up the baby and rug and was hurrying inside. Dear God, Alice thought, if she doesn't turn up tomorrow I'm calling the police. Pat opened the door and Alice practically fell inside she was so preoccupied with what she had just seen.

Pat grabbed the bag and feeling the weight said;

'Oh dear, I'm not sure my head can do two nights in a row.' Then looking at Alice's face also said. 'Still maybe we can give it a go, you only live once.'

Alice steadied herself on the wall, it had been a shock to realise what was happening next door, the poor, poor girl. I must help her. I will help her.

'What's wrong Alice, you look like you've seen a ghost.'

'I have Pat, not my ghost only one similar. I hate to tell you this but I think you are living next door to a monster!' With no other warning Alice burst into tears and Pat wrapped her arms around her while she sobbed.

Number 3 BonBon Street

Monique and Harry

Monique saw Alice go into Pat's house again. Alice had been there yesterday and Harry had seen her and Lisa, stumbling home across the road quite late in the night. She wished they would include her, she could do with some female company.

It wasn't as if she had a shortage of friends, only this pandemic had been hard, mainly because when her friends did meet up they chose others with children. It was killing two birds with one stone, adult conversation for them and a friend for their kids to play with. Monique couldn't blame them at all, she had been the one to choose this life and those who had thrown the words sugar daddy their way, did not know of the sacrifices both herself, and Harry, each had to make. To do this only for money would be soul destroying. To do it for love was the only reason anyone would give up so much for one person. Looks like they are having another girl's night, maybe one day they will ask me.

Harry was organising a date night, he had seen it on the television and said he wanted her to dress up and put makeup on, like they were going out, he had said he would do the rest. Moni could not love him more at this moment for him wanting to make her happy. Her only worry was she had tasted his cooking and secretly hoped it was salad for dinner. Tucking the thought away she went back inside and into the garage. Harry had made half of it into a little studio with mirrors on the wall so she could practice her dance. Turning on the music its rhythm soon caught her up and moved through her body like the blood through her veins. If only she hadn't had the accident, this was her great love, and Harry of course, if she could not have danced at all, she did not think she could have lived, it was such a big part of her life.

Moni had cancelled Brodie for the morning, between the exercises and teaching him to dance, she was worn out and needed a day off to relax. He was so keen it was hard to do, and being a perfectionist he wanted to have every move right so the whole routine would be go without a hitch at Lisa's birthday. Harry's face, when she told him she had cancelled, made it worth the disappointment she had felt from Brodie.

Brodie was planning a surprise for Lisa's birthday, and Moni was secretly teaching him some dance steps. Brodie had sworn her to secrecy, even from Harry, as he didn't want his little surprise to leak out. In return he was giving Moni some free classes as payment. Maybe Lisa was distant to her as Moni did spend a lot of time holed up in her garage with her husband.

Oh no! Monique suddenly realised how it must look, oh dear. Brodie had mentioned they'd had a small tiff about his time spent in private classes, and it suddenly dawned on her how it must look. Harry had been saying things as well and she had dismissed it as his insecurity about their age difference. Lisa's party couldn't come soon enough, as then maybe the women in the street would be more welcoming.

Doing a final stretch Monique glanced at the clock and realised she should be getting ready for her big date. Her heart melted, her darling Harry was so thoughtful, Moni wished his children could see how happy he was. If only she could make them see, it would complete Harry's world to see the grandchildren again.

Harry heard Monique head into the shower, he had planned everything for tonight and was excited to see her face when she came into the dining room. He had set the table carefully even measuring how far the knives and forks were from the edge of the table. He knew she would be worried about the food, he was no cook, however the butcher had assured him he could not go wrong with this peppered beef puff, some whole potatoes and lightly steamed broccoli. *You can't go wrong mate, not too fancy for you. A good hearty winter warmer I'd call it*, he'd said and Harry had trusted his word and followed his instructions to the letter. It smelt good anyway and Harry only had to remember not to overcook the broccoli, he really wanted it to be perfect.

Harry had seen on the television, on one of those morning shows, people were doing all kinds of things to treat themselves and feel normal in these crazy times. When he saw the date night he knew how special it would make Monique feel and also thought it might lift them out of the bit of a slump they had been in.

Harry heard a noise and looked out to see Jason heading out his gate with the dogs, he was a bit late tonight, must have been caught up trying to finish the fence. Harry had offered to help and Jason thanked him for the offer and said he was happy to do it on his own as it helped fill in the days as well. Harry understood.

Harry double checked everything for the hundredth time, table set, flowers arranged, soft music ready to play, and dinner in the oven. The vegetables were ready to cook after their pre-dinner drinks and for dessert, he had an apricot pie from the bakers, ready to slip in the oven to warm while they ate the main. Harry had bought the whipped cream in the can to go with it, it looked easy and he thought it would look fancier than if he tried to do anything more. Satisfied he hurried to the bathroom for a quick shower and hoped he would be all dressed ready before Monique was finished with her makeup. He had asked her to wait in their room until he came to escort her to dinner, although he didn't want Moni to wait too long and become impatient. Harry, a towel wrapped around his waist, tapped on their bedroom door and made his announcement.
'Your taxi will be arriving in five minutes Madam.'

He heard her chuckle and went into the spare room where he had hidden his clothes earlier. It is a long time since I've worn a tuxedo, he thought, as he clipped on a bow tie and ran his hands over his hair one more time making sure it was smooth and neat. Shoulders back, silly grin on his face Harry went to pick up his bride for what he hoped would be a memorable night for both of them.

Monique actually had butterflies! Harry had tapped on the door as he went passed from the shower and as she was putting the final touches to her outfit. She had chosen a fitted floor length gown she had not worn in years.

Yesterday she had noticed Harry's tuxedo missing from the wardrobe. Not wanting to give away she had noticed, Moni instead had made sure she chose something as elegant to match. He was going to so much trouble it brought tears to her eyes. Enough silly, she thought, stop it or you will ruin your makeup.

Harry knocked at the door and opened it slowly, Monique stood in the middle of the room a gentle smile on her face which grew broader as her husband let out a whistle and the only word he uttered was 'Wow!'

Pulling himself together, he offered her his arm, told her she looked stunning and escorted her to the lounge room.

The smells from the kitchen were wafting through the house and making Moni's mouth water. Set on the coffee table were two glasses along with an ice bucket cooling some very expensive champagne. Harry gallantly poured it, the bubbles overflowing the top of the glass as he dropped a strawberry in each one. He raised his glass.

'To the most beautiful woman and the most wonderful wife a man could wish for.'

He kissed her gently before they both took a sip and turning, opened the doors to the dining room.

Monique could not believe her eyes, it was beautiful. Harry was fumbling on one side before standing proudly as gentle music filled the air wrapping around her like all the love in the room. Drawing out a chair he excused himself to check on the meal and Monique held her hand over her heart thanking any greater being for blessing her with this man, she was so very thankful.

Number 4 BonBon Street

Maisie

Maisie had only ventured out once or twice, mainly to get supplies. She now thought she had a handle on most of the residents, they, like most people, soon conformed to habit and it was exactly what she had needed them to do.

This job was pretty easy really, there was nothing happening at the moment or anything which looked out of place to her. To have her here, keeping an eye on things, and to see if her suspect made any wrong moves, plus to ensure the equipment didn't fail was the main priority. Her boss had been vague about the details on this job, which was not unusual, something, somewhere, had triggered a need for her to be here now and with everything else she had been dealing with lately, Maisie was happy to know as little as possible.

It was so weird, a job, in this street, at this time, had come up. It was almost stranger than fiction, yet, they did say the truth always was. Maisie was a big believer in fate. Fate had given her this job, being in the office at the right time, her boss knowing she needed a place to rent long term, and also a less stressful case, due to her now having Savannah to care for.

Maisie was grateful for most things in her life, even when her wayward mother had finally succumbed to drugs, it was actually a blessing. It made it easier for Maisie to take over guardianship of her little sister, releasing her from a life of foster homes and uncertainty. Maisie, although young to take on the task, had a secure job and her boss had backed her with statements of her integrity, and also of her reliability, to take on this child.

Even though she was only little, Savvy had already learned to stay quiet and be good, whining or crying had only ever earned her a good hard smack or no dinner, neither of which a four year old understood. In the few weeks Maisie had spent with her full time, the changes were obvious. She still slept a lot, suddenly having good nutritious meals, which Maisie thought would boost her energy, actually sapped it as her little body absorbed the goodness and seemed to store it away in case this was not a long term thing, Maisie was delighted to see her smile and hear the giggles as she played with the new toys they had chosen. A social worker was going to do regular checks on them and Maisie was determined this little girl would only know happiness from now on. She had made a vow over her dead mother's body, never would either of them be made to stoop to the depths their mother had dragged them both to at times. Maisie was determined to erase as much as she could from her little sisters head and replace it with a world full of wonder, excitement and love.

The house was perfect, and over time Maisie wanted it to be a home. The beauty of this job was she did not have to come in contact with the client as a work thing, and therefore could continue to live here even after the job was done. So far she hadn't even spotted the client and the comings and goings at the house appeared to be normal for these times. Maybe he was holed up in there unable to come out, time would tell, she knew these things were always complicated and the outcome was hard to predict. Maisie thought it was one of those insurance fraud cases though her boss had indicated another agency would be receiving the footage as well.

It was known to boost their cash flow, mining companies made fraudulent claims and continued to pay their workers without them even knowing they had a workers compensation claim in and the company collected the money. Maisie had heard there was more to this case than what she knew, so she did her job, maintained her equipment and kept her mouth shut.

Part of her wanted to think he was innocent so forever more she could live here in a normal street, with normal people, and fingers crossed re unite with family who did not, as far as she knew, know she, or Savvy existed. With her family issue she would bide her time, get to know them first, see if they did know or what they were like as people before she would help them join the dots, as they say. The equipment saved a copy for her and also live streamed to unknown suits in an office in the city. So far Maisie was happy with what she saw and decided today she would take Savvy for a walk, apparently there was a creek nearby and Maisie could imagine her little face lighting up in amazement at such a thing. These little joys were giving as much to Maisie as they were to Savannah, Maisie was feeling the joys of a childhood she had never had.

Savannah eased herself into the room, Maisie wondered if the sneaking, for safety's sake would ever leave her, she could only hope.

'Hey Munchkin, are you hungry?'

Savvy nodded vigorously.

'I was thinking, would you like to go on a little walk? I found out there might be a little creek and we could take your little bath boat and see if it floats, what do you say?'

Savvy's eyes lit up, Maisie didn't even know if she knew what a creek was, their mother had not introduced her to many books in her little life.

'We won't get lost will we?' Savvy looked concerned. 'I like it here Maisie, will we find our way home?'

'Of course we will and we can even leave a little trail to follow back if you like, you know like in Hansel and Gretel.'

Savvy looked at her blankly, so Maisie covered her smile and led her to the kitchen for a snack, making a mental note to add story books to the shopping list.

Savvy's little body was shaking as they stood at the door.

'It's ok Savannah, it's like going to the shops and we are not scared going there are we? Now remind me next time we go, to get you a hat, you should be alright for today. Are you excited, I hope the creek is there, fingers crossed eh.'

Maisie smiled as she glanced down and saw her sister trying to twist one finger over the other, such little things to learn and it made the ball of anger she held inside twist slightly. It's ok Maisie, she has you now which is a lot more than you ever had, and you turned out ok.

Double checking she had the key they both waited for the door to click closed, then hand in hand made their way across the street towards the laneway which they could see the start of next to the big hedge which surrounded the last house. Both were chatting excitedly for their big adventure. As they passed the house at number seven, two labradors rushed out, tails wagging and tongues reaching out to give sloppy doggie kisses. Savannah screamed and flew into her arms wrapping her legs around Maisie's waist and lifting her toes as high as she could away from these scary creatures. A man rushed out and grabbing the dogs, roused on them sternly with the command of sit, which they obediently did, their tails still going ten to the dozen and their eyes pleading for forgiveness.

'I'm so sorry, did they hurt her. Is she ok?'

'Yes, yes, no, so sorry, she is a bit scared of dogs and I think they took her by surprise is all.'

'I'm Jason, by the way, I'm building them a new fence so I was letting them play while I'm outside with them. They must have heard you coming, they love kids.'

'It's no trouble really, they are lovely. Look Savvy the dogs only wanted to say hello, and I'm sure these two won't hurt you.'

Savvy sneaked a peek and a tiny smile pulled at her mouth, Maisie put her down slowly kneeling next to her whilst reaching out a hand to the dogs to show her not to be afraid. One long tongue then another snuck out to lick her hand and Savannah giggled. The dogs turned their gaze on her and the chocolate one inched forward, stretching out its nose to touch her hand, Savannah giggled again and within seconds was patting his head while the golden one nuzzled her other hand.

'They're cheeky, and a bit naughty. They won't hurt you.'

Jason knelt so he could talk to Savannah at her own level.

'The brown one is called Clyde and this pretty girl here is Pippa.'

Savannah looked in his face weighing up if she should speak to this stranger with the nice dogs or not. Easing back she moved behind Maisie and as Maisie stood up, clung to her leg, peering out from behind to get a better look. Jason stood too, and Maisie put out her hand.

'I'm Maisie, and this is Savannah, we not long ago moved into number four.'

'That's great. Say, if you ever want to come and see the dogs you are most welcome. Did you move far?'

'Not really I suppose, but it feels a million miles away from the city here. Our mother passed away and I thought it would be better for Savannah if we moved out of an apartment. There is so much more room for her to play and she is supposed to start school next year so it was good timing too. We were lucky this house was available, especially with everything else going on.'

Maisie and Jason chatted for a few more minutes then both grinned as they saw Savannah feel a bit more confident and stretch her hand out again for another sloppy lick.

'Well nice to meet you Jason. We are off to discover the creek we heard is over there, and, if it truly is ok with you, I might bring her over again to meet the dogs, I don't want her to be afraid anymore.'

Jason frowned slightly at her comment, obviously deciding to let it slide and Maisie wanted to get going, not only anxious for their walk, but also to stop herself from slipping out things she did not want people to know. For a bit longer she wanted to have her guard up. With a wave they moved off then Jason called out.

'Maisie, nice to meet you and, um, sorry about your mother, if you need a hand, don't hesitate to ask.'

Maisie raised her hand and continued walking, turning the corner onto the path she looked back to see him still watching her, not in a bad way, in a way which brought tears to her eyes and she felt like she had made a friend.

Savannah's head drooped and her chin dropped on to her chest, the dinner cooled on the plate as Maisie hurried to swallow hers before lifting the sleeping child off the chair and carrying her into her makeshift bed. They'd had the best afternoon, Savannah was mesmerised by the water running between the rocks then bubbling over them like mini waterfalls. They had forgotten in the end to take her boat instead making ones out of leaves, cheering them on as they rushed through the tiny rapids, sometimes getting wedged between the stones, while at other times, rushing off and disappearing out of sight as the creek widened and flowed on down the gully. Exhausted they had retraced their steps back up the hill, hungry from the exercise and exhausted from the fresh air which had purged their lungs ridding them of the last of the stale city air.

Maisie tried to hurry with dinner. Savannah didn't last, only getting halfway through before sleep took over, and her body gave in. They had passed Jason again as he took the dogs for a walk. Savannah, not as afraid as she had seen them coming, actually gave cheeky Clyde a kiss on the nose, much to their surprise. It had been

nice to have a conversation with an adult and Jason seemed like a
decent man, probably lonely like everyone else during this
pandemic,

Maisie knew he lived alone, as no one else showed up on the
recordings, and he seemed to be a normal bloke, two dogs, a ute and
a nice smile to go with it.

Maisie lifted Savannah on to her bed and with a damp
flannel wiped the little girl's feet and used a handtowel to pat them
dry. It was enough for tonight, kids were allowed to be dirty
sometimes. I think I've been a bit too squeaky clean with her, trying
to wash away both our pasts.

A quick tidy of the kitchen, a shower and she was ready for
bed herself. Maisie knew sleep would escape her no matter how
hard she tried. She picked a novel out of her small collection and
read the title, *a Million Stars*. If only we could get lost in a million
stars she thought, where no one can ever hurt us.

The red light on one of the motion cameras turned a steady
green. It was the house straight across, Maisie had seen a silhouette
of them slow dancing in the lounge room, Harry holding his wife
close as they swayed to a tune she could not hear. The light behind
them and the curtain hid their features from view but Maisie could
almost see the love which was swirling around them. I'll have that
one day she vowed, all or nothing, I won't settle for less, not like
our mother did, I will aim for the stars and try, try, try, to hit the
moon.

The book tipped to one side as her eyes closed and Maisie
dreamed of a better life, both for herself and her sister.

Number 6 BonBon Street

Claire

Claire had been on tenterhooks all night, Mark did not even mention what had happened outside yesterday so she was unsure of how to bring it up. Alice had said if she didn't turn up she would come over to get her, and this whole thing had Claire's insides wound up tighter than a clock. The thought of getting out of the house, with Sophie and maybe, having a chance to ask for help, even to escape, was turning her tummy in excitement. She felt lighter however was being extremely careful to remain calm and follow the usual routine.

Alice had looked at her bruise and Claire had seen the faint horror run across her face. She was so grateful for how Alice had covered her expression and pretended to Mark as if she hadn't even seen anything out of the ordinary. Alice had recognised her situation immediately and Claire felt Alice had carefully chosen her words, as if sending a secret signal to Claire, letting her know she was not alone.

The clock on the wall ticked over to five minutes to ten and Claire pushed the pram towards the door. She had tucked a book in between the mattress and the pram wall and popped a normal nappy bag in the tray underneath. Claire knew today was not the day, just hopeful, fingers crossed, it would be a huge step in her plan. If Alice would help her and Claire could get away without Mark knowing anyone else was involved, it would be perfect. Alice looked tough, like she could hold her own against him. Claire's thoughts were getting away and she had to rein them in as Mark stepped in the back door.

'So you're off then.'
Claire let a tiny breath escape her lips.

'Yes, you'll be able to see me the whole time, I won't say anything, I promise.' Claire's fingers crossed behind her as she fed him the lie. 'I'd better hurry.'

She reached the door as his arm went around her and the blood drained from her face.

'I'll be watching. The bitch thought she was smart, I'm not stupid, I'm on to her you know, don't get too friendly or you won't be the only one seeing the end of my fist.'

They both heard the latch on the gate and the squeak it made as it slid open. Mark turned the door handle with one hand and pinched her hard on the back with the other making her flinch.

'Don't forget what I said,' he whispered as the door swung back and Alice's face appeared on the other side.

'There you are, thought I'd come over and help with the pram, can't wait for a cuddle, oh goodness she is absolutely adorable.'

Alice prattled without a breath and practically pushing Mark out of the way, had the pram almost out the gate before either of them had moved. Turning she looked at Mark.

'Come on Claire, let's go.'

Claire pushed past Mark. Not quick enough to avoid him, he pinched her hard on the fleshy part of her underarm, she almost cried out, bit her tongue, and hurried after Alice. It would bruise up fairly quickly there and at least as long as she didn't raise her arm up, no one would see. He knew it too, he planned every move she realised, it was getting more frequent and he was less sorry each time for his actions.

Tears filled her eyes by the time she was in the middle of the road and she squeezed them closed refusing to let them fall. Tonight she would not think about. He would be angry, and not only at her, but at Alice too, she suspected. If she could survive a bit longer the escape would be perfect. Once gone she could never again risk him getting her back.

Alice waited for her at the other curb. Pretending to have trouble getting the pram up the gutter Alice bent down whispering rapidly as Claire tried to help.

'You come to me or to Pat whenever you can, just bring the baby, we'll fix the rest.'

Claire glanced back, Mark was standing at the gate watching her carefully.

'Yes, thank you it is nice to get out,' she said loudly.

Inside, her heart was doing a happy dance yet it seemed every nerve in her body was tense. Alice slid the pram inside her gate and motioned for Claire to take a seat. Claire heard Pat speaking to Mark as she walked past their house and saw her cross over, joining with the new girl from house number four who was holding the hand of a small child. They both entered the yard taking seats next to Claire. Lisa from the end house emerged with a tray full of cups followed closely by Alice who had ducked inside to get the teapot and a cake.

Alice did not have much of a garden, the bare ground was quite compacted and Claire decided to leave Sophie in the pram. She hoped her baby wouldn't grizzle as she wanted to stay as long as she could. The feeling of someone watching over her was almost too much, and she tried to suppress the growing glimmer of hope she felt. Claire knew there was still a long way to go, and did not want anyone else hurt in the process or to be put in harm's way. She pulled her cap low and with one eye on Mark, who was trying to look busy in their front yard, accepted the tea and a slice of cake. If she was eating he would know she was not talking.

Alice cleared her throat and started to speak, talking loudly at first then lowering her voice so it would not carry further than the fence line.

'Thank you ladies for coming today, for the inaugural meeting of the BonBon Street book club. Now I think we should meet once a fortnight and once we all get to know each other I know I, for one, wouldn't mind if we changed the time occasionally to incorporate other beverages with our meeting.'

Alice winked and even Claire had to smile.

'Now let's all introduce ourselves properly before I set out the basic rules of the club, and then we can get down to business, how does that sound?'

Everyone nodded, then in turn said their name, and pointed to their house in the street. Of course they all knew where each other lived, it was to help Claire feel like one of them, as if they were all setting off on a journey together. She kept her head low as the bruise on her cheek was still slightly visible even though she had tried to conceal it with makeup. Sophie stirred and Claire stood and picked her up, apologising as she did, involuntary tears springing to her eyes as she saw Mark start to head towards them.

Pat jumped up taking the baby and calling out loudly.

'Oh we're fine Mark, stop worrying and go inside. I'm not going to let you steal this baby back now I have her.'

Pat moved a hand like she was shooing him away and sat down, smiling and talking baby words to Sophie, completely dismissing Mark before he knew what had happened.

'I'm sorry, maybe I should go, you don't want a crying baby here.' Claire apologised, panicking Mark would make a scene.

'You sit, no need to go.' Pat said it firmly, squinting her eyes as she watched Mark hover then disappear around the back of the house only to emerge again with the whipper snipper.
Alice held up a book and spoke softly.

'Now I have made this a ladies only group for a reason. None of us want to live in each other's pockets, yet with the world the way it is, I think sometimes, for many different reasons, each of us needs some support.'

Alice flicked the pages of the book as if she was describing the paper quality.

The new girl Maisie looked a bit confused and Claire's face started to blush as she realised all these people were about to be told of her predicament. Pat was still acting as if Sophie was the best thing she had ever seen, and Sophie was amusing Maisie's girl by blowing bubbles in reply.

Alice continued.

'Ladies I know some of you are thinking I'm acting a bit looney and I am. Please, please, listen and do as I say, as this is important.'

Lisa leaned forward in her chair.

'Claire… Lisa, don't look at her!' Alice scowled at Lisa and continued.

'Claire's husband seems to think it is ok to take his frustrations out on her face.'

Claire felt like they suddenly each had a hundred eyes which were burning into her, even though they weren't looking at her at all.

'I haven't spoken with Claire about this fully, I can tell you I have seen that look before, and I know how hard it is to get away from a life you no longer want. Believe me Claire, you are not alone.'

Alice continued to wave the book around and nod towards different ones as if they were asking her a question. To anyone watching it all looked normal. Claire's eyes welled up as Maisie snaked a hand across and squeezed her arm gently. The whipper snipper stopped and Alice again raised the book and looked squarely at Claire.

'So do you like crime stories too Claire, ones which might involve the police or detectives?'

Claire shook her head.

'Oh no please, I can't risk not being believed, I have to protect Sophie.'

'Right then, if we all put our books in the middle we can each take one of someone else's to read until we get a system going.'

Alice spoke swiftly as Mark started the small motor again.

'Is everyone willing to take Claire in if she can get away?'

They all nodded.

'Make it soon Claire, because I can't guarantee I won't take to him myself with a baseball bat.'

Lisa looked shocked. Maisie seemed to take it in her stride reinforcing Claire's original opinion she may once have been a victim too.

Pat was holding Sophie up in the air above her head, jiggling her and smiling to try and make the baby smile back.

'I will be leaving my front door unlatched each day, if you come at night, slip through the side gate and I'll leave a key under the pot at the back door. Wake me up and we'll go from there.'

Claire nodded. The others tried to tell her things swiftly as Mark came over calling her, saying her mother wanted to talk to her on the phone, and before they knew it he was in the gate and pulling the pram across the street. Claire looked at them all and taking Sophie in her arms mouthed the words thank you and followed him, stopping once next to Alice to whisper.

'I don't have a mother.'

'Don't forget.' Pat called out loud enough for Mark to hear. 'Next meeting is at my place next Saturday. Don't let her forget will you Mark.'

Mark slammed the door behind her and Claire trembled in fright, holding Sophie tight, the colour drained from her face as she fought within herself about whether to put the baby down or keep holding her as some kind of protection. Mark turned and Claire realised she was trapped in the front entrance and backed away towards the door.

'Good girl.' Mark came closer and squeezed her face between his thumb and pointer finger, twisting her mouth to an odd and hurtful angle.

'Keeping the neighbours friendly is probably a good thing after all, don't get too friendly though, I'll be watching you, and them. Mark my words.' He laughed then at his own little joke about his name and thrust her away heading towards the kitchen.

'I'm hungry, no one gave me any cake.'

Claire stayed frozen for an instant, then rushing to set Sophie in the cot, also made her way to the kitchen to make him some lunch. Claire heard the ring pull sound as he opened his first beer of the day. Today Claire, today, this might be it, don't upset him and maybe he will pass out long enough to get away. You have somewhere to go now, a few places, and people to help. Keep calm, keep normal, dear God I might be saved!

Mark demolished the sandwiches she made and with no thanks went out to the shed and came back with some tools. Claire nibbled at her lunch and wondered if a cake might soothe him. Sophie whimpered as he flicked on the drill and noisily started to do something to the front door.

'What are you doing?' Claire looked and bit her lip as she saw the deadlock in his hand and realised he was installing it. With no key to it she would not be able to get out. He had put locks on the gates and most of the windows were keyed as well. Claire backed away. Now she was very afraid. Stay calm, think girl, with his back to her she seized the opportunity to get the secret bag out and holding it in front of her made her way to the back door, silently thanking the heavens it was open. As she slid the screen he called.

'Where are you going?'

'To the clothes line.' Claire hesitated as she called back, listening to hear if he was coming.

A deep breath and she rushed over to the side fence and with all the force she could muster threw the bag over the fence into Pat's yard. The handles hung low as it skimmed the top and she half closed her eyes willing it to not catch, then let out the breath she had not even realised she had held, as it slid over and disappeared from view. Glancing back, Claire ran to the line and pulled the few towels off it, bundled them under her arm and sprinted to the gate. It was locked. Not wasting a minute Claire was back inside the door as Mark came around the corner.

'There job done, should keep us safe, you can't be too careful these days, watch the crime rate go up with all these people out of work, you mark my words they'll be looting any place they can get into.'

Claire stepped back to let him past. He was sick, she could see now how he had hidden it from them all, however this was heading towards delusional. She could not help him, he needed professional help. All Claire could do was keep herself and her daughter safe, whatever direction Mark's life took after this would be his decision, Claire knew she had to be strong and make her own.

Claire vacuumed the wood shavings off the floor, there was no key in the lock and she tried to turn it to see if it would open. Mark stepped up behind her.

'I put the key in a safe place, can't have the baby turning it and wandering out.'

Claire looked at him in amazement.

'She's a baby Mark, she can't even sit up by herself. How on earth could she open a door?'

Instantly she knew her voice had been raised, she backed away. Too late, the blow struck the side of her head and knocked her back against the door and she hit it then slid towards the floor, the kick caught between her now bent legs and her belly and it threw him off balance at the same time as he wriggled it free. He swung it back again and Claire turned more towards the wall shielding her face and tensing her body trying to make herself as small as possible, subconsciously trying to protect her vital organs. His boot hit her back and she cried out, the pain seeming to penetrate every part of her. She could feel blood start to drip out of one ear, the sound in it was like the roar of the ocean and she turned her head again, instinctively listening for her baby's cry with her other ear.

Claire felt him move away, the heat from his body was like a radiator and over the pain her body felt sticky from the heat. She risked a glance and saw him back away wiping his eyes then looking at her with a glazed expression. Part of her wanted to believe the Mark she knew or had known, hoping he could see the hurt he had caused, and realise he was ill. The other part of her knew an adult was always responsible for their actions, no excuses.

Mark backed away, she knew it was over for now and stayed still, not wanting to break his trance and alert him again to her presence. She heard him open the fridge and the familiar noise as he cracked the ring pull on another can. Her body was stiffening quickly yet she held on a bit longer before stretching her legs out and rolling over onto all fours. With the help of the wall she pulled herself upright. She rested there, every nerve alert to his movements, the television blared and the football commentator's voice called the kick off. If she kept quiet now he would drink himself into a stupor and she might get a chance. She had no idea where he had hidden the key, Claire knew she could go into the backyard and yell out for help, then hope someone heard her. Her main concern was Sophie, she needed to get her out safely and she couldn't throw the baby over a fence.

Claire tippy toed into the lounge room, he was fully engrossed in the game now and she slid into each room feeling in dark corners looking for the key or any clue which might give her a way out. The baby stayed quiet and Claire wondered if she knew today, might be the day, which would change her life.

A million thoughts raced through her head as she followed routine by preparing dinner in between holding an ice pack to her back whenever Mark was occupied and thrusting it under a tea towel when he came in the kitchen to get himself another beer. The game finished and his cries told her luck was on her side, his team had won. More beers were downed and his head sunk to his chest several times over dinner which he ate from a bowl whilst still sitting on the lounge. Claire bathed Sophie and tried to stay calm, it had to be tonight, tonight or never. Each of her ideas had come up against a brick wall. Mark had built a prison, a prison too hard to escape from for a woman holding a baby.

Claire's mind went over every piece of their property. The ladder was locked in the shed so she couldn't use it to get Sophie over the fence, the front door was deadlocked, again no key, the side gate was locked and the phone was in his pocket. Claire went over and over it, there must be something, she checked the baby again, her beautiful lashes resting on her cheeks as she slept through her mother's turmoil. Claire hoped she would never remember. Did babies remember stuff from before they could talk? She hoped not and she would do her best to erase them anyway, and give her precious daughter a better life than the one they were destined for at the moment.

Claire had wrapped Sophie up in a way which made it easy to grab her and hold her securely if she saw a chance to get away. She knew she would have to move quickly without letting panic take control. Claire sat by the cot listening as his breathing steadied and a slight snore escaped his lips. Once she was sure he was out to it, she sneaked into each room testing the windows and watching the darkening sky. He would not sleep for long and this nap would keep him awake long into the night, she had to find the way out soon.

Panic started to rise as she again checked all the exits. The door into the garage was open, he had the car keys and it was so long since Claire had driven a car it would probably be a disaster to take it anyway. She wasn't sure she could get it out of the garage before he heard it, and didn't think she was strong enough to push it, plus knew she had to keep Sophie close no matter what.

Something was gnawing at her brain, the car, what was it, the car. He would hear it she argued back silently, the car and the garage door. Oh my god!

She pulled the door handle of the car and it opened. Quietly she opened it further and there it was, the remote for the garage door sitting right there in the console, she almost flung herself in but stopped herself, no mistakes now Claire, you only have one chance. Careful so as not to touch the button she withdrew from the car and moved its door back so it was still slightly ajar, then made her way to the back of the car putting the remote on the floor on the side nearest to Pat's house. Be smart Claire, don't mess up now. On her

toes again, she slipped back in the house thankful she had thrown
the bag earlier as it left her mind clear to grab the baby and run.

Pausing for a moment, she ran a plan through her head, she
would go to Pat, as he would think of Alice at first. She was sure
they had a plan if she was able to get away, so could only hope the
boys would be there to protect Alice. Claire checked her own
clothes and for a split second wondered if she had time to get some
things for herself. Mark stirred on the lounge, turning slightly and
opening his eyes, her heart sank then soared again as they closed
and he seemed to settle again, the noise from his throat rumbling
louder than before.

Claire had to move. Sophie whimpered for a moment then
settled as Claire slipped her into the baby sling which held the baby
high up near her heart. Claire hoped its racing sound would settle
her and keep her quiet.

Here we go my precious girl, I wish you could have a father
only this is not the one I am choosing for you to have, and I hope
you don't ever hate me for it. Claire slipped out of the room and
down the short hallway into the garage. Two hands on the door, she
closed it slowly and took steady even steps around the car to where
she had put the remote. She hoped he would sleep through it as the
door rumbled open and planned to be in Pat's yard before he could
even get out of the chair. She would go straight to the gate in case
the door was locked for the night already. It was time and Claire felt
the adrenaline start to pump through her veins. Go girl go, it's time.
Crouching as low as she could with Sophie at her chest she pressed
the button and the door slowly started to rise, she cocked her head
listening for him then ducked underneath it, hitting the button again
to stop it in its path and again to make it descend again. As it
lowered she threw the remote under the door and saw it slide
beneath the car. Scrambling to her feet, Claire vaulted across the
drive smashing through a few bushes and without looking back, slid
into Pat's yard shutting the gate quietly behind her. She paused for a
moment then inched her way along the house and around to the back
door. Pat seeing the movement rushed to open it and ushered her
inside, drawing the curtains behind her as she did.

'Does he know you are gone?' Pat's voice was barely a
whisper.

Claire shook her head.

'Not yet, he's asleep. I don't think it will take long once he wakes, to know I am gone. I was hoping you and Alice had a plan.'

Pat touched her arm.

'We do, he won't hurt you again.'

As she spoke Pat was noting the dried blood on Claire's neck.

'I'll pop out quickly and put a lock on my gate before I fill you in.'

With a quick hug Pat was out the door and securing the gate.

'I couldn't hear anything so we will go with plan *A*. We have a safe house for you, one he won't suspect. I think we should drive, if he comes out I don't know if the police could get here quick enough, for you, or for him.'

Claire could see the anger on Pat's face, the adrenaline was still racing through her body as Pat had her crouch in the back of her car covering her and the baby with a blanket then locking the doors before starting the car and backing out into the drive.

'It looks all clear.'

Pat tried to look in each direction without moving her head too much, flicking her eyes as she triple checked her mirrors.

Claire started to shiver violently as the shock of what she had done took hold, her mind went blank, and the only sound she heard was the tick, tick of the blinker as Pat's car turned the corner. Sophie stirred as the tears from her mother's eyes dripped onto her face.

Number 8 BonBon Street

Pat

Pat was struggling to keep her feelings in check. Even though all her thoughts had been on Claire and the baby since she had found out their secret, she was still in shock it had been going on right next door and she'd had no idea. The poor girl, thank goodness Alice had noticed, and acted. Pat knew some of Alice's story and now Claire was safe, it may stop Alice committing an act of violence of her own on Mark.

Pat had turned away after checking out the front window when she heard the gate click closed, a tiny sound yet loud enough for her to know to scurry to the back door and usher the fugitives inside. Closing the curtain swiftly she had given them a quick cuddle before ducking out to securely lock the gate.

Pat had found the bag in the backyard when she went out to get her washing in. She had known then, the time was close. Claire must have had her own plan and today had given her both opportunity and a destination, something Pat was sure was a tipping point in the decision of today being the day. If only she had known, she admonished herself, even with everything going on in my life I should have noticed, or heard something, I should have known another woman needed help.

Pat knew it was a silly argument, no one ever knew what went on behind closed doors, she had to snap out of it and appreciate the fact she was here now for Claire, when she really needed it. Mark had no idea what he was up against. Even if Claire didn't go to the authorities, she had a growing army of people to help her now, both to keep her safe and to help her fight back if he came at her again.

Pat drove around the quiet streets, her aim was to look like she did not have a runaway girl in the rear seat. She stopped at the local garage and filled the car with fuel, reassuring Claire the coast was clear and it was all good, she was safe. Pat was making sure she had an alibi for being out in the car tonight, a fuel receipt and the carton of milk she purchased would be the proof she needed if questioned. What Pat didn't tell Claire was she was also checking they weren't being followed.

Pat's tummy was jumping all over the place as she tried to remain calm and act like it was a routine stop. Pulling out from the service station she turned back towards BonBon Street. One short stop and she would be home again to keep an eye on Mark's movements, Alice would be his first port of call. Pat knew the boys were home so Alice should be fine for now.

Pat pulled to the side of the road and made a quick call. Reassuring Claire again they were nearly there, Pat pulled back out and within a few hundred metres turned into an open garage. The door closed slowly behind them before she let Claire raise her head. The baby stared out of her tiny blanket with wide eyes. The poor little pet, Pat thought, I hope she never remembers the things she must have witnessed in her short life.

Two figures stood quietly at the door which led into the house and the woman moved forward swiftly scooping the baby out of Claire's arms as the man put his hand out to guide Claire into their home and take the bag from Pat. Pat nodded and slid back into the car. The garage door slid silently up and Pat backed out into the street, one more lap of the block and she turned into BonBon Street scanning both sides of the street as she slowly pulled into her own driveway and waited for the roller door to go up.

Pat jumped in her seat. Mark's face filled the passenger side window and she could hear the door handle pop back into place as he tried to open it. Unconsciously she had placed her hand on her heart and knew he would be able to see the startled and frightened look on her face. Pat recovered quickly and pushed the button to lower the window.

'Mark! You scared me.' She laughed nervously. 'I nearly jumped out of my own skin, what's up?'

'Where have you been?'

Pat frowned

'Is Claire ok? Is it the baby? Do you need help?'

Pat motioned to get out of the car hesitating as Mark spoke.

'No, no sorry, have you seen Claire, she went out earlier and I thought she may have popped over here.'

Pat felt the bile rise in her throat as he gained some self-control and spoke so smoothly as if he was out for a regular nightly stroll.

'No sorry I haven't seen her, I had to pop out myself for some milk.' Pat indicated to the carton on the seat in front of him. Mark glanced at it and she saw him thinking hard. He reached in and picked up the carton.

'I'll help you carry it inside shall I?'

Pat's eyebrows shot up, he was a clever piece of work.

'If you want to Mark, though I am sure I am perfectly capable of carrying a litre of milk.'

Pat had to choose her words carefully, she also felt nervous about being alone with him in her home and was trying to balance fear and bravery on a knife's edge at the same time, as well as thinking sensibly so she didn't give him the slightest indication she may know something. Pat felt if she failed now, the whole plan would be jeopardised and the unseen weight of it on her shoulders, an extra burden to bear in these crucial moments.

'Well if you insist, Mark. Could you put it in the fridge for me and I'll get the car in.'

Mark hurried into her house through the internal door. Pat knew he would be rushing to search every room before she came in, so she took her time hoping he would exit, before she had to. He wouldn't find anything of course and as they now knew, he had kept his true personality hidden, so she wasn't willing to trust him or his temper. Added to it all, the strong smell of alcohol as he leaned in her car had been almost overpowering, an angry drunk was something she was too old to fight off.

Pat moved forward into the garage and clutching the door remote in her hand, climbed out of the car and fussed about a bit near the boot, stalling for time, while also remaining visible to others in the street. Mark came out filling the doorway before making his way towards her.

'Milk's in the fridge, anything else I can do for you?' He looked smug as if he was goading her to say something.

'No thanks Mark, although next time I have some heavy milk, I know who to call.'

Pat saw him scowl slightly as some of his toxic ego drained out of him. Pat felt suddenly like she was the stronger one in the room and recognised Mark knew it as well. Turning on his heel he skirted around to the other side of the car and headed out. Pat pushed the button and didn't move until the roller door hit the ground blocking him completely from view. He's a coward after all, he picks on women to make his ego big. Look out Mark, I think your life might have taken a turn for the worse and I for one, am happy to watch it spiral out of control.

Pat went inside. She could tell he had been in the spare room, the door was always kept closed and was now slightly ajar, she felt dirty almost and a shiver ran down her spine. Claire and Sophie were safe, she had to concentrate on the positives, now to check on Alice and fill both her and Lisa in on what had happened tonight. Somehow Pat felt they would already know some of it, anxious, as she had been, to be ready, and watching out for any signs Claire may need help.

As she entered the kitchen she saw the outside light from next door glow above the high fence and heard Mark curse loudly and throw what sounded like an empty beer can against the fence. He would drink himself to sleep, and his muddled brain would try to work out where his wife had escaped to and how he was going to explain her absence to others. Pat had to keep her own head on alert and along with the others, they would save the lives of both Claire and her baby daughter, of that Pat was very sure.

Number 9 BonBon Street

Lisa and Brodie

Lisa watched closely as Mark and Pat exchanged words through the car window. She had squashed herself inside the hedge and with one finger held back a few leaves so she could see out the other side. Mark disappeared inside and she could see Pat pause before pulling the car into her garage.

Lisa wriggled slightly to try to get a better view as a hand touched her shoulder and she let out a brief squeal and turned, relieved to see it was only Brodie.

'And you talk about Harry spying.' He said it with a light tone to his voice. 'What are you up to my girl?'

'Shh!' Lisa put her finger to her lips. 'Mark is at Pat's and I'm keeping an eye on her. Claire escaped!'

Brodie immediately crouched next to her outside the foliage.

'Did she go to Alice? Do you want me to go over to Pat, make sure she's ok with him there. Wow good on her, so brave. How do you know?'

Brodie's thoughts tumbled out in a million questions.

'Shh!'

Lisa put her fierce look on and he closed his mouth tightly, and with his hand imitated turning a key and throwing it away to lock his mouth shut.

Lisa grinned as she turned her attention back to the scenario across the road in case she missed anything and whispered to Brodie.

'She went to Pat and then Pat took her out to the safe house before he even knew she was gone. Pat came back and he turned up. They rang me to say Claire and Sophie were safe. I wanted to check Pat was home safe too. He turned up almost as soon as she pulled in.'

Lisa's eyes were squinting now in the dwindling light as she continued.

'I don't know what's going on, he went inside Pat's house on his own and has come out again now, so I think it's ok. I didn't go over as I thought it might look a bit suspicious, and it might twig with him we could all be involved. Fingers crossed he hasn't worked it out.'

She glanced back at Brodie and reached for his hand.

'It's awful isn't it, the poor girl, and the baby.' Tears welled in her eyes and he gripped her hand tighter.

'We were only over here yet she couldn't call for help, what a monster. How could a man hurt his wife and child?'

Brodie stroked her arm gently.

'We couldn't have known, my love, and now we do, Claire and little Sophie are safe, thanks to you, Alice and Pat.'

The sound of the roller door touching the ground made them turn back and they watched as Mark pushed through the shrubbery and stomped his way into his own house. Even from here they could sense his frustration by the tense way he held his shoulders and clenched his fists. Lisa hoped he had a punching bag to release some of his anger, at least tonight it would not be Claire he used for the purpose.

Brodie helped Lisa as she untangled herself from the hedge then gathered her in his arms.

'I'm proud of you. It takes brave women to stand up for each other and I'll do whatever I can to help you all keep them safe.'

Lisa hugged him close, she could not imagine Claire's pain or terror and she was so grateful for Brodie and the love he gave to her. At times she could not believe any man would hurt a woman, when he held her safe and warm in his embrace. Her sister Sally had known, and Mark had better watch it, as Lisa would never forgive or forget a man who hurt a woman, it was not only women either, anyone who would hurt another human being. She could never help them all, she knew that, if she could only save one, and see them on to a better life, it may help her forgive herself for not being able to be there to save her sister.

Brodie kissed her forehead and gently steered her inside as the darkness spread its fingers across the yard. Once there he handed her the phone and moved to the refrigerator to get them both a drink, tonight they both deserved it. He heard Lisa as she spoke to Pat and opened a bag of crisps deciding, you couldn't be healthy every day.

Lisa's shoulders were slumped and the stress of the day showed on her face. It was not even quite twenty four hours since she had arrived back from Pat's to tell him about Claire and the plan they had made to turn the book club into a rescue plan for a woman and her child.

Brodie had wanted to storm over there, punch Mark's lights out and rescue Claire, Lisa had cautioned him and said they had to stick to the plan. They had let Claire know they could help her and she had to be the one to decide to leave.

Brodie didn't really understand how all the women knew what to do, it was like they had all been there yet none of them had. All had a sixth sense for a plan of escape if they were ever in need of it. Lisa told him it was because he was, and always had been, a strong healthy male so he never really had to think about his personal safety. Women did this every day, no matter what situation they were in. As Brodie shook his head at the thought of having to decide things like which street to walk down, or which public facility to enter, Lisa again complained of the injustice of it, it was so wrong. To feel safe should not be a daily issue.

He handed Lisa a glass of wine and she sipped it gratefully allowing the alcohol to settle her nerves and relax her muscles.

'Pat is fine, Mark carried her milk in for her. He needed an excuse so he could check the house in case she had hidden them there. No wonder he looked sour, Pat said he went to Alice's as well and the boys told him to well … you can imagine. I think we've put him off the trail anyway and hopefully we can keep their whereabouts a secret for a while. She did say she was a bit nervous, it's why she fussed around putting the car in, she was stalling for time, didn't want to get caught inside the house with him on her own. I told her we were watching out.'

Lisa drew breath and took another sip.

'Pat had word from Harry to say Claire had eaten and they convinced her to take a sleeping tablet so she gets a good rest. They are going to bottle feed Sophie for the night.'

Brodie nodded.

'They say it takes a village. I think Claire is lucky, as in spite of everything, she landed in this village.'

'I can't help thinking about the baby, the poor little thing, she will have to grow up knowing her father is a monster and probably having to go through horrible custody battles. I hope they are both strong enough to get through it all, today is only the first step.'

'So what happens now, tomorrow? Step one is done and so it would help to know step two.'

Brodie waited as Lisa licked the salt from her fingers, and washed the chips down with another mouthful of wine.

'Claire will have to make some decisions. Also, according to Pat, they took photos of her bruises, and the ones he gave her today will be fully out tomorrow, so Moni will take more then. If she will go to the police and get a restraining order, then if he does find her we will at least have legal paperwork in place. It's all a bit close to home, isn't it? We didn't have much time to pull it together. We will all have to be careful and do our normal routines or he will catch on to us, tomorrow he will be sober and have all his wits about him as well.' Lisa paused for a moment to gather her thoughts.

'If you can check up on them on your morning run I don't think it would look out of place. Alice and I are going to go for a walk in the afternoon so by then I'm sure we will have some ideas. A few days of being looked after will do Claire the world of good and make her strong in both mind and body. Pat's going to do her normal routine as we think he will still suspect her for a bit.'

Brodie cleared the glasses and started to make a salad for dinner. As he reached into the cupboard for the salad bowl Lisa spoke.

'I hope when we have a baby it feels safe and knows how much it is loved.'

Brodie froze and closed his eyes as a surge of joy raced through him. A baby, she was thinking about a baby, he wasn't sure how to react, he didn't want to scare her by showing how much he wanted one, he would be fine if she couldn't handle it and would accept her decision. If she could, wow he would not be able to suppress his happiness. Turning slowly he replied.

'I'm sure it will, with you as its mother I have no doubt.'

Brodie tore the lettuce and threw it in the bowl, with one eye on his beautiful wife. He saw her smiling to herself as she stared into space. A slow grin crept onto his lips as for the first time in a while he knew they were both dreaming the same dream.

85

Number 7 BonBon Street

Jason

Jason had seen the women of the street gather at Alice's place and part of him wanted to go and join them. He loved the company of women and liked to have them as friends, they always seemed more accepting. He had a few mates, mainly from work, although he did not push the friendships, afraid of what they would think if they ever found out.

His little secret had set him apart from other kids when he was younger, they had liked to dress up as dragons and superheroes, not their mother. The past reactions made Jason wary and anxious therefore adding to his loneliness.

Jason hadn't fitted in with any of the alternative groups at school either, they didn't dress up like their mothers. Jason had now come to terms with the fact he had a lifestyle which was different to other boys he knew. He liked girls, he just had to find the one who would allow him to dress like them and was not worried about frock shopping for their husband.

Jason knew it was a hard thing to do, and to ask of anyone. Kylie had tried, although he now realised at the heart of it, the foundation of their relationship had been wrong from the start, she was looking for freedom from her parents and he was trying to conform and fit in, show his father he was really a regular bloke. Jason knew the anxiety and guilt he felt were uncalled for, his father's inability to parent and show sympathy were the problem. Jason acted out in a subconscious way, aching for the love of a mother who had been torn away from him at a young age. Jason now felt, if his father had been the one to have counselling, they probably would have been better off. The more his father expressed his horror at Jason, the more Jason withdrew and acted out, often purging his wardrobe and going through cycles of accumulating wigs or makeup or clothes. If only, was a wish Jason always had, if only his mother had lived, if only his father had been able to see beyond his own grief, if only his dad had not seen him on that particular day and made a fuss about something which may have, in its own time, faded away. If only his dad had said, *I miss her too.*

Jason had seen Claire almost roll under the roller door, baby in arms and bolt into Pat's yard. He had stood shocked for a minute and was unsure whether to interfere or not. Claire looked afraid, so as much as Jason wanted to run to her, he decided to wait it out as he suspected Mark would soon follow if they'd had an argument, and it could be then, he would be able to help the most. He didn't know Claire very well, she always seemed to have her head down when he saw her, he thought she must be shy and Mark always did the talking. They had moved up from central Victoria was all he knew, somewhere near where Lisa came from he thought Mark had said, though it didn't seem as if they knew each other.

Jason busied himself in the front yard, keeping one eye on number six in case Mark decided to make a move in Pat's direction. The dogs could be secured in their own space now, so he wanted to fix up the garden a bit and get some shrubs established enough so they couldn't dig them out. A noise at Pat's made him pause and he saw her car pull out of the garage and she raised a hand as she passed him though he could tell it was an automatic gesture. Pat was by herself so Claire must be still in the house.

Jason continued digging and weeding as the sun slowly started to disappear over the hill and had almost decided to call it a night, when Mark stormed across to Alice's house demanding loudly to speak with his wife. The boy's stood shoulder to shoulder at the door and told him to, well, take a long hike, she wasn't there and he backed away again crossing the road as headlights swung their way around the corner. Pat was back and Jason saw an angry looking Mark approach her car.

Jason dusted his hands and watched. Mark was talking to Pat through the passenger window, there were no raised voices, so he kept his distance. Mark entered the house on his own and soon came out again empty handed and departed, stomping his way home while cursing to himself. Jason stood for a minute as the setting sun fanned her last rays across the sky then turned and made his way inside. Something was not quite right and Jason decided he might slip over to Pats later, to check all was well with her. It's what neighbours were for and both Pat, and Keith, had always been kind to him from the moment he moved in.

Jason had a quick shower to wash off the sweat and dirt from the garden, made a toasted sandwich and checked the dogs. Their loud snores always amused him as they lay flat out exhausted from their exciting day and with their bellies full from a dinner eaten much too quickly. Checking up and down the street he sprinted across to Pat's door and rang the doorbell. The porch light sprang on and he called softly.

'Pat, it's me Jason.'

Pat opened the door and ushered him inside, sticking her head out and looking at number six before closing and dead locking the door after her.

'What's going on Pat? Is Claire here? I saw her run in and I've been watching all afternoon in case you both needed me.'

Pat burst into tears and Jason stood awkwardly then reached out his arms. Obviously there was a lot more going on than he knew.

Number 5 BonBon Street

Alice, Jay and Charlie

Mark had stormed up to the door, yelling loudly from the time he entered the gate. Alice had hung up the phone a few minutes previously and knew Claire and Sophie were now safe. She had felt relieved the boys were both here and glancing out the window was in time to see Mark come out of his door. Alice had run to the lounge room and the boys, seeing her face had jumped up with questioning looks on their faces.

'I don't have time to explain. Mark is coming across the road, he's a wife beater and I arranged for Claire to get to a safe house. He likely thinks I'm hiding her here.'

Alice's shoulders were tense and the boys both wrapped their arms around her as they digested her words. The sound of his fist banging on the door made it seem like the whole house was shaking and Alice was suddenly very afraid. What had she done, had she put her boys in danger? Charlie pushed her gently aside as both he, and Jay, stepped towards the door hissing quietly in unison.

'Hide!'

Alice crouched behind the lounge hidden from view, her body starting to shake as she realised her phone was still in her room if she needed it. She heard the door open and Mark's angry voice echoed around the room.

'Where's my wife, I know she's here.'

Surprisingly it was Jay who spoke next and she could hear their bodies as the muffled sounds of them obviously pushing against the door jamb, standing their ground, shoulder to shoulder against Mark.

'Piss off you scumbag, she's not here and even if she was, we would never let you near her.'

'You're a pathetic piece of shit.' Charlie wasn't holding back. Alice inched forward. The sounds of pushing and shoving made her pull back trying to make her body as small as possible, it was a feeling she remembered from her childhood and one she knew Claire would recognise as well.

The door slammed shut and Charlie raced in to watch Mark's retreat out the window. He was gone, to curl up and lick his wounds. Alice knew he would be back she would have to be careful.

Jay drew her out gently and they both sat on either side of her as she told them the story of the last few days. Alice told them about going to Pat's and how she had found out about the abuse on Claire, the fake book club, and their hastily made plans which had thankfully resulted in Claire's escape.

'He has a baby, did he hurt her too?' Jay felt his anger rising.

'I don't know, it's crazy. All we really know about Claire is she had a bruise on her face which was unmistakably caused by a human hand and didn't know how to get help. We may never find out all of it. I'm so glad she is safe for now, and thank you, both of you, for what you did, I don't know what would have happened if you had not been here.'

She squeezed their hands tightly and saw a look pass between them.

'We know we are not always the best sons to you, Alice, we do love you, and are truly grateful for everything you do and have done for us.'

'Without you we don't know where we would be, because Dad's bloody useless.'

As usual they both talked as one, each finishing the other's sentence. Alice put one arm around each of them and promptly burst into tears.

'I was scared when you answered the door, what if he had hurt you, you have to be careful, people like Mark don't forget and he probably thinks she is here still. He'll be watching us.'

'Don't worry, we will hang around the next few days, one of us will always be with you. If he comes again we should call the cops, take one of those restraining orders out against him. Don't worry Alice we won't let him hurt you or Claire. Where is she anyway?'

'Not far, maybe the less you know the better for now. If any of our neighbours call for help, know we are all aware of the situation and are helping in our own way.'

Alice considered these two young men in front of her, she was proud of them, they were overwhelming at times, and it wasn't their fault, it was their fathers. It was his lack of attention which burdened her with the responsibility and the harder parenting of these two, plus the fact she wasn't even their mother, instead someone he had married to look after them. It had all combined to increase the pressure she felt. Even though Alice may not have been there at their birth, she was proud of herself for getting them through these teenage years, especially as she had no previous experience and had been pushed in head first.

'I have to go to out for a while to check on things and I want to spend some time with Pat because she may need both the company and the support. Pat was the one who took Claire away, so he might realise and target her too. Keep your eyes open boys and don't hesitate to call for help, we all have to stick together to save them.'

They both nodded and one of them said, or was it both.

'Don't worry Alice, he's a bully and we won't let him hurt anyone else in our street, don't you worry.'

Charlie heard Pat return and they all watched from behind the curtain as Mark approached her, entered her house for a few minutes, then left to return to his own home. They could see Pat had positioned herself away from him and visible to others if need be. Alice hoped he didn't start drinking as it could result in him being irrational, as well as violent. They each nodded as they saw Jason watching on and realised he must of heard the commotion here earlier. Alice made a mental note to fill him in properly, the more man power the better.

With the boys help, Alice made a hasty meal and they had decided a night driving lesson was in order. Charlie elected to stay behind and keep his eyes open for any movement at number six while Alice and Jay went for a lesson and a secret check up on Claire. They would not tell Charlie until they came back so he would not be lying if asked by anyone. Alice wondered if Mark would report Claire missing, probably not, and part of her wanted to keep the boys out of it.

They pulled out of the driveway and onto the street. There were no lights to be seen at Mark's, and they had fussed about when putting the learner plates on the car, in case he was watching, so he would know their intention.

Charlie waved them off then slipped over the fence to Jason's to give him a brief rundown on the events of the day. One of the dogs barked as he tapped on the door and called quietly, but getting no answer he retraced his steps, and returned inside to watch the television. He felt restless and found himself frequently getting up to check the street searching for any movement. What a low life, he had better not come near Alice or he'd cop it, he and Jay would not hold back. If their father was not here to protect his wife, his sons certainly would. They gave her a hard time but lately Alice was standing up for herself and by doing it, was holding a mirror up for them to see their behaviour towards her. Neither of them had liked the look of what they saw and talked about why they seemed to set out to hurt Alice the most, when at the end of the day she was the only one who really cared and had been there for them. Charlie wondered what would have become of them if she hadn't. His father never altered his life for them and their mother hadn't cared at all, it seemed two boisterous boys were too much for her and so she vanished herself from their lives, never to be heard from again.

Charlie wandered through the house, he wasn't often alone and it felt quite strange. He opened a few cupboards and drawers not really knowing what he was searching for. From his parent's room he could see clearly across the street, there didn't seem to be any movement over there at all. Charlie checked up the street and with no sign yet of his brother and step mum returning, he slipped out the door and into the garage.

Pulling down an old wooden crate he could see it hadn't been touched since the last time, though a layer of dust had settled on the old piece of cloth he had thrown over the top. Glancing over his shoulder, in case someone was watching, he pulled back the cloth and delved deeper into the box. This is where he had found the camera, part of him wished he hadn't and he knew there was no going back. He hadn't even told Jay about it and he wasn't quite sure why, whether it was to protect him from any knowledge of it or something else, he wasn't sure.

Scratching through a few papers his hand caught on a square velvet box like the ones they give you in a jewellery store. He pushed it open with his thumb to see a small diamond ring nestled inside. Charlie was confused, he snapped the box shut and as he placed it back in the crate, an envelope wedged in the side caught his attention. Unsealed and folded in half he opened it slowly to look inside. Caught in the corner was a delicate chain, a small flower charm swung from it as he took it out and he caught it in time as it fell free, realising the chain was broken in two places. A tiny letter was engraved on the back of the charm, the grime on it and the fading light made it hard to make out. Charlie thought it was an *S*.

Charlie heard a car and lifted the box up sliding it back into place, he slipped the chain into his pocket and wandered out into the yard trying to look relaxed even though his insides were jumping all over the place. He made his way to the front gate as the street light flickered into life and looked again. Even though there was no car in sight, Charlie decided he did not want to risk returning to snoop any more tonight.

The box was a mystery and after seeing what was on the camera Charlie felt frustrated and was trying to work out what it all meant. The worst of it was he had sneaked off with it the first time for a lark, wanting to test it out and see if it still worked, also thinking he would then maybe surprise Jay with a few cheeky shots. It had whirled into life as soon as he flicked the switch and the photos had flashed before his eyes. He had been horrified more and more by each one and fumbled in the rush shut it down, his head reeling from what he had seen. Charlie had not known what to do and was somewhat dazed when old Harry had stormed up, grabbed the camera and demanded to know what he was doing hiding in the hedge.

Charlie had taken off, his mind not making sense of any of it and the next day, as he mulled it over, he hoped Harry would not look. If he did, he would certainly not be happy and would blame Charlie straight away. Charlie felt it would be hard to prove he didn't use it, it wasn't him, if he could get it back and check the dates as well as all the photos stored on it he might be able to work out who it belonged to. It certainly wasn't Alice's and he hoped it wasn't Jays, they were so close surely he would know. Jay was quiet, much quieter than him, they were the same yet different and they had an understanding, a twin thing. Charlie was sure he would know if it was Jay. Other than him, it would have to be his dad's, and the thought made him feel sick, the bile rising up in his throat, wondering if a member of his family could enjoy doing this, and be able to hide it on a daily basis. It was sick.

Charlie had tried to make reason of it over and over. He tried to recall exactly what Harry had said, could it be his and he had hidden it in their shed? Harry was always coming in the yard putting the bins in or some other such excuse. If it was true, how could there have been shots of him? Then again, the ones Charlie had seen of house number three were mainly of Harry's wife Monique, dancing in a leotard, her legs extended as she stretched at different angles. Charlie's mind went over everyone in the street, rubbing his forehead as the images he had seen flashed in his head and he ticked off each residence. You never knew what people were up to behind closed doors he thought.

The headlights startled him as they turned in the driveway and he moved forward to open the door for Alice. He would keep it to himself a bit longer and hopefully would get up enough courage to ask Harry for it back. Yes, it's what he would do, the less people who stumbled on those photos, the better. I'll take a deep breath and do it tomorrow he vowed.

Alice was smiling as he ushered her inside, it was probably relief as he had turned down the offer for his lesson. Today had been long enough, for all of them.

Number 3 BonBon Street

Harry and Monique

Monique had picked up her phone and saw Lisa's name flash up on the screen, it took her by surprise and she hesitated for a moment before answering. She had been feeling down all day after Harry told her he had seen the other females from the street gathering in Alice's front yard having some kind of meeting. Harry had assumed she must have forgotten about it, however he soon realised when she burst into tears, once again she had been excluded from a group and he had done his best to console her. Seeing Lisa's name brought it straight back up to the surface. Monique's voice cracked as she answered and she felt for the table to guide her into a chair as Lisa spoke.

'Moni, it's Lisa, I have rung about a delicate matter and I hope and pray you can help, can you?'
Monique didn't even get time to answer.

'I don't know if you saw today, we had a book club meeting at Alice's this morning. Look, it is not like we didn't want to ask you, but Moni, something terrible has been going on and we couldn't, not if you were to be part of the plan.'
Monique was still wondering what on earth Lisa was on about, a book club, she likes books, what thing was terrible?

'Lisa, Lisa slow down, you are not making sense and anyway I'm getting used to not being included in things. You know it's a bit upsetting not to be asked, then again, what do you care? … And now you want me to help you? It's not exactly the way to go about things you know.'

Tears welled in her eyes as she spoke, the build-up of the day letting loose on her tongue.

'No, no Monique, we did want to ask you, please listen, we needed it to look like you weren't involved. Please, I knew it would hurt your feelings but it was the only way we could do it. Please say you will help, please, we are all counting on you especially Claire.'

'Claire, what has she got to do with it?'

Monique was really confused now and turned the phone to stare at it in bewilderment. Lisa continued.

'Claire is a victim of domestic violence. It's Mark, he's been hitting her and Alice found out. She doesn't want to call the police so we invited her to a meeting, spur of the moment thing, and we were able to tell her we would help her if she had the chance to get away. By the look on Mark's face when they left we are hoping she does it soon. This is where you come in, please Moni, we need your help.'

Moni was shocked.

'What! Oh my god, is she ok? The mongrel, oh and the baby, he didn't hurt the baby too did he. I'll call the police now, he has to be stopped.'

'No she doesn't want that, she's scared he would get off and come after her. We want to hide her somewhere if she can get away. I'm so scared Moni what if he's hurting her now? What if we are too late?'

Lisa started to sob on the end of the phone and Monique softened and allowed her a moment for the tears to flow.

'Right, so what do you want me to do, do you need Harry?'

'We need both of you, this is our plan.'

Lisa almost whispered as if she was worried her voice would float across the street and alert Mark to what she had devised.

'It's a bit close to home isn't it?' This was Moni's first reservation when Lisa had finished. 'What if he hears her voice or the baby cry?'

'We can work more out later. For now can you help? You and Harry? We have to keep a united front on this, he will be looking for any cracks, once we have her out safe we can make new plans, with the virus and the restrictions we thought it best for little Sophie to keep them close.'

Monique's head was still reeling as she hung up. Lisa's voice thanking her and telling her to be on alert, as Claire's opportunity could come at any time, was still bouncing around inside her head. The poor girl, how could any man hurt the woman he loves. Moni shook her head to clear it and hurried outside to find Harry so he could help her prepare in case they received some precious guests.

Harry heard Monique calling and checked his watch, it was nearly five and he was done fiddling around for the day anyway. He sensed urgency in Moni's voice and when he saw her face, his concern grew, he had no idea what she was going to say and would never have guessed it once he did.

Harry was as shocked as Moni, and the father in him wanted to march over there now and show Mark a thing or two, mainly with his own fists. Harry was struggling to keep his temper in check as the rage filled him and desire surged to rescue a defenceless girl and her tiny baby.

'We have to stick to the plan Harry.' Moni spoke firmly to make sure he listened. 'The best thing is for Claire to get out herself if she can. It will give her time to make decisions and for him to calm down. It has to be her decision or she will end up back in the same situation, with him promising he will never do it again. Claire has to be convinced herself there will be no going back, it will be her inner determination which will save her now and in the future. We have to trust her and hope she gets out before it's too late.'

Harry knew it was true, they would be ready. Mark had better watch it, if the dirty mongrel found out where she was, Harry would not hold back and he would get the police involved no matter what Claire said. He wasn't sure about the plan, it was all a bit too close to home. Then again it might put Mark off, as he will think she will run further away. It might be the best idea after all.

The women had done a good job, one, for Alice to notice and then act so quickly, and for the others to back her up, no questions asked. The men too would rally, as this was not a gender issue, it was a human rights issue, as every person had the right to feel safe, no matter what.

Harry followed Moni's instructions and they soon had everything ready. He then made a pot of tea and staring into space as the tea went cold in the cups, they both sat worried and anxious discussing the different scenarios swimming around inside their heads. Harry felt pleased as Moni confessed.

'I'm so grateful they rang me. It is a good plan for now, and Harry, is it terrible to say I'm also glad they had a reason for not asking me to the book club, not they didn't like me?'

'Not at all my sweet, I told you, they are good people and making you feel sad for one afternoon may be about to save someone's life, no, two someone's.'

Harry leaned over and rubbed her arm gently.

'If I was you, I would think about it. My darling girl, they thought you were the perfect person for the job and I think that alone should tell you all you need to know about what they think about you, you are one special lady.'

Monique put her hand on his.

'Thank you Harry, you are right again, and I have been a bit quick to jump to conclusions. Now let's get a meal together and hope we get some visitors soon.'

Monique's phone rattled as it vibrated on the table.

'She's out. I'm leaving now. I'll call soon. Be ready.'

Those four quick sentences contained all the information they needed, and they were ready. A bed was made and Harry had washed the old cot he had in his shed and they had fashioned a makeshift mattress for it out of some foam, fresh towels and clean sheets, it would do for today. Monique stood wringing her hands and watching her phone, she had prepared a light meal and now all there was to do was wait.

Harry paced up and down like a restless tiger. Three times he approached the internal garage door then turned back. They had to wait for the call.

It seemed so long until the sound of the ringing phone made them both jump.

'By the time you push the button I'll be there.'

Pat's voice sounded in control. Monique nodded and Harry hurried, pressing the remote as he did and again as the car drove carefully in so the door was closing before the car even came to a stop. Pat motioned to the back door and Moni hurried to it gathering the baby in her arms as Claire, eyes wide, extracted herself from the car. Harry took a bag from Pat and once she was back in the car gave her a nod and the door slid open again and she reversed out disappearing from view in seconds.

Harry ushered Claire in placing his hand on her back for a moment then removing it swiftly as she flinched. He apologised quietly and could have kicked himself for his insensitivity, a man's hand is the last thing this girl would need touching her.

Claire went straight to Moni reaching out her hands for little Sophie. Sensing Claire's need to keep her baby close to her, Moni relinquished her hold and pulled a chair out for Claire to sit.

Harry moved towards the window in the front room. 'Don't move the sheers Harry, each of us has a job and if he spots us looking over there he might get suspicious, we have to bide our time and let everything go along like normal. You could probably draw the curtains anyway, it's dark enough now to not seem out of place.'

Harry stepped away, although not before glancing through the side window and seeing young Charlie from next door loitering around his front yard. He had his eye on that one. The camera was still something he had to consider, he'd been thinking about it when Moni called him this afternoon then had put it to the back of his mind. At the moment, he had more important things to think about. It was not a priority, but it could go to the top of his list for him to bring up the subject with that young fellow very soon.

Harry turned back. Claire was trembling and Moni knelt at her feet holding Claire's knees and imploring her to stay calm, she was safe, they would protect her, everything was going to be alright. Now they were here Harry was unsure of the next move and decided normality was the best bet so clearing his throat, he spoke.

'Now young Claire, let's have a cuppa eh? Don't worry child, we'll keep you and this beautiful girl safe, but first I have to ask, do you need any medical help, this afternoon, did he hurt you some more?'

Tears spilled over and ran down her face and again Harry felt the rage try to fight its way to the surface. Claire shook her head slowly.

'No, I'm ok. He did hurt me. I think it will be ok. It does hurt though, now I'm here.'

Claire lifted the baby as high as she could and twisting awkwardly, raised her shirt to examine the injury and show them the damage.

Harry felt the bile rise in his throat as he saw the ugly bruise had already spread its thick blue and black fingers across her body, the centre of it deep and dark.

'I'll get some ice first before I make the tea, what about some cake too, are you hungry?'

Harry tried to give her a cheerful grin, it didn't make it to his eyes and he turned away, glad to have something to do.

'Here Claire, let me have Sophie, I won't hurt her, I promise.'

Moni's calm sweet voice seemed to seep into Claire and she allowed her to take the baby.

'We'll have a cup of tea then we might give her a bath, what do you think? Alice is bringing some baby formula over later and I thought we might give it a try, only for tonight, so you can catch up on some rest. It won't hurt her and you have some big decisions to make so a clear head will be needed.'

Moni seemed to keep her hand on Claire at all times in one way or another and it brought tears to Harry's eye's as he watched his gentle wife say and do all the things Claire needed right now, and most of all earn her trust.

The kettle boiled and the icepack started to drip as Harry wrapped it in a towel and placed it gently on Claire's back. He held it there as her shoulders shook and she sobbed silently into his wife's shoulder.

Number 4 BonBon Street

Maisie

Maisie had turned up at the appointed time for the inaugural book club meeting. She had felt a bit awkward when Pat had knocked at her door and relieved when she had only introduced herself, issued the invite then left not indicating at all if she would have liked to be invited to come inside. Even in those brief minutes, Maisie realised Pat was a no nonsense type of a woman and when Savannah, eyes wide with curiosity at someone being at their door, poked her head around the doorway, Pat's easy laugh set them both at ease.

'So I'll see you tomorrow then, and bring the little one. Everyone is welcome of course…except the men of the street!'

Pat's jolly laughter seemed to echo around their foyer long after she left.

Maisie could see Savvy was nervous and excited at the same time. She was not sure if there would be other kids there but it would do the little girl good to mix with people. Maisie was nervous herself. To meet Alice face to face was going to be huge and keeping her surprise to herself would be hard work. Maisie still wanted to suss out the whole scenario and be really sure of her actions before she approached her with the truth.

Maisie hurried Savvy to the door before she chickened out and was glad when Pat joined her on the curb to cross the street with them. Although Pat was talking to her, Maisie was very aware she was also noting the movements of her own neighbour Claire and her husband Mark. It all seemed a bit mysterious, as if something was not quite right or as it seemed.

Books, she discovered, were the cover for a far deeper problem. Maisie had been confused at first as Alice babbled on, although as soon as she caught on to their hints, her insides churned, and she struggled to contain her feelings. Savannah was naturally drawn towards the baby and Pat encouraged her to hold baby Sophie's hand and sing her little songs. It also helped to cover their voices Maisie realised. The women had already hatched a plan and

Maisie of course, nodded her agreement, if she was needed at all they should call her. Maisie snaked a hand across to touch Claire's arm lightly to let her know she was there for her.

Amazingly with few words, though the right ones, they all understood what was happening and swiftly formed a tight bond to protect Claire and the baby. The husband had been the one to break up the party. He had stood glaring at them most of the time between trying to look busy in the garden. They all saw the change in Claire as she was led away, her shoulders hunching forward curving her body around the baby and hanging her head low as he steered her through their gate and into their house, closing the door with, what only could be described as a strong push, as if warning them away from it.

Maisie had piped up first.

'What if he hurts her now?'

Alice looked directly at her, her eyes made Maisie feel unbalanced, they were her mother's eyes right down to the last fleck. Alice only had one thing on her mind, so even though she seemed to be staring, Maisie knew she wasn't registering the eyes looking back, the familiar turn of her face or the colour of her hair. Alice did not know she was looking at her sister.

The women tried to remain looking relaxed in case Mark was watching, flicking through the books and talking quietly amongst themselves. The plan was brief, a start if Claire chose to get away, the rest could be worked out later. Everyone in the street would be told, so if she noticed even a tiny thing Maisie could speak to anyone for assistance.

Maisie thought it was a good plan and they asked if she could befriend Monique and Harry, so it would not look odd if she went over there. Pat gave her a scrap of paper with all their numbers on it and Maisie scribbled hers in the front of one of the books before passing it to Lisa. One way or another they would all get messages and updates.

Savannah was playing happily in the dirt, drawing a trail for ants to follow as she placed cake crumbs on the ground along it. Alice raised her voice and declared the meeting over and also suggested they meet again the following week, at Pat's place, around the same time. They all agreed and after Alice refused her help to clean up, Maisie took Savannah's hand and headed home. As she closed the door, the little girl looked at her with big eyes.

'I liked the baby Maisie, can we get one too? Then I would always have someone to play with.'

'No, not at the moment Savvy, though maybe one day. I'm sure Claire will let you play with Sophie another day and Pat did say for us to come over tomorrow as she has some toys you might like to play with.'

Savannah's eyes lit up even more, her little world had expanded tenfold since she woke up this morning.

'Come on then Miss Socialite, let's make some lunch if you can fit it in after having cake.'

Savannah giggled as Maisie tickled her belly and they made their way to the kitchen.

'Why are you smiling?' Savannah looked at her intently as Maisie lifted her up on to the bench to help make their sandwiches.

'I think I did the right thing at last Savvy, I think we picked the right street, fingers crossed we get to stay here forever.'

Maisie smiled as Savannah pulled one finger over the other.

'Me too Maisie, I love our new house. Can a baby be a friend Maisie?'

'The special thing about babies Savvy, is they are everyone's friend, because they don't know how not to be.'

Savannah nodded, satisfied with the reply, she herself was excited and couldn't wait to see what the nice lady Pat had at her house, maybe she would let Savannah borrow some toys if she promised to look after them very, very carefully.

Finishing their lunch Maisie set Savannah to do some colouring-in while she checked all her equipment and cleared away the lunch utensils. Standing at the sink her mind wandered back to the events of the morning. Alice appeared to be a kind person, to do this, to get involved with the situation of someone she hardly knew was brave. They would all have to be careful and if Claire ever changed her mind there would be hell to pay from Mark. Maisie hoped Claire would not weaken. She had gone out to the fence between them several times listening for any noise of disruption. If she heard something she would act she decided, she had enough backup in the street and would never forgive herself if something happened to Claire and the baby on her watch. It all seemed quiet, the only sound a television, and it wasn't blaring so hopefully she would be able to hear anything over it.

Somehow Maisie felt Claire would not be one to call out in case he threatened Sophie as well. Snapping out of her daze she realised she could no longer hear the scratching of pencils and turned to see Savannah's head drooped over the page, pencil still in hand. It had been a big day in their little world and possibly, hopefully, they would have many more. Maisie smiled at Savannah's drawing, it was a picture of their street and the bright colours displayed how happy her little sister was since moving here. Quietly she lifted the little girl and laid her onto her makeshift bed. Savannah stirred slightly and smiled before rolling over to dream her four year old's dreams.

Number 6 BonBon Street

Mark

Mark was furious. He knew the bitch next door had something to do with Claire escaping, he was sure of it. She wouldn't get far. Anyway, where would she go? He had been going to get in the car to look for her but he'd been drinking and didn't need to get pulled over, not today. Stuff her, she'd be back, wouldn't be able to live without him and she had no money, he had been careful to keep an eye on his wallet and nothing had ever been missing. Cops would probably pick her up and bring her back, woman with a baby wandering around at night confused, yes that's what would happen and she wouldn't tell, she'd be glad to get back to her bed and have a roof over her head.

Thoughts rattled around in his head, he had searched the bedrooms and it didn't look like there was anything missing. Claire couldn't go far, the baby would need things, maybe she had snuck out for a walk, her little social outing this morning making her bold. He'd show her! She can't have gone to the police or they'd be here by now. Besides, it was not as if he had done anything wrong and those bruises well, she was clumsy, she said so herself. He would wait her out. Let's see how sorry she is when she gets back, it won't be long. He cracked another beer open and took a swig. The woman next door seemed so smug, though he had searched her house as best as he could in the time, and there were no signs of Claire, and there had been no other milk in the fridge when he put the carton in. It was something though, it niggled at his brain. Maybe another drink would bring it to the fore, who knew? He'd give it a try.

Mark settled back in the chair as the news bulletin flashed across the screen. Shit this bloody virus, he'd had enough and wished they'd shut up about it. Probably wasn't even real, yeah, probably a conspiracy made up by the government, frigging scare mongering so they could get total control. Well stuff them. He threw the can at the television and watched its contents splash across the screen and run onto the table below. He would give her another hour and he would go to pick her up. She's probably waiting at the bus stop for a bus that never came anymore. Stupid bitch he thought, then, as if someone had snapped their fingers his eyes closed and a loud snore exited his mouth.

Number 8 BonBon Street

Pat

Pat switched on the porch light and heard Jason call softly to her as if his face was pressed up against the keyhole.

'Pat it's me Jason.'

She opened the door and glanced next door to make sure Mark was not lurking in the shadows somewhere, then ushered Jason inside. His kind face and worried look was the end of her and she promptly burst into tears soaking his clean shirt as he held her gently. Not rushing her to stop, Jason carefully guided her to the lounge and settled her before searching for a box of tissues.

'I'm sorry Jason, it has been a big day and I was so relieved it was you, I've been so wound up and since I dropped her off I have felt, um, afraid yes, he frightens me. I'm glad you're here. So sorry you must think I'm silly.'

Jason placed the tissues next to her while making soothing noises before turning back towards the kitchen. Pat heard the tap running and the flick sound of the kettle as he turned it on. By the time he returned with not only the promise of tea but also a glass of water, Pat felt she had pulled herself together enough to apologise properly.

'Thank you Jason I'm so sorry, I think I needed to let go and I am grateful of your support. Now let me fill you in properly.'

Pat ran through the details of the day and explained they hadn't told him, one, it had happened so fast, and two, they thought if Mark attempted to ask him anything, it would be better for Jason to look surprised and not involved.

'I was so scared when he came up to the car. All I could think of was thank god, as without really thinking earlier, I had hidden the bit of milk I had, in a jug at the back of the fridge and put the carton in the bin. I had no idea he would go into my house, I was

careful not to leave any trace Claire had been there. I'm so glad she is safe now.'
Pat paused.

'Seems like I haven't drawn a breath' she admonished herself, 'now let's have our cup of tea while it's hot.'

Pat's admiration of Jason grew. As the tea soothed her nerves and she felt the anxiety of the day slip away, she was glad of his company and so glad he was close by if she needed assistance of any kind, it gave her a feeling of safety.

Jason asked all the sensible questions and even offered to guard her house all night outside, or grab his swag and camp in the hall next to the front door. Pat almost agreed, then the strong (and maybe foolish) woman inside reassured him she was fine, she had a phone and would not hesitate to call the police if needed. Jason still insisted on checking all the windows, the gate and the doors were locked. Finally he held out his arms again and gave Pat a big hug.

'I'll pop over again in the morning Pat and don't hesitate to call if you or anyone else needs a hand.'

Pat let him out the door and knew he stood for a moment to hear the click as the deadlock fell into place. Flicking off the light, she returned to the lounge room to pick up the empty cups and thought again how lucky she was to live in this street, even Claire was lucky in a sense, at least here someone had noticed, at least for tonight Claire was safe.

It seemed a million plans swirled in her head and Pat thought the quicker she showered, and hopped into bed, the quicker sleep may become her friend. If she let it, the fear Mark was trying to spread would come seeping under the fence to tie her up in knots, and she too would become a victim. It was one thing tonight Pat could control, and she was not going to hand it over to a low life. Bring it on she thought as she stepped out of the shower and glowered at herself in the mirror. She had to smile at the image.

'Yes go on bring it on and never underestimate an overweight woman in her sixties.'

Pat spoke out loud then cheekily poked her tongue out at herself. With a big grin she marched to the bedroom, slipping between sheets and loudly calling out to the universe.

'And if you wake her in the night she'll be a naked, overweight woman so look out, it won't be pretty.'

Take that, was her last thought as her friend called sleep rolled over her, closing her eyes and leading Pat away to the land of dreams.

Number 9 BonBon Street

Brodie and Lisa

Lisa was up early, she touched Brodie's face lightly as she slid out from between the sheets and quietly shut the door so he could get some extra rest. They had talked a lot last night, their concern for Claire and her sweet little baby made the questions of having one of their own come out and their discussion had been frank as well as heartfelt.

Lisa wandered out into the yard, the air seemed somehow sweeter and the dream of holding a child close filled her head. It was time, Brodie was right. Lisa could see it took a village and yesterday had shown her what a wonderful village she had. Everyone in this street, except for Mark of course, would help her protect her child. It would be hard for her, yet surely the joy should overwrite the fears she had. Lisa looked up enjoying the warmth of the sun's rays on her face. It certainly did feel like a new day.

Leaning over the gate Lisa glanced up the street. It seemed everyone was up early, busying themselves in their yards, calling out hello and waving. Lisa knew they were all secretly checking on each other while silently letting each other know they were there for help and support. Squinting she saw movement at Harry's and willed everyone not to all turn at once. Harry pulled the cord of his hedge trimmer and it was like a ripple as shoulders lowered and the invisible tension eased slightly as Harry acted as normal. The message was loud and clear, they had gotten through the night and all was well.

Lisa saw Alice disappear inside and Jason rally the dogs to play fetch with them in the street, glancing across to Pat's repeatedly until seeing her come out and wave. He then leashed Pippa and Clyde and strode off on his usual morning walk.

Lisa's mental checklist was now all ticked off and plan *B* was to wait until lunchtime, then herself and Brodie were going up to Harry and Monique's to speak with Claire and try to work out the next safest option for her. It was almost like a willy-willy had spun up the street yesterday throwing up dust and turmoil before disappearing, leaving no visible sign it had even been there, though the things it had dislodged were hiding, waiting to decide which way to fall.

Claire and Mark's house was silent. Lisa wondered if he was there sleeping off a drunken stupor, or if he was out looking for his wife and daughter, a new day making him realise what he had lost. Lisa decided it wasn't even a question, his only thoughts would be how he was going to explain her absence.

Lisa felt Brodie's warm hands slide around her body and melted back into his embrace as he whispered in her ear.

'Come back to bed my sweet we have babies to make.'

'Babies? My, my, we will be busy, I wonder how fast you'll be able to run pushing a double pram.' Lisa grinned at her own playfulness.

Brodie spun her around and with horror she realised he had nothing on!

'Brodie, what the? Thank god we have a hedge. What if the neighbours see?'

'They would think you are one, very, lucky, woman.' Brodie emphasised each word, his eyes wide as he tried to make it sound like a serious statement.

They both dissolved in giggles and Lisa pushed him towards the house, the laughter now filling the garden as Brodie strode, like a model in heels, pulling her by the hand as tears of joy filled her eyes and ran down her cheeks.

Harry opened the door at their first knock. Lisa thought his greeting was a bit loud and appreciated the effort he was making to make it look like a social call. Monique came into view raising her finger to her lips whilst half scowling at Harry.

'Shh! Sophie is sleeping, come on through, I have the back windows open, though our voices shouldn't carry far. Pop the radio on low Harry, it will be enough to cover our conversations.'

Brodie took in the disarray of the kitchen. Used cups and utensils were stacked haphazardly on the sink and the remains of a long forgotten breakfast remained on the table. Claire was huddled in a large chair covered in a crocheted rug, her eyes looked heavy but clear and she smiled at them shyly before glancing away as a faint blush rose up her neck, spreading across her face. Lisa went straight to her, kneeling down, and taking her hand.

'How are you Claire? You are so brave, the whole street has pulled together to protect you. Mark can't hurt you anymore.'

Claire's blush deepened.

'The whole street! Oh no, does everyone know? They will think me such a fool.'

A tear rolled down her cheek and Brodie searched his pocket for a handkerchief.

'No they don't Claire, not at all. We all think you are brave. Don't blame yourself. This is Mark's fault, not yours, and we want you to know we are here for you, all of us. This is only your first step and I don't really know how you feel, I would think the rest is certainly not going to be easy either.'

Claire reached out her hand to him.

'I'm not going back and I'm so grateful.'

Claire's eyes welled full of tears and as she spoke, they overflowed and rolled in big droplets down her face.

'I don't have any family to turn to and for all of you to help me, a complete stranger, I don't know how I can ever repay you. You, all of you, have saved my life, and Sophie's. I hate to ask for more help, but what do I do now?'

The tears turned to sobs and Lisa leaned in holding her tight, whispering in her ear, *it's ok, it's ok.*

Brodie and Harry exchanged looks across the room. Moni too, was weeping quietly, she looked drawn and unkempt as if sleep had evaded her as they guarded their precious visitors for the night. Harry put his arm around her and sat her down.

'Looks like it's time for a bite, eh, let's eat before the little one wakes up, she's quiet as a mouse she is, hardly heard a peep last night. Now Claire why don't you come and show me what you would like, I'm not much of a cook but I can butter a mean piece of bread!'

They all felt Harry's little joke ease the tension and worry in the air enough for each to take a deep breath and gather their feelings and thoughts together. Lisa felt a part of her soften. Her anger at Harry about the camera abated slightly as she watched him care so gently for Claire, and Moni too. Maybe she had jumped to the wrong conclusion, she might do a few subtle investigations before accusing him.

Claire seemed eager to help and take the focus off the problem at hand, and herself for a moment. Lisa watched as Harry slipped up and brought a smile to the girl's face, like a grandparent guiding and reassuring, yet teasing and almost making her giggle.

They ate in silence, each selecting, or trying to select, the right words in their heads before letting them out to help Claire make, what they all hoped, was the right decision.

A cool winter breeze glided silently in swirling the drapes and making the shears billow across the room before settling them back into place. Brodie stood and pulled the window closed then collected the plates as he also broke the silence trying to prepare them all for the discussion ahead.

'Now I'll wash up, while we come up with step two. We can't keep them here forever and Claire, no matter where you hide it is no life looking over your shoulder for ever. I think the first step should be a strong positive one, so Mark knows you won't back down. I think a visit to the police for a restraining order and a solicitor are the way to go Claire. That's my two cents worth and I am only putting it up for discussion, the longer you hide the harder it will be.'

Lisa opened her mouth.

'But.'

Brodie raised his hands.

'I know, *but,* it would be better for them to see the bruises and know the truth. All I'm saying is, it should be in the discussion.'

Harry agreed yet Moni thought they should give it another day, to let Claire settle down. In the end they all saw the sense. Claire looked empty and had an almost vacant look as her fate was discussed by them all. In the end she was the only one who could decide.

A faint gurgle from the next room told them all Sophie was awake and Brodie watched as his wife held the little girl close for a moment before passing her to her mother. Sophie's big blue eyes surveyed them all and Claire spoke at last.

'Thank you all so much. I have no family, nowhere to go, and I am scared, scared of Mark and what he might do. What I want most though, is, I want Sophie to be happy and safe, safe most of all. I'm also angry. Angry at Mark for doing this, angry at myself for taking it and I'm not going to take it anymore!'

'That's my girl,' cheered Harry.

'So what now?'

'I want to go and speak with him, tell him to get out of my house. One thing my parents did for me was leave me enough money for a house deposit, and when Mark lost his job, he told me he took the payment exemption from the bank because of the pandemic and hasn't paid an instalment since, as far as I know. The house is in my name. Even though I loved him, my parents always instilled in me to look after what was mine, and now, as it has all turned out, I'm glad I pushed it with him.'

Her eyes were wide and she slammed her fist on the table.

'So I want him out.'

The few things rattled as she hit it and an apple toppled out of the fruit bowl and rolled slowly across the table.

Sophie, thinking it was a game, slammed her rattle on the table too then looked around waiting for a reaction, a big dribbling smile on her face. They all laughed and leaning their heads in together started making firm plans and decisions on her future.

Brodie raised his hand in a final wave as Harry and Monique stood at their door.

'We must do it again soon, thanks again.'

Taking Lisa's hand they slowly strolled down the street, murmuring quietly to each other. Glancing across at number six they both drew in a breath as the curtain moved and they knew Mark was watching them.

They both spoke at once.

'She is so brave.'

'He's alive in there.'

'She is brave, I'm a bit scared for Mark now, and I think he will get a shock when he knows how determined Claire is. I bet he's a coward and will run away with his tail between his legs. Good on her for not backing away and it will be good riddance from our street.'

Lisa laughed.

'Claire's going to ring his family and send them the photos of the bruises! I can only hope he cuts all ties and leaves.'

'Well I know a good Italian family if we need back up. *The Mafia on Bonbon Street*, mmm, could I suggest it for a television series? I could play the hit man and…'

Brodie stopped as his arm tugged and he realised Lisa was standing still staring at him.

'A hit-man? Who is this man I married? He is certainly full of surprises today.' Lisa spoke in a light hearted way and with a smile on her lips. 'I hope nothing happens to Mark now or I'll be looking at you sideways mister.' Lisa was laughing again while poking him in the belly.

'Oh dear, it feels wrong to be laughing about a situation like this doesn't it?'

'No' he said grabbing her about the waist. 'It's a way of coping with something we can't even begin to imagine.'

The dogs barked as they passed number seven and they heard Jason call to them from inside. A frown shot across Brodie's face and Lisa stopped again.

'What is it?'

'Nothing, well nothing I want to talk about yet. Have you ever thought you never know what's going on in people's lives? You go along thinking everyone is living the same sort of life as you, and when something happens it shocks you into knowing they're not? For me the thing which is hard to understand is everybody seems to be wearing some kind of mask, which they hide behind when they step into the street. It makes it hard to know the truth don't you think?'

Brodie looked her full in the face.

'Does it make sense, to you?'

'Yes, I know what you mean. You never know what people are up to, at the end of the day, as long as they are not hurting anyone, does it matter?'

Lisa wondered what he was thinking about and knew he would tell her in his own time. Her own thoughts flicked back to

Harry and the camera, knowing again, today was not the day to confront him about it, or to tell Pat and Alice what she had found.

Brodie took his wife's hand again before glancing back at Jason's. What he had seen was something he was still trying to get his head around too, today was not the day for it, and he tried to push the image of Jason in the dress and wig out of his mind. Tomorrow would be soon enough to work out how he felt about his friend, what Mark did behind closed doors was unforgivable however, what Jason did, well really it was none of his business.

Number 7 BonBon Street

Jason

Jason felt restless, the word was seeping along the street about Claire and Sophie. They were fine and she was going to confront Mark about his actions. Jason marvelled at her bravery and it surprised him a bit as he thought she would have snuck away, gone to another state or back to family. Seems she was tougher than she looked.

Jason had seen Lisa and Brodie walk home last night, and pondered how he would approach Brodie to try and explain. Half of him argued he didn't have to, he was just sick of the war in his brain and wanted to get it over with. He had slept fitfully and wasn't sure if it was because of Mark, wanting to keep one ear open in case anyone needed him or if it was the Brodie thing, it had been laying heavy on his shoulders. It was guilt. He felt guilty, and ashamed as well, he didn't want to be different, it was something he had no control over. As simple as it sounded it didn't solve the battle raging in his head.

Leashes in hand he opened the back door, a heavy dew lay on the grass and the air had a chill to it. The days were getting longer as spring seemed within their grasp yet winter still stood firm reminding everyone it was not done.

The dogs seemed subdued too. It was a bit early for them and Jason had to urge them out of their kennel. Jason wanted to be back ready to support Claire and hopefully, throw Mark in his car, he would push it out of the street himself if he had to.

'Come on you two, I know it's early. How about I give you the rest of the day off, what do you think, come now, Pippa, Clyde.'

They wagged their tails and sat while he clipped their leashes on and their enthusiasm returned as he turned down the lane and the reserve came in sight. Once things settled bit more he might ask Maisie and Savannah to come with him, he had enjoyed the company when they stopped to talk. Jason had always had more women friends than men, a lot of them had been Kylie's friends, and he never quite fitted in with their footy loving husbands. The fact they also believed him to be a cheater, meant the friendships had drifted away, as they thought they should take sides. Maybe also, it was Kylie, who had finally delivered a bouncing baby boy and he felt the final tie to her slip as he looked at the happy photos of her new family.

The dogs splashed in the creek and bounded back to him hungry for their breakfast and as Jason's tummy rumbled loudly, he realised he was too. He let the dogs wander back unleashed until the final turn and they both sat obediently for once while he caught up. Clipping Pippa's first a faint call brought his head up, and before he knew it, Clyde was off bounding up the street as young Savannah clapped her hands in delight at the sight of them. Clyde responded with a drooling sloppy smile, knocking her over and licking her face. Running as fast as he could Jason was waiting for the crying to start, all he heard were chuckles of laughter as the girl stood up and encouraged Clyde to come in the open gate and play.

'Miss Savannah, I think you might be as naughty as Clyde today, are you?' Jason smiled as her big eyes looked up at him and he could see the change in her face as she realised he was teasing. Maisie called out loudly.

'Savvy where are you?' She appeared through the door a look of astonishment on her face as she was confronted by a giggling child and two damp labradors.

'What! Savvy, um sorry Jason I didn't hear you knock.'

'Don't be sorry, because I didn't. Clyde decided on his own he would come for a visit, didn't he Savannah?'

Jason gave her a conspiratorial wink and she slipped her hand into his in agreement.

'Can they stay and play Maisie, pretty please'
Maisie looked between the two.

'Well I think there may be more going on here than I know, you had better come and finish your breakfast, and explain why you were out the front without permission first young lady.' Maisie faked a fierce look which only made Savannah giggle again. 'Maybe then, I might consider it.'

'Actually if you don't mind Savannah, the dogs need their breakfast too so what about I bring them over when they are finished and we can have a play out here, I think the sun is going to stay out for a bit. What do you think.'

The little girl nodded and pulling Maisie's hand commanded;

'Come on Maisie, they'll be back before you know it.'

Jason and Maisie burst out laughing.

'Seems she is four going on twenty four today, see you soon and I'll make us a coffee.'

'Thanks Maisie, I thought if we play out here I can keep an eye on him.' Jason jutted his chin towards Mark's house. 'You heard the news?'

'Yep, yes I mean, Pat called. Fingers crossed he does the right thing.'

Holding her hand up with the crossed fingers, Jason watched as she closed the door and he wrapped the leads loosely around the dog's necks to get them across the street.

'Well that goes to show naughty doesn't always turn out to be a bad thing, does it Clyde?'

Clyde turned and looked at him as if he understood every word and even looked a bit smug, as if he had planned it.

It was good to be out talking with people again, not about work either, just about whatever came to mind. After all this was over he might even thank Claire, it might help her understand good can come out of a bad, terrible event, her courage was bringing them all together to be a real community. If a slip of a girl could do this then he should have the courage to tell people the truth, be more open and not hide behind the curtains any more. His mind now set full of determination, Jason dished feed into the bowls and felt a weight slip off his shoulders, he had a plan now. With either decision there would be consequences, a life of guilt and fear of being found out, or a life of honesty and acceptance. Although he would be judged by some, they would never be the ones important in his life.

'Eat up you two. I'll have a shower and some toast and we can head off to our playdate.'

Both dogs looked at him anxious for their food and shivering with a kind of excitement as if they too, knew today was a different kind of a day.

Number 5 BonBon Street

Alice

Alice was ready, a bit nervous, yet very determined. She was going with Claire to confront Mark, everyone else would be watching and the police had been informed.

Claire was so brave and even though Alice knew this would not end today, at least it was a step forward for her, and knowing she had so much support and showing it to Mark, would blindside him for sure.

The police had been kind and Monique said they had spoken at length with Claire about her plan. Claire was determined not to hide and they were going to issue the restraining order this morning at eleven, giving her time to confront Mark. The police showing up to present it, and tell him the conditions of the order, would show Mark, Claire was not going to back down and would pursue formal charges if he broke the conditions.

Alice hoped he would slink away into a hole somewhere never to reappear, relinquishing all rights to his daughter as well. Alice knew what it was like to have a bad father, several in fact, the memories blurring until she couldn't really remember which one had been her real one.

Alice's phone rang once and she didn't have to speak as Harry's voice relayed a brief message. They were keeping Sophie with them and Claire was slipping out of their yard onto River Parade at half past ten. Alice was going to meet her there, leaving the house in the car then coming back to park out the front as if she had Claire hidden somewhere else, not in BonBon Street at all.

Alice put down the phone and reached for her purse. Sometimes you have to step outside the square, stand up for what you believe in, protect other people because it was the right thing to do, and most of all help another woman when they needed it the most. The consequences would be dealt with later, whether good or bad they were in the future, now was the time to act.

With this determination in her head Alice strode out to the car, if Claire could escape this monster then Alice could take control of her own life and start living. Jonathon was never going to change and it was time Alice moved on too, with her boy's support they would all benefit. The engine kicked over and without even glancing across the street she pulled out and drove carefully to the corner, pausing only to check for traffic. Alice turned the wheel to the slow tick, tick, of the blinker, glancing back over her shoulder she made sure her car could not be seen from BonBon Street, and slowed almost to a stop checking her mirrors, as she rolled the car half off the road, to reassure herself she was not being followed.

Claire stepped out and glided into the car sinking low in the seat, Alice could see the strain in her face and reached over to pat her arm as she pulled back out fully on to the street.

'Are you ok?'
Claire nodded.

'I don't want him to find Sophie, seems crazy we are only a few houses away from him. I feel safe with them, and Monique is so kind.' Claire began to straighten up.

'Are you sure you can go through with this? You have the photos Claire. Do you need more time?'

Claire shook her head and as Alice glanced over she could see the glint of determination in her eyes. So young and so brave, Claire had a lot to get through. This would change her whole life and Sophie's too, as she would always be overprotective of her. It was not such a bad thing and it was something Sophie could live with, Alice thought. Alice pulled into a drive-through and ordered two coffees, taking a last few minutes to evaluate what was about to occur before it would be time to head back. She pulled into the car park and turned off the motor.

'We don't have to talk unless you want to, I just have to say, no matter what happens, I want you to know we will all do everything possible to keep you safe. Hopefully Mark will do the right thing, get some help and move on. It's all I can hope.'

Claire was pale but she nodded.

'Yes, I hope so too. I think deep down there may be a good person underneath, he needs to learn a better way to deal with stress.'

Alice knew her mouth had dropped open as Claire held up her hand.

'Don't worry, I've had months to think about this, I'm not softening, I hope he is man enough to seek help so he never does this to anyone else. I have thought about this from every angle Alice. I think the shock of it happening so soon is what has thrown me, I knew it had to be soon or I don't know what would have happened to me. It's why I had been hiding Sophie's clothes, one piece a day so at least I could keep her warm. I somehow knew time was running out.'

Alice watched as Claire turned to look out the window.

'It's time Alice, now or I spend the rest of my life looking over my shoulder. I'm ready.'

Alice squeezed her hand and started the motor, the clock ticked over and as long as things went to plan the police would show their presence before Mark could react.

They hadn't gone far, yet far enough to take Mark's attention away from Harry's house if he saw them. It all seemed ok as they pulled back into the street, and Alice drove to the end before turning around and parking in front of her house facing the escape route if needed. She squeezed Claire's hand again and they both noted Harry raking the verge on the road and Jason, with Maisie, talking in Maisie's front yard as Savannah threw balls for the dogs, her laughter sliding through the air cutting through some of the tension which seemed like an invisible curtain hanging over their street. Pat was seated on her front porch. She rose and walked to the gate as they opened their doors.

Alice saw Claire take a deep breath and straighten her shoulders as she stepped around the car and they joined hands to cross the road. Brodie and Lisa were standing on the far corner of Pat's block and Alice saw them embrace as they watched them step up onto the kerb. The curtains fluttered and she saw a shadow as it moved behind them. Fear suddenly gripped her, what if he had a gun. She had never thought to ask Claire, did he only threaten with his fists? Claire stopped at the gate.

'Leave it open,' she whispered. 'I'll go ahead.' Alice stood with her bum against the gate, her eyes darting to and fro, searching the ground for a rock or stick to hold it open as Claire approached the door. It seemed so trivial yet she could feel the panic rising as if finding the prop was more important than anything else going on here today.

The door flung open and Mark's body seemed to fill the doorway like the Incredible Hulk rising up larger than life. Alice saw Claire straighten and hold her shoulders back as he spoke.

'Claire I was so worried.' He glanced at Alice and she could feel the hatred rush towards her. 'Come in, where's the baby? We'll sort this out, I had a few too many is all, you know me, come in and we can talk.'

Claire stood firm and he reached out to take her arm. Alice stepped forward, it seemed to incite him and he spoke in a low and threatening manner.

'You stay out of it bitch, this is my wife and my family, none of your business.'

Even though she knew what he had done Alice was still shocked at the sudden change, and the anger he was displaying before her. Claire flicked her arm out of the way and stood firm.

'I called your mother. I told her what you did, what you've been doing Mark.'
The shock of her words registered on his face.

'You did what!' Mark shouted as he glanced up and down the street, now noticing the movement in every yard. He lowered his voice.

'You shouldn't have Claire. I'll explain to her you made a mistake, come inside and we will sort this out, I'll stop drinking, it was a bit of frustration, you know, losing the job, this virus thing, and with the baby crying, it was all a bit too much. You know Claire, you could've been a bit more understanding.'

Alice saw Claire throw her head back and Alice herself was shocked. He had tried to blame Claire, oh my goodness, the man was so arrogant. Mark grabbed Claire's arm, this time getting a firm hold and pulling her roughly.

'Come in, we'll soon sort this out.'

'I wouldn't do that if I was you.'

Alice felt a movement behind her as Brodie pushed past and at the same time the police opened their car door, she had not even heard them arrive.

Brodie went to speak again as the officer stepped forward to intervene.

'We'll take it from here Sir.'

Brodie stepped back.

'Are you alright Miss?'

Claire nodded.

'Yes and thank you.'

Mark started to backtrack.

'No need for you fellas to be here, the missus and I had a bit of a blue is all, I'm sorting it now.'

Alice could see Mark was worried, yet his arrogance made him confident he would be able to talk his way out of the situation.

'Sir, we are here to present you with an apprehended violence order. I will explain the full terms to you, so you understand. The most important thing to tell you is the minute your wife and I walk away from here, it comes into effect. Do you understand what I am saying Sir?'

Mark's mouth had dropped open. Alice could see he was fighting back words.

'Claire, you called the cops! Are you serious? Honey, come on, we can work this out, I only had a bit too much to drink.' He held his hand up to the policeman as if to say can't you see I'm innocent.

Alice's stomach churned in disgust, there were so many emotions fighting within her, she was rigid with the fear, afraid one of them would escape. The main one wanted to smack Mark in the mouth, and it was the hardest to keep down. Alice knew if she acted on it, it would make her exactly like him.

'If you are finished now Claire, we might have a word with your husband. I will be in contact with you as a follow up, later on today, to see how you are, and to run over the conditions again. Ok?'

Brodie had stepped back and was ready to escort Claire out of the gate. Claire and Alice had already planned to do the reverse of their trip here, the exception being Harry was going to pick up Claire at the coffee stop, in case Mark was still around. Alice's consciousness now registered who was looking out for them. Maisie was standing on the edge of her yard. Jason had moved in closer, probably to give assistance to Brodie if it had been needed. Lisa with Pat were standing together outside of Pat's front gate, trying not to stare, yet both wanting to be a sign of support for Claire.

Claire took one step back and turned. Her face was so pale Alice wondered if she was about to faint. The officer reached out as a support, then indicated to his off sider to step forward. The police woman took Claire's arm and moved back towards Alice and the gate. Claire turned once more.

'Do the right thing Mark, I'm not coming back and my lawyer will be in contact with you. I gave her your mother's number as well as a copy of the photos of the pain you inflicted on my body. Do the right thing, go back home and get some help. Don't ever come near me, or Sophie, again. I'm not pressing charges yet, though don't think I won't. It's over Mark. Goodbye.'

Claire allowed herself to be led away, the officer whispering quietly in her ear. Alice thought she would be crying, however the determined young woman was showing her last ray of strength for today, fighting back against the bully, a lioness protecting her cub. There would be time later, for the tears to fall and the fear to creep back to haunt her nights.

Alice felt her brain suddenly click back into gear and she hurried across the street, thanking the officer as she went. Jason and Brodie were standing guard as Claire sank into the car, the energy seeping out of her body almost visible as the reality of what she had just done took hold. The female officer crouched and took Claire's hand.

'Don't hesitate to call the station if you even suspect there will be trouble, we are here to protect you. Always remember we can't help you, if you don't tell us. Do you understand Claire?' Claire looking even paler now, and drained of emotion, nodded she understood. The police woman shut the door and signalled to Alice now would be a good time to leave.

As Alice pulled away from the curb she realised her hands were shaking. The policewoman, she also realised, had never once taken her attention away from what was happening at the house, always watching her partner whilst looking after everyone else as well. Alice felt a bit crazy, although also knew she had to say it out aloud.

'I'm proud of you.'

Alice felt Claire's silent acknowledgement rather than saw it. I'm proud of you she said again in her head, not only of Claire, the bravest of them all, but of the police, her friends, and her neighbours, everyone in BonBon Street.

The blinker ticked its repetitive noise as they rounded the corner and headed hopefully towards Claire's new life.

Number 3 BonBon Street

Harry and Monique

Harry was raking the verge again even though there was not even a leaf on it to pick up, he didn't know what else to do and felt he should be outside keeping an eye on things while Claire was resting. The solicitor had called with the message Mark's mother wanted to speak with her again, Claire needed a rest before she felt she could return the call.

Harry couldn't quite grasp how he felt, the father in him boiled with anger, the grandfather in him showed the maturity to beg him for calm, only do what could be done and let others take their roles to fill in where he couldn't. The conflict was real and it reminded him of an old song about a father and son both seeing the world through different eyes. Both those people were inside of him and the conflict was real.

Harry had gone out to pick Claire up and returned as soon as he could, again thankful his garage faced the other street. It had been a funny decision when he built here at the time and he had made sure it blended in with both street scapes. To Harry, and his first wife, it made sense to face the house itself towards BonBon Street to give them a chance of making friends with a smaller group of people, than with the long stretch of houses which seemed so impersonal along the Parade at the time. It was different now trees had grown and gardens bloomed, here at least in their tiny street people waved as they went past and it felt more friendly, at least to Harry it did.

Harry sighed, he felt a bit tired, the baby was so good, no trouble at all, it was only both he and Monique had stayed up late with Claire as sleep eluded her and they didn't want her to feel alone.

It had been a big day. Harry was pleased with how it had all gone. Mark still was unaware his wife and child were so close across the street. They all knew this could not go on for too long, as little Sophie would need to get outside and Claire would need to breathe the fresh air and start to rebuild her life.

Harry had left not long after Alice and hurried back with Claire wanting to have her safely inside before Mark left the house, if he was going to. It had all gone smoothly. Claire was quiet and withdrawn and Harry could still feel the tension in her as she, and they, waited to see what Mark's reaction would be.

His dear sweet Moni had coffee and cake out when they returned. Holding Sophie, Moni was singing softly to her as she swayed gently from side to side in a movement Harry felt all women were born with, whether they eventually had children or not, it was a movement they carried within.

The police car was still parked at number six and Harry left the girls to rest, even persuading his wife to have a lie down for a time while the baby slept. It felt good to have them in the house, he missed his family, and having Claire here made him realise how much. Maybe he would try to contact them again and let bygones be bygones. Yes, he would try one more time, as maybe they were hesitating as well, Harry knew bad words had been spoken on both sides.

Harry turned as he heard a car start and as the police car went past, the male officer in the passenger seat raised two fingers to the side of his forehead in a kind of half salute. Harry dipped his head and turned back towards the house, he might pop the rake away and go for a wander to the reserve, it might help him lose the restlessness he was feeling. It would be a waiting game now with Mark as the key, his reaction would let them know how easy or hard the next steps would be, Harry was happy to be here for the long haul. Until Sophie was grown, he silently pledged to protect her.

Harry wandered up the street glancing at each house, his hands pushed deeply into the pockets of his shorts. He had wanted to be friends with everyone here, and since Moni had moved in he thought they would have been friendlier with people than they were. Maybe this brave little girl, and it's what she was to him, would be the glue which brought them all together. He was proud of them all. Harry contemplated the events of not only their street but the state of the planet at this time. Even this virus thing was bringing people together. The world was a strange and wonderful place, humans think they are so smart, and then Mother Nature gives a push and shove to remind us what's important.

Harry stopped at the top of the incline and took a deep breath, he had gone far enough and the tension in his shoulders had eased slightly as he let his mind work through the events of the day, the past and the future. Tomorrow was another day and Harry hoped it was going to be a good one.

Number 4 BonBon Street

Maisie

A loud crash and what seemed like things being thrown around made Maisie jump. She slid the door closed to lessen the sound, then pushed it again to leave it slightly open as she still wanted to know if Mark was out of control.

Savannah was quietly watching *Play School* on the television, waiting for her favourite part where they looked through a window to come on. She was learning fast and could recite the days of the week, months of the year and count to thirty. Maisie supposed she should be asking about preschool, yet with the pandemic having nearly everything shut down, she had put the idea of it aside, no use worrying about some things for now.

The job was proving to be easier than first thought. The surprise was Maisie had not expected to be feeling emotions about the neighbourhood so soon. The situation with Claire had really brought people together and so far taken the focus off Maisie being new here and also awkward questions being asked. All the focus was on her next door neighbour's house and as bad as the situation was, Maisie was thankful. This was where she wanted to stay, put down roots for both her and Savannah. Jason was nice and she had been glad of his visit this morning, the fact they had met out the front also meant, so far, no one had been in their house as yet, so her equipment and questions about it were yet to be dealt with. The non-appearance of Jonathan meant she was really filming a normal street with people going about their days in this new social distancing society. Maisie had received word from her boss about her new position, and the thoughts which had been cast around the office were another week should see her winding this one up, whatever other information they were getting it must be from somewhere else. Maisie had asked if she could be filled in on what happened, or a few more details. As usual she felt her request had been glossed over with the old, *need to know basis*, reply. Seeing as Alice was her sister, or half-sister at least, was the only reason Maisie wanted to know. In her other jobs she had never cared, as long as her section of the system was correct and allowed justice to take its course. She didn't mind, although occasionally months into another job something would crop up on the news, a side story or a gap filler which rang bells in her head, and she would know somewhere along the line she had made a difference and a funny kind of satisfaction would fill her for a time.

The goings on in the street had caught her up and made her a part of it, and in some ways Maisie was grateful. Claire's situation, bad as it was, had allowed her to jump the first awkward meeting stage with everyone and simply become one of them. One of her foster mothers once told her good could come from bad, and she had never really understood, somehow now she could see how it could work.

Maisie was glad Claire was safe, she seemed nice and Savannah had taken to the baby at the book club meeting. It would be a long road ahead for her. Mentally some of it would never go away. A thought occurred to Maisie. If she could live through what she had, and if Alice, once she knew her better, told her story, they would probably not be far from Claire's. Abuse came in many ways and forms and often from the people you least expect. If you are strong enough you could get through it, and she, Savannah, and most likely Alice, were proof of it.

The banging seemed to have stopped and she realised Mark was moving about in the yard, the banging had come from the shed and she crossed her fingers hoping he was packing his tools to leave, not building a weapon to take them all on. Maisie smiled, well you never know, when something snaps in a person's head, they could be capable of anything.

Jason's company this morning had been good, she could see they would be mates, and there was a gentleness to him which defied his tradesman knockabout looks. Savannah was especially taken with Pippa and Clyde and had pleaded afterwards about getting a puppy. Maisie had told her she must learn to take care of Jason's dogs first to make sure she was ready for the responsibility.

They had agreed to a bbq dinner at Jason's so she intended to ask him then, about maybe them joining him sometimes on his walks with the dogs and letting Savannah feed or wash them sometimes. Maisie had thought about getting her a little kitten, now she was thinking, maybe a dog would push them out into the world more as they would have to socialise it, as well as themselves, it was something to consider in these strange times. Maisie also knew it was a serious thing to add another permanent change into their little family.

Maisie had been watching the boys, they were like one person split into two and Maisie had yet to meet them properly. To even watch them walk together was a strange thing, it was if they were joined in some way. Alice had done well considering her husband was never there and Maisie thought this was probably the toughest age, independent yet still so dependent. They would get a shock when they found out the tiny four year old across the street was really their aunt!

This street was certainly full of untold secrets. It would be good to get this one out in the open. After Claire's bravery everything else seemed almost insignificant and Maisie wondered why she was worried about telling. What was the worst case scenario? Alice might reject her? Well, her mother had already been awarded that trophy, it may open old wounds yet at the end of the day she would survive. Part of her was eager to get it done, tell the tales and start getting life sorted, the only thing holding her back was Alice.

At the moment Alice had a lot on her plate in helping with Claire. Maisie thought the timing was bad right now, it may overload her, and Maisie wanted Alice to have a clear head when she made their relationship known. Although there seemed to be plenty of time, Maisie knew, with each passing moment Savvy missed out on someone who would genuinely love her, and she had already missed so much.

Maisie's surveillance camera whirled and she glanced at the screen, Alice was out taking one of the boys on those endless driving lessons and Maisie had seen the other one walk toward Harry's. She had a pretty fine angle on this one, and it was fine-tuned only picking up objects of a certain size etc. so if say, a cat ran along the fence, it wouldn't go into melodramatics about it.

Maisie stood at the window and gazed through the curtains, she could still hear the goings on next door so she knew it wasn't

Mark sneaking over, in some kind of revenge for Alice helping Claire. A slight movement caught her eye and she pressed a few buttons to see what the camera had initially picked up. Without zooming in or running it through the analytics program it was hard to tell, yet with her trained eye she could see a shadow slip into Alice's shed and disappear in the shadows. Savannah called for a drink and Maisie stalled her, promising a biscuit as well if she could wait a moment. Torn between her normal routine, her instructions and the emotional attachment she had to this job, her professional mind reassured her, whoever went in, had to come out, and it was then she would get a clear shot. If she saw he was stealing something of value she would confront him, otherwise at least she would have the evidence to turn in if she had to. Maisie adjusted some angles on the other cameras and punched numbers in the computer making it sort and match different movements and angles to form a full clear picture. Savannah called again and she pressed the last button so it would alert her phone within milliseconds of his exit.

Savannah gave her a stern look.

'Can we go now?'

'It's not dinner time, Savvy. Jason said about six o'clock. I know you're excited only you have to learn to be patient. We can do some other things until then, would you like to play a game or do some more drawing?'

'Not Jason, Maisie, the nice lady who laughs a lot. She said she had toys.'

Maisie smiled remembering when Pat had mentioned it.

'I'd forgotten about her saying it, what about we go tomorrow?'

Savannah lips tightened not knowing whether to frown at her sister, or smile, to get her own way.

'She said tomorrow and we had a night-time so that means today.'

Maisie had to smile at how she was being explained to about nights and days. She checked the clock

'Ok then, we can go and ask now. Remember Savvy, if Pat has forgotten, don't be disappointed alright, we can always go back another day.'

The little girl jumped up in excitement.

'I know, but we can ask … in case she did forget.'

Her eyes glowed in anticipation and Maisie told her to pop to the bathroom then they would give her hair a quick brush before they left.

'Remember Savannah, we are borrowing, so we must look after whatever it is and give it back another day, ok?'

'Ok,' Savvy's voice echoed out from the toilet and Maisie knew Savannah would have a glum look she put on when things weren't exactly how she would like them to be.

Closing the door Maisie glanced across at Alice's, squinting her eyes she could see no sign of anyone lurking there. Mark was at the front of his garage, the door was open and the back of his car was too. Maisie didn't know whether to speak or not and the problem was solved as he firmly turned his back on her. Savannah half skipped ahead and waited at Pat's gate, the crimson petals of the fallen camellias squashing beneath her feet. Maisie hurried her in the gate and lifted her slightly so she could ring the doorbell.

Pat opened the door tentatively, and on seeing who it was, she threw it wide open, her laughing voice welcoming them in.

'Now this is what I call perfect timing.'

Pat's eyes twinkled along with her big smile.

'I was washing the rocking horse and could use a helping hand.'

Savannah's eyes almost exploded and she pushed Pat out of the way in her excitement to get inside.

'She's going to make my day,' Pat said giving Maisie a quick hug.

'Oh no Pat, I think you are about to make hers.'

The two women hurried after the little girl, her squeals of delight already echoing back through the house.

Number 6 BonBon Street

Mark

Mark felt no remorse, Claire had become a whiny little mouse since they got married. She had to be shown who was in charge. Her business degree, no, economics degree, as she always corrected him with a smug look on her face, made her think she was all fancy, stupid bitch. The baby had been a big surprise and before she came, Claire had always fired up against him, he'd liked it. With the job offer, and her parents will, it had all come together to get them this house with the sizeable deposit they'd left her. He had been a bit pissed off when she had stood firm about the house being in her name, but whatever…, he always knew he could change her mind if he had to.

Claire had been the pretty but quiet one and had always seemed surprised when he, the tough guy at school had chosen her, he enjoyed her adoration and they had slipped into a sort of routine as the *it* couple in their group. Mark had roughed her up a few times early on, although not enough to scare her away. With the pregnancy announcement in her last term of university, he had bottled up the feelings of rage and anger he always felt and tried to change and steer his anger in a different direction. A couple of his mates had told him to back off and get a grip so he had started going out without them, lurking around the streets late at night looking for something to ease his frustrations, whether it be kicking in a door or picking up some scrag in a lowlife bar and showing her who was boss.

The pressure to do the right thing and the fuss about a stupid wedding and a baby had kept him in check for a while, his mother over the moon about the impending birth.

Claire had glowed with the pregnancy and Mark had enjoyed all the attention, it fed his ego. The pats on the back and the, you're the man, comments had made him feel important and he had started to look forward to his son being born, he could teach him to be a real man, footy, beer, he'd teach him how to fight, stand up for himself. Mark had even felt himself softening about the whole thing and his acceptance of their future had made Claire feel even more secure as now, she again, would have a family.

The wedding, the move, the job, had overfilled his days and all had been going well, Mark had thought, and he even was starting to have a few mates, blokes he had met at the pub a few times before this damn pandemic shut everything down. The pandemic had saved him in a way. The job loss was more a sacking, although he hadn't enlightened Claire with that news, then everything started shutting down, so he had told her his job disappeared like thousands of others around the country and access to government money became almost too easy.

At first he hadn't minded being at home then once the baby arrived, and Claire became a constant bore about how tired she was, she had worn him down. All she had to do was keep the place tidy and cook a meal. It was not like it was bloody hard, and she had been on the phone half the day, his mother constantly ringing, checking in. What did it matter how often the kid pooped, seriously they would discuss it for hours! He'd fixed that, taken her phone away and told her they couldn't afford it anymore, then whenever his mother rang he fobbed her off telling her Claire was busy or out on a walk. The day she kept calling insisting on talking to Claire had been the last straw, he wanted her to butt out. Aww, how's my precious little girl she'd say, it made his blood boil, another bloody female to mess up his life, he honestly didn't think he deserved it.

Claire had put a plate of mush in front of him and called it dinner, what was he, a dog. It looked like muck, oh boo hoo she was too tired to make anything else. He'd shown her.

He was surprised when she turned up at the door with the nosy bitch from across the street. He had seen them all, every one of them pretending to be busy in front of their houses or casually walking the street. He knew they were all involved. Finding the remote on the garage floor let him know how she had escaped. He had forgotten how smart she was, as the baby brain had been in place so much it had become the norm. It was the book club crap that had been the undoing, she had been smart for sure, probably waiting for the opportunity. Couple of bruises he had assured himself, he could explain those away, although the one sober morning he had woken up and seen her face swollen with purple bruises lining her cheeks like roughly applied makeup, he had been shocked himself. Claire must of done more damage to herself in the night, no way he had done all of it, he'd only pushed her around a bit. She was setting him up, making things his fault, when they had time to talk he would sort her, yeah, he would make her understand. The way the world is, being cooped up, away from the crowd, he had been kingpin at home. Here, restricted from going out, everything closed, he was nothing. The dead beat job they had all been so excited about and the fresh start they apparently had needed, had turned into nothing except four walls and two whinging females. Christ!

He had snuck out a few times, stalking the streets, restless for some action of some kind, there was nothing, no one, streets were empty and curtains were drawn.

His mother had rung. He had tuned out, the clever little bitch had even sent her photos. So what if the olds had got him out of a scrape years before, they didn't know the half of it, this was his life not theirs, all the rules growing up when they thought they had him locked in tighter than a noose. They had never known, or suspected some of the things he got up to. When he had squeezed the life out of the guinea pig wanting to see its eyes pop out, he had then placed it under the wheel of his dad's car and they had never realised the torture it had endured in the last hour of its life, the car tyre would have been a blessing if it was still alive to feel. It had been the first. How he had laughed when he saw a poster for a missing pet in the neighbourhood, he had been the only one who knew it would never return.

His mates had looked up to him, he was fearless and unafraid of authority of any kind. The gang had matured though and he had been careful to cover his anger at the world, deep down inside only letting it show in the earlier hours of the morning as the riff-raff of society circulated the streets, scavenging and pillaging the footpaths like rats in a rubbish bin.

He had been watching out and saw the car pull up across the road, he wondered where they hid her. He couldn't make out the baby seat in the back and he briefly wondered which house his daughter was in. It was not as if he wanted her, though she may be the tool he would need to set things back in place and keep him appearing to be a part of society, she would be the cloak to hide his true self from the world, as Claire had been.

Mark opened the door, he pulled his body up tall and straight, filling the doorway with a show of strength ready to grab his wife and draw her inside so they could talk away from the prying eyes and ears of her companion.

'Claire I was so worried.' Mark had glanced at Alice and a surge of hatred rushed into his mouth, a vile taste of stomach acid, mixed with saliva, making him hold his mouth firm in case it all came rushing out.

'Come in, where's the baby? We'll sort this out, I had a few too many is all, you know me, come in and we can talk.'

Mark felt so confident. He glanced up and down the street trying to assess which one of them could be his ally, see his side of this, she was his wife after all, and this was none of their business, he needed her to toe the line, he was the man of the house and she was going to show him some respect.

The police car shocked him. Was she serious. It was a bit of roughing up to let her know who was boss, she had gone too far now, he had to get her inside to talk before they started to persuade her otherwise. He glanced up the street again wondering which nosy neighbour had called them. The minute the officer spoke he knew it was Claire, her meek, cringing attitude of late had obviously been hiding what a scheming bitch she had become, he would show her, making out like it was all his fault, time would tell and time was one of the only things Mark had at the moment.

Mark paced the hallway after they all left. Cracking a tinny on the second round, his mind soothed as the golden liquid ran down his throat. The headache which had been silently knocking on his brain all day, slid behind a door refreshed by the amber fluid. Hiding away it was like a wild beast, satisfied for now by the sustenance it had received. He would have to bide his time, Claire would soon realise her place was here, looking after him, who did she think she was, won't be long before she comes crawling back with the kid under her arm. Oh the baby, the baby, seemed she was all anyone thought was important any more. What about his needs, did she think they could be tossed aside. The queer across the road, bet he put her up to it, oh yes Mark had seen him all dressed up in his fancy clothes at night looking like a trumped up tart in his makeup and wig. People were so caught up in their own secrets they forgot to lock doors or close a back shade. He had seen him.

Mark cracked another beer, crushing the previous can in his hand and throwing it across the room aiming for his wedding photo on the side table. It wobbled backwards and wedged against the wall, held there slightly by the heart decoration on the top corner of the frame. He would get it next time, he had all night to aim, shoot and watch it smash into tiny pieces on the floor. Yep, he had all night to figure out how to make Claire realise how humiliated she had made him feel, telling the neighbours and his family, making a mountain out of a molehill. He'd show her.

Number 8 BonBon Street

Pat

Savannah's squeals of delight had warmed Pat's heart. She had kept the old rocking horse from when she was a child, Keith had pulled it out not long before he died, thinking it would be a nice little project and had set about sanding it back and delicately painting it again. He had chosen a pale grey with a darker grey for the pinto like spots on its rump, the blonde mane had a few chunks missing and she could see how he had combed it out carefully. Pat remembered the daydreams, as a little girl, when to her it was a real horse and she was galloping across a paddock with the blonde mane flying back in the breeze like her own hair. To and fro she had rocked for hours with her head full of dreams.

Pat hadn't touched it since she lost Keith. In the days afterwards when she had wandered the house aimlessly, restless for answers to questions in her head which had none, she had seen it there in his shed, the paint brush dried on the bench, waiting for the next time he would need it. It was not to be, there was no next time, and the small shed seemed to still hold the essence of him. For a moment this morning it had caught her by surprise, and all the whys, and the anger at the grief she was feeling for him being taken too soon, plus the loneliness she felt, came crashing in. It had been too soon for him and too soon for her, they'd had so much more life to live and experience together.

Pat had pushed the horse gently and watched as it rocked smoothly, its face seeming to come alive with the movement. Pulling the door wide open, Pat had dragged the horse out onto the grass. With a bowl of warm water and a cloth she had only begun to wipe it down, while also wiping a few tears away, when she felt his gentle hands cover hers to help her.

Some days she couldn't feel him at all, and at first she had searched for him, longing to feel his presence. On other days he surprised her, and she would feel a warmth on her face or would stop suddenly, for a moment in time to think of him in a busier day.

The doorbell startled her and she'd had to shake herself wanting to hold him there, yet knowing she had to let him go.

'I needed you then, thank you my love.'

Pat hoped he heard her as she made her way inside to answer the door.

The little girls face was a picture. By the time she and Maisie caught up to her, Savannah was standing with her eyes wide and her hands cupped over her mouth. Pat grabbed a dry cloth and gave it to Savannah.

'After you help me dry her off I thought you might like a little ride while I make us some afternoon tea, what do you think?'

Still with her mouth open Savannah could only nod and took the cloth tentatively wiping the horse's face, her own face glowing in excitement. Maisie and Pat exchanged grins and Maisie mouthed thank you over Savannah's head.

'Right let's get to work then, because I'm busting for a cup of tea and to cut a yummy slice I made this morning' Pat said.

The little girl started rubbing furiously which made them laugh and Maisie leaned over and whispered to Pat behind her hand.

'This is like all her Christmas's have come at once. She hasn't had much of a life Pat, and I will fill you in some other time. I only managed to get her into my care a few months ago and she is coming along in leaps and bounds.'

Pat hid her surprise, she had presumed Savannah was Maisie's daughter, it didn't matter as there would be time for their story on another day. This afternoon was for enjoying their company and making new friends. You could never tell what went on in other people's lives and with what had been happening in their street already, Pat felt a need to reach out and help those around her. It was what she thought this world should be about, especially with the shutdowns and social distancing, it was important to help those people who were close to you.

Pat couldn't contain her delight when Maisie helped Savannah mount the horse. Placing one foot carefully in the silver stirrup then hanging on both to Maisie and the slight pummel on the front of the saddle as she threw her leg over, Savannah then sat proudly holding the reins. Maisie helped her get her other foot in then pushed her slightly to start the rocking process. Pat could see the dreams in her eyes already and a smile so big which threatened to break her little face. Pat's joyous laugh filled the yard and she hoped it was something she would never forget, both for herself and Savannah, it was such a simple joy to hang on to.

Pat broke away to make some tea and the doorbell sounded again.

'Goodness, it's like Pitt Street today.'

Pat said it over her shoulder and made her way towards the front of the house to answer its call.

Number 9 BonBon Street

Lisa

Lisa stood with a camera in hand and couldn't stop her face lighting up when Pat opened the door. Lisa had been half expecting Pat to be feeling a bit down, or worried by the events next door, instead her face and voice both boomed a big welcome.

'Come on in, ooh you have a camera, goodness I wish you had been here a few moments ago to capture the look on young Savannah's face. It was a picture, come in, come in.'

Pat was gesturing her through before Lisa had a chance to say a word. Once the door closed she tried to splutter a brief explanation about the camera in her hand as Pat bustled past.

'We're out the back, I dragged out my old rocking horse and I think we might have to ask Brodie to carry it up the street with Savannah on it, she hasn't stopped!'

Lisa greeted Maisie and Savannah slowed long enough for a shy hello then called to her.

'See how fast we go, faster than anything.'

With a grin she was off again pushing the pony to its limits, her smile wide and her eyes focused on some invisible thing in the distance.

'Maybe I should come back some other time, I can see you are busy.'

'Not at all, sit and have some tea.' Pat insisted. 'Any news from down the street, how did they get on today?'

Lisa filled Pat and Maisie in with what she knew. Harry and Moni were having a quiet day with the baby and Claire. So far, Mark had not contacted anyone, not even his mother as far as they knew.

A friend of Moni's had a holiday house which, with everything going on, was empty right now. After Moni had enquired about it, and on hearing it was empty, Moni had told her friend some of the story and straight away the friend had offered it to Claire as a short term hideout. It was far enough away Mark was unlikely to go near there and yet still within the current travel zone for their area. Lisa explained it would give Claire a bit of free space while they all waited for Mark to make some kind of a move, or at least indicate which way he was going to act and Claire could begin to plan her next step.

'It's kind of a waiting game at the moment. Moni assured me Claire is still determined he should get out of the house and she is remaining strong. It's all hard to take in isn't it? I can't imagine how she feels, I feel so angry for her. Does it make sense to feel useless at times like this, even though doing nothing is the best thing to do?'

Pat nodded.

'It does. I do think she is doing it the right way though, and I hope Mark does the same, otherwise Claire will be running scared for the rest of her life. It's like a sickness I suppose, an unforgivable sickness.'

As they all paused for a moment, Lisa tried to feel what it would be like if Brodie ever hurt her in any way. It seemed unimaginable and in the past few days she'd had to remind herself she did not really know how it felt, she did know she was going to try and support Claire in any way she could. It was a promise Lisa knew she would keep.

'I didn't know you were a photographer?' Pat glanced at the camera changing the subject, while smiling at the happy child at the same time.

Lisa glanced across to Maisie, unsure if this was the right time. The poor thing had been thrown in the deep end since she moved in, and none of them had gotten to know her very well yet. The last few days they had all been so focused on Claire, and before that, the pandemic and the lockdowns which ensued because of it.

'Look I'm sorry Maisie, I don't really know you at all, and I'm not sure if I should involve you. With all that's gone on you seem to have been pushed into this and …' Lisa trailed off as she realised nothing was making any sense.

'I'll go if you like.' Maisie began to rise as if to leave. 'It seems like this is personal.'

Pat leaned in and covered Maisie's hand with her own.

'What is it Lisa, I'm getting confused, there's been a few secrets let out in the street lately so why not another one? Come on, out with it, you've caught someone doing something on this camera have you? Mm, it's not Harry is it, what is he been up to now?'

Pat looked at Maisie.

'He's a kind man, a little bit too much of a sticky beak at times, although what he and Moni have done for Claire these last few days, I could nearly forgive him for anything.'

Pat had winked at her as she spoke and Lisa couldn't help but grin as she remembered Pat's confession about her cabin and her friendship circle there.

'Well yes and no, the camera isn't mine, I snatched it through our hedge and sprayed Harry with my hose.'

They both looked at her in astonishment.

'I thought Harry had been spying on me, you know how he gets around Pat, popping up in your yard when you least expect it. He always has an excuse, you know like, popping your bin away for you luv, or need a bit of help with the hedge.'

Pat nodded.

'Yes it's hard for him to get in, or see in my yard for that matter, though when Keith died I did give him a set of my keys and every time I ask for them back he seems to evade the question.' Pat looked at Maisie.

'When my Keith died Harry was a huge support, he helped me with lots of things I couldn't cope with at the time. Sometimes I feel uneasy though when I get home, like someone's been in the house, nothing has ever been missing so I've started to wonder if it is me, getting nervous now I'm on my own. I still want my keys back though, I think it would make me feel easier.'

Savannah called to Maisie she needed to use the toilet and they hurried inside heeding Pat's directions.

Lisa leaned forward, whispering loudly, wanting to spill the beans before Maisie returned.

'Pat, there are pictures of you on here! I understand them now you told us about your lifestyle, and now I'm certain you didn't know they were being taken.'

Pat looked shocked.

'What! Show me!' Pat reached for the camera and Lisa pulled it away.

'Pat, no! I have to warn you there's other photos too, of everyone in the street, well the women at least, and other women too, people I don't know. Some are them in a street, walking or at the park, some of the others are …um, sick, because you can tell they don't know they are being taken.'
Pat was looking at her, mouth open and eyes wide.
Lisa suddenly felt emotional.

'They sort of give me the creeps. Pat, you know about my sister, so I'm not sure if it's me and my past, but it makes me feel, I don't know, well actually, they make me afraid.'

Maisie returned after setting Savannah happily riding off into the sunset again.
'What happened to your sister?'
Lisa took a deep breath.
'She was taken on her way to school and killed, they never caught him. They found some photos, and it was so random, it was like he had left them to be found, no fingerprints on them, he was careful. They were photos of her at school and home, some at the shops. He had been following her, stalking her without her knowing. It was like he wanted us to know he had been watching.'

A sob escaped her and they both leaned in and she felt a comforting arm circle her back. Maisie's face was shocked, Lisa had seen it before when she'd had to tell people, it was hard to take in and they had no words, sorry always seemed inappropriate, not a big enough word to convey their shock and sympathy at the one time.

'So what's on this camera?' Maisie spoke softly.
Pat filled her in while Lisa composed herself.

'I hate camera's Maisie, it's like someone being afraid of heights or spiders, my insides churn and I have a kind of panic attack. It depends on the situation, sometimes I lose it completely. Brodie is good, he has helped a lot. At one time I wouldn't touch the mobile because it could take photos though it's mainly cameras.'
Lisa smiled weakly. 'Sounds crazy I know.'
Again Lisa paused.

'Pat with everything going on the last few days I didn't want to upset you, it's not why I'm here. I think I should take this to the police. I wanted to show you first so you know what others will see.'

Pat took the camera and flicked it on, the first photo was of Lisa's hedge and the path next to her house. As she scanned through, Pat's horror grew and she paused looking up at her back fence trying to work out the angle it had been taken. Although Pat may be a nudist, Lisa knew, it didn't make her an exhibitionist. It was up to Pat if her image should be shared, or even taken. Lisa could see the anger starting to rise in Pat's face.

Maisie had leaned over and she too was shocked. Savannah sidled up exhausted now from all the activity and they hurriedly shut the camera down.
'So you think this is Harry?'

Maisie had to admit it shocked her a bit, she wouldn't have picked Harry as the culprit. He was a busybody, but this? In her head Harry didn't seem to fit the scenario.

'I did at first, then I found photos of Moni too, so I'm confused. The ones of most concern I think, are of Alice. Some are of women I don't know and whoever it is has been in Alice's house, whereas the others are taken from a distance.'

'I'm hungry.' Savannah crawled onto Maisie's lap, rubbing her eyes.

'Oh dear look at the time, we are supposed to be heading over to Jason's for tea. Look I can't fully explain.' Maisie chewed her lip as she sought the right words without giving too much away. 'Could I have the camera, I know people who may be able to help.'

Lisa felt a bit annoyed at Maisie taking over yet the idea of picking up the camera again repulsed her.

'Trust me ok, I'll contact them tomorrow and get some advice, I'll come over as soon as I know something. What did your husband say about them?'

Lisa frowned.

'I didn't tell him, I started to. I was worried he might think I was overreacting. I wanted another woman's opinion, plus I trust Pat, and I know she will look at it from all sides.'

Maisie nodded at her.

'I know you haven't known me long Lisa, I do truly think I can help, and in a discreet way too. The advice I get will help you decide which way to go with this. I need you to know you can trust me and I promise I'll fill you in tomorrow.'

Lisa could see the child getting impatient so they all said good bye and made their way out the gate with Pat promising Savannah she would find someone tomorrow to carry the horse up to her yard.

Lisa glanced up the street and shivered slightly, she was glad it was now a secret shared and hoped Maisie was true to her word and her friends would be discreet. It seemed there was more to Maisie than met the eye. Lisa hurried across the road and shutting her gate firmly somehow made her feel safe, the lights were on and the smell of onions frying wafted around the garden. She wouldn't tell Brodie yet. I'll wait and see how tomorrow pans out first she thought, as she opened the door calling to Brodie, she was home and silently thanking the stars for the man of her dreams.

Number 7 BonBon Street

Jason

The dogs sensed Jason's excitement and watched with interest as he set up a table outside. It was only for the pre-dinner snacks as the nights were still cool and he had decided it might be warmer inside for Savannah once the sun dropped completely out of sight. He glanced at his watch and hoped for a second they hadn't forgotten. Jason heard Pat call out and moved to the corner of the house to check, she was turning her back and closing the door as he looked. Savannah suddenly seemed to burst out of nowhere making him laugh out loud at her excited face.

'I got a horse Jason, Mrs Pat gave it to me. It's just to lend, it's not really mine. It is so beautiful, wait until you see it. Can you come and watch me ride?'

She took his hand half dragging him towards the dog pen as she rattled on with all the details.

'It has a saddle and reins and those things you put your feet in, and you should have seen me Jason, I was going very fast.' Savannah paused for a second to catch her breath as the words tumbled out.

'Can you go and get it tomorrow and bring it to my house? Please?'

'Well of course I can, how exciting. Now are you hungry, or do you want a quick game with these two before it gets too dark.'

Savannah tilted her head giving the question great consideration.

'The dogs please, but I'm starving.'

Jason laughed and opened the gate, the dogs bounded out licking the girls face and dancing around her, their tails going ten to the dozen.

Jason looked up to see Maisie round the corner of the house holding a bottle of wine high as the dogs raced to greet her as well.

'Sorry Jason, we were at Pat's and I wanted to duck home first for this.' She looked across at Savannah. 'There certainly was no stopping her when we saw you poke your head around the corner, so I thought it would be ok to let her come in.'

'No trouble at all, welcome, Savannah has been filling me in, seems she has had a very exciting day.'

Maisie nodded.

'You should have seen her face, she was so excited, it's a beautiful old thing too, it's one on the swinging mechanism thingy?' She laughed. 'Now you know how technical I am, I mean it's not on rockers.'

Jason laughed too.

'Yes I do, and anyway I will see it tomorrow because missy here has assigned me the job of carrying it to your house.'

Maisie put her hand over her mouth.

'Ooh no, she didn't, well she is really coming out of herself.' They laughed together as they watched Savannah throw a ball and Pippa and Clyde race then scuffle with each other, each wanting to be the one to proudly bring it back to her.

Jason found Maisie easy to talk to and she filled him in on Claire and the next lot of plans. They then bounced from one subject to another as they sipped the wine and shared the platter he had prepared earlier. The dogs came to flop exhausted at his feet and Savannah crawled into Maisie's lap yawning while licking the salt of the crisps off her fingers.

'I'd better put this meat on before someone here falls asleep.'

'It has been a big day, but we are so glad to be here with you Jason. Our life, and especially Savvy's, has been an emotional roller coaster and to be welcomed here the way we have been by everyone in BonBon Street is amazing. I finally feel like we could become part of a community, a safe and solid one for Savvy to grow up in.'

After locking the dogs in, they made their way inside. It only took one sausage rolled up in bread to fill her tummy and Savannah's eyes could not be kept open anymore. They settled her on the couch and continued their meal.

Jason could see Maisie looking around, taking it all in.

'You have a nice home Jason. Tell me about how you came to be in BonBon Street. Did you grow up around here?'

Jason hesitated as he thought again about his decision to be more truthful in the future, far back in his mind he could see a therapist waving madly urging him to do so.

'Not that far really, a bit further out, on the rural fringe. My mother died when I was young and my father struggled with her death.' He paused and stared into the past for a few moments. 'I can see now how much he did.'

Jason could see the sympathy in Maisie's eyes and a weak smile on her lips, she leaned forward urging him to continue, her hand clasping his forearm in silent support.

'I struggled too, I missed her terribly, and I used to go into their room, while Dad was at work, to smell and touch her clothes.'

'That's so sad,' Maisie whispered.

Jason hung his head, he felt he could trust her so continued quietly.

'I started to put her clothes on. It made me feel safe somehow, and it wasn't long before I would go the full hog trying her makeup and walking around the house all dressed up.

Although he saw Maisie's eyes had widened slightly, she remained silent.

'Dad walked in one day. He was so mad.' Jason put his head in his hands, his elbows on the table trembled as he spoke. He felt a hand rub his back gently.

'I'm sorry Maisie, I decided recently if Claire could be so brave I should be too. I still dress up sometimes, it makes me feel … I can't explain it, …safe or maybe it feels closer to Mum, I've had therapy, Dad never understood how much I was hurting inside. I sometimes think if he had held me close we could have grieved together, instead he shut me out like he was the only one who loved and missed her.'

Jason paused again, not game to look at her and see the horror on her face, he had gone this far he now almost couldn't stop himself from continuing.

'I'm not gay, bi or transsexual, and there is nothing wrong with any of them, they are just words to describe who people really are. I'm what they call a cross dresser, and for me, it has nothing to do with my sexual orientation. The therapist said I could grow out of it, it's an emotional thing. I suppose nowadays people would call it a mental health issue, really it is my way of coping. Whenever I'm stressed or lonely I tend to do it more.' Jason tried to explain better. 'It's not quite the same, but if you think about a smoker reaching for a cigarette, it's like a stress reliever. Although this is not really an addiction either, I could get over it or I could be someone who does it forever.'

He took the chance now and looked up, expecting her to be slumped back in the chair and trying to find an excuse to leave with a look of rejection on her face. He was wrong. A single tear rolled down her cheek and she adjusted her chair so it was closer to him.'

'I'm so sorry Jason, so sorry for your mother, and your father who didn't know what to do, and you, you must have felt so alone. Don't worry your secret is safe with me.'

Jason was stunned.

'Thank you Maisie I was so afraid to tell you. Somehow these last few days something has switched inside of me, and I want to take control of my own life. My ex-wife, Kylie tried hard, but at the end of the day it was too much for her to keep my secret, it became a burden she didn't want to share. I don't know what I would have done without her though, and we are still the best of friends. I'm happy for her and she just had a baby with her new partner.'

Maisie reached out and clasped his hand.

'I'm sorry you must think this is such a crazy street you have moved into. I hope we can be friends, I like you Maisie, and Savannah brings a spark into my day whenever I see her.'

'She is special. I didn't have the best upbringing and Savannah, well her story is for another time. All I want now is for her to smile every day of her life as before, before here, she didn't have much to smile about. She is so resilient, and I'm so glad I have her with me, you're right, she is a spark of happiness.'

'Coffee?'

'Yes please, and Jason.'

Jason went to release his hand as he rose from the chair. Maisie held it firm, reaching out her other hand urging him to take it.

'Jason, I am where I am today because someone reached out a hand to me. I believe in paying forward, so if you ever need it, I'm here for you.'

Jason hung his head and took her other hand in his. Deep inside he could feel a ball of suppressed emotion rolling and moving trying to find a new place to hide away, yet releasing slightly as he looked at his new friend. A tear dropped to the table and she stood putting her arms around him as he sobbed.

'You know there are two bonuses from what I can see.'

Jason pulled back, drying his eyes and searching her face for clues.

'Well, one is I have two hands, so if you ever need more than one don't worry I have another.'

Jason smiled.

'And two?'

'Well now I have someone to help me with my makeup, as I'm really, really, bad at it.'

Jason laughed out loud and hugged her again.

'It's so nice to meet you Maisie, so very nice.'

His voice trailed off as emotions welled again and he said a silent prayer as he turned to fill the kettle. Maybe he was right, those who would be important in his life wouldn't care and anyone else didn't matter.

Jason carried the sleeping Savannah across the street, Maisie had run ahead to turn on the lights and he went in and laid the child on a makeshift bed. It was late so with the promise to return with the rocking horse the next day, he made his way home, pausing at the front gate to look up at the stars. Thoughts of his mother filled his head and he hoped one of those twinkling lights up there was for her.

Tonight he had made the right choice, tonight, no matter who or what he was, he had made a new friend and felt he could start to put his trust in people again, and let them decide how they felt. Jason scolded himself for not asking more about Maisie's life, he would, there would be time for questions in the weeks ahead as their friendship grew.

Pressing two fingers against his lips, Jason raised them to the heavens.

'I love you Mum,' he said in a whisper before turning and making his way inside. As he closed the door and looked around his home, a thought occurred. There had not been much furniture in the house across the street, the rooms he had passed through were rather sparse. In fact now he was thinking about it, Savannah's bed looked no better than a camp bed. In the morning he would have a look in the shed or even in Jonathon's garage. With a bit of research he might be able to make a bed every little girl would dream of. Maisie was right, paying it forward would feel good, it was about time he started to think of others and stopped wallowing in his own self-pity. Tomorrow he would start to live again, not only exist. He would go and see Brodie, as friends were too hard to come. If Brodie was ok with his confession, it would be good to have him as a mate again, if he wasn't, at least they would have talked it out and wouldn't be playing the cat and mouse game of late.

Turning off the light Jason slid into bed and pulled the covers up around him. Tomorrow is the first day of the rest of my life and I can't wait to see Savannah's face when I deliver the horse tomorrow. She was a funny kid, she really was.

Number 5 BonBon Street

Alice, Jay, Charlie and Jonathon

Alice surveyed the kitchen. The boys were trying at least, dishes were now put on the sink and she simply closed their door after putting their clothes in their room and left them to deal with it. It made her smile to see Jay's side was much neater, whereas Charlie still seemed to have the whole 'floor robe' thing going on while his actual cupboard was open, clearly displaying mostly empty shelves.

They were talking more too, arriving home to have proper meals at a reasonable hour and setting their precious phones aside and including her in the conversations. Alice hoped they kept it up, there were still a lot of chores to be done yet it somehow all seemed so much easier than a week ago.

Their reactions to Claire's situation had relieved her in a way and being able to discuss it openly with them had shown her how mature they were getting. Alice felt like she had taken a step back and was seeing them both with fresh eyes, the individuals not just the daily chaos they created. By taking a stand she had made them take a good look at themselves, and thankfully, broken down some walls of false resentment which had been slowly building in each one of them.

The boys' anger at Mark was still simmering. Alice wondered how they would see the whole situation, their mother leaving, as she did, had often made her consider how this would affect them in the future. It had only been a slight concern, one which had played at the back of her mind as she watched them grow into teenagers. Alice realised now their rough and tumble style was boys being boys, each a rival yet also a protector of the other with their unique twin code thrown in. They were good boys, they actually were, and their words now expressed to her their feelings for her as well. In a way, Alice realised Claire's terrible situation coming to light, had helped them as a family. Coming together to try to protect her had opened up those deeper conversations more, and not only about Claire and Mark, as their own feelings and insecurities within this family were expressed. Also, the boys had told her how their lives would have been different if not for her. With their mother's rejection and an absent father, they saw how things could certainly have played out in a much different way.

Alice could see it now. No matter how the noise, mess, and scolding had upset her at times over the years, her loneliness with Jon away and with these two towering bodies bumping down the hallway, somehow her lessons and morals had been taken in. They would all still have their ups and downs, there was no doubt, however now, these boys were forever truly hers. They did see her as more than a slave, and saw how hard it was for her as well as what she had sacrificed to keep them all together as a family unit. They appreciated her and at last felt confident to say so. It made her heart sing. They were growing up, and she loved them yet also now realised how much she liked them. By sharing some of the load they could see she was happier and so now they had started to share some of the fun too.

Alice was washing up as she stared vacantly out of the window. Her hands moving automatically felt warm and soapy, she paused, a cup in one hand and the dishcloth in the other, and now I'm going to break us apart again, she mused. When Jon returns they would talk, and talk was all it would be, as Alice now knew it was over. Alice loved the boys, she no longer loved their father, and thinking back knew she had not loved him for a long, long time.

When Jon returned he might get a bit of a surprise, as the boys had certainly expressed their disappointment in him. It wasn't only him being away they said, it was the emotional detachment, as if, when he played ball with them or showed them how to fix the car, they had always felt it was a chore for him, not knowledge sharing of life skills passing from parent to child. Jay had explained it.

'Alice, it's like he wanted to be somewhere else, somewhere more important than us, it took us a long time to realise it wasn't you Dad wanted to spend our time with. We were both jealous of you for a long time and for all the wrong reasons.'

He had then reached out his hand.

'Not always, just sometimes, there have been some good times.'

Alice had been touched it had been good to hear both the good, and the bad. Now when they walked in the door, she knew they wanted to be with her, talk to her and have her support. Things were definitely looking up, and as for Jon, emotionally she had dealt with him too. Alice was sure there would be a few more tears to come, but mostly it would be getting down to the small print. Jon could have whatever he wanted, she only wanted this house and she wanted her boys, somehow she didn't think he would argue.

A knock on the door startled her and she placed the cup on the draining tray and shook the cooling water off her hands. Taking the tea towel with her, she hurriedly dried her hands and flung it over one shoulder as she opened the door.

'Jason, hi, come in, I could do with some company.'

'Thanks Alice, I will come in, only for a minute though. I actually came to ask a favour, then I have to get over to Pat's or Savannah will have my head.'

Jason grinned and Alice laughed.

'So a four year old has you held for ransom does she?'

'Oh yes,' he said as he slid past her making his way to the kitchen. 'There is a rocking horse involved and she is probably chomping at the bit now for me to knock on their door.'

Alice smiled again, he looked happy, and he usually was, there was a change though, a shift somehow which seemed to bring a deeper glow from within. She shook her head, maybe it was her, or maybe by reaching out to help someone had lifted a cloud off everyone on the street, who knew?

'Look I won't stay long.'

Jason explained about Pat's donation of the horse and Savannah's excitement for it.

'I had them over for a meal last night and Savannah fell asleep so I carried her home for Maisie. I don't know their full story yet but it seems they have had a hard time of late and I noticed they don't have much stuff, you know it's pretty bare of furniture. Savannah's bed looks like a camp bed and there's an old table and lounge, not a lot else. Look anyway, it got me thinking, and I wondered if I could borrow some of Jon's tools and maybe scratch around the shed for some bits of timber and I'll make her a bed, a proper bed. It will keep me busy and well, she is a good kid and I'd like to do something nice for her.'

'Of course you can, that's so sweet of you. Hey, I saw this cute doona cover on the internet, let me show you and I can get it for her as well?'

Jason's smile said it all and Alice felt a twinge of jealousy as his face lit up as he spoke about the new neighbours. It shocked her a bit, then again her feelings toward Jason were mixed between her own situation and the kindness he had always extended to her. Alice was not sure what she felt about Maisie, it was not as if she knew her very well and had only met her at the book club meeting. There seemed an air of mystery about her.

Looking into Jason's eyes she swallowed the emotions which were rising to the surface and smiled. Showing him the doona covers, they both ooh'd and ahh'd over the pretty colours as if they were watching a fireworks display, and as each also, tried to ignore the spark jumping between them. With the selection settled Jason thanked her and left to head over to Pat's. Alice had told him the shed was always unlocked anyway and she didn't care what he took or used, Jonathon had never used half the stuff in it so he could feel free to use it all.

Alice watched him cross the street and sighed as she turned away and shut the door. Would she even want another partner she pondered? Well yes she answered back, I really haven't had one, the absent Jonathon had grown so distant it was the whole reason for the split, she wanted companionship, someone to laugh with every day, not just when they felt like being around. Whilst part of her was happy for Jason if he had found his someone, even though it was early days, a tiny bit of her wished it was her table he would be coming to sit at. A tear of sadness crept out of her eye and she brushed it away suddenly annoyed again at her situation and wishing it was done so she could move on. If Jonathon would answer his phone she might be able to start the process sooner, for some reason he seemed to have forgotten how to do that lately as well, communication was definitely not his forte`. Part of her wondered if he was a player, if he'd had other women. It had never really occurred to her before, lately though, looking at the relationships in this street alone, she could see how things were different to what you expected, if you only scratched the surface. Alice shrugged, well if he had some other woman up at the mines, so be it, she knew she was done, and it was time to move on. At least I will have Jason as a friend and I'll try to get to know Maisie better, like Claire I may need all the friends I can get.

The day seemed to loom ahead empty except for chores and after finishing the dishes Alice wandered out to the shed, Jason's visit making her curious as to what actually was in there. The boy's old car was covered in a tarpaulin with the lawn mower jammed in behind it in case they ever needed to shut the door. The shed was often open as they didn't see the need to close it. The boys rattled around playing with the tools occasionally, as did Jon when he was there. Alice rarely ventured inside. Alice poked about and saw several pieces of timber leaning up against the back wall she hoped Jason might find useful. This could really do with a good clean out she thought and pulled down several boxes to see what was in them. One box in particular looked like it was more used than the others and Alice was manoeuvring it to the bench when a deep voice startled her.

'Now what are you up to in my shed?'

The shock of his voice as she spun around saw the box fall and several items tumble out onto the dirty floor.

'Jonathon! What, um wow what a surprise.'

He held out his arms to her though did not move any closer. With the box at her feet Alice could falter and stumbled slightly avoiding the embrace. Bending to pick up the scattered contents of the box she was surprised when Jon knelt to help her.

'When did you get back, you said with the pandemic it would be too hard?'

'I thought I'd surprise you, I've been in hotel isolation for a few weeks. It was about time I came back to sort some things. Are you pleased to see me?'

Alice was troubled by the look on his face and the intensity of his tone at the question. Stalling for time she threw the last few things in the box and stood while he lifted it back up onto the shelf. A few scraps of crumpled notepaper still remained so she scooped them up pushing them down into the pocket of her jeans as she turned away to exit the shed.

Jonathon grabbed her hand.

'Well? Cat got your tongue?'

'No, no, it's a shock to see you, I've been trying to call. Look Jon, we have to talk so I suppose now is as good a time as any, before the boys get back. I'll put the kettle on.'

Alice busied herself making the coffee and rummaging around to find any snack left unconsumed by the twins. Jonathon sat looking deep in thought, and Alice again felt like she was looking at things through different eyes. The man she had fallen for all those years ago was ageing, his hair now peppered with grey and his skin bloated from what she suspected was too much alcohol, there probably wasn't a lot to do locked in a room for two weeks except drink. His arms were thick and she could tell he was still working out, although his hands showed his age where his body did not. Jon enquired after the boys and Alice for once felt her heart surge as she praised them and told him of their achievements over the past few months. Laughing she told him she would be happy to relinquish the driving instructor job to him. Alice watched him closely, he remained reserved and said little about his own time away. The coffee made, she sat down both hands circling her cup and after a deep breath decided, now or never.

Jon was looking at her expectantly.

'I'm sorry Jon, it's over, this marriage for me is not what I want.' Alice closed her eyes and continued. 'It's more than you being away, I haven't been happy for a long time and I want something more than waiting around for you to come back.'

Alice opened her eyes and looked straight at him.

'I'm happy to keep the boys with me and I'm sure they want to stay. I want the house. You can take everything else, I won't ask for part of your superannuation, your car or anything I promise. I only want the roof over our heads.'

Jonathon's mouth drew back into a firm line.

'So that's it then is it? You've made all the decisions and I'm to what? Disappear. Who is he?'

'What! Are you kidding? How would I even have time between running around teaching the boys how to drive and home schooling and the pandemic! Think about it Jon, we haven't been a couple for years, I actually sometimes wonder if we ever were.'

'And what's that supposed to mean?' His voice was low and it came out like a growl.

'Jon please, I'm being realistic. I did love you at first, and I also needed a family, I wanted security after the life I'd had, and don't get me wrong I was grateful, you gave me exactly what I wanted. Admit it, I also made it convenient for you to continue living the way you wanted to, so you didn't have to feel guilty about abandoning your kids, like their mother did!'

Alice realised she had pushed herself up, her arms straight and tense, her shoulders rounded as she leaned towards him across the table. Jonathon had pushed himself back in his chair as she released her pent up emotions.

'I am sorry Jonathan that was a bit of a low blow, unfortunately I do see some truth in it. I'd rather end it now and let both of us get on with our lives. The boys are old enough to make their own decisions, I would like them to finish school and I think being here in their regular routine is the right place for them, especially with restrictions and the uncertainty.'

Alice couldn't quite judge how he was feeling, his hand pumped in and out of a fist, other than that he made no movement nor showed any outward emotion.

'You can stay here for now of course, although I will be making up the spare room, I don't have a problem with it Jon, I do want this to be as amicable as possible.'

Jon sipped his coffee, his fist had uncurled and Alice felt the table vibrate as his leg tapped unconsciously against it. A rumble at the door and the boys tumbled in, a ball of energy with four legs which pulled up short at the sight of their father.

'Dad.' They cried in unison as Jon stood and hugged his sons. Charlie and Jay both leaned over to hug Alice as well, a new experience she had valued the last few days as their talks had deepened and their appreciation of each other was restored. Jon watched the banter as they filled both him and Alice in on their day, questions overlapped each other as well as answers. Alice could see he was surprised by the shift of loyalty in the room and the muscles in his face twitched as if she was watching the thoughts flick through his head.

'So how long you here for Dad.' Jay asked.

Jon paused and Alice felt his reply would tell her how easy or hard this was going to be. She felt a sort of release now she had told him, and like Claire, vowing to hold firm and move forward, Alice felt the same strength rising inside of her. Jon had been a good provider however the more she looked at him across the table, the more memories crept in of his absence from this marriage even when he wasn't physically away.

'Not long. I came to get my things. We have a bit to talk about. Look boys, to be straight with you, Alice and I won't be living together anymore.'

Alice looked at him in surprise, he seemed to have worked it all out very swiftly and made some decisions of his own. Alice could only hope it all would go smoothly.

Alice reached out and took both Jay and Charlie's hands.

'I don't think this will really surprise either of you and you know, even though I'm not your mother, this will always be your home.'

Jon raised one eyebrow.

'Alice wants to stay here with you boys until you finish school and as I said, we can talk about everything else later.'

As Charlie and Jay hung their heads each gave Alice's hands a squeeze. Jay spoke first.

'Thanks Dad. We want to stay here and this is between the two of you. Alice has always been here for us and no offence but, we like things the way they are.'

Alice's heart filled and she saw a shift in Jon as he realised he had found his boys a mother, one thing he doesn't know Alice thought, he doesn't know I'm also their friend.

The gaps in the small talk widened and Jon rose to leave.

'I'll be in touch boys, and you to Alice. I'll look at the finances though I think this place will have to go, you get things in motion we might as well make this.' Jon flapped his hands about as if the material goods were what mattered. 'Official.'

Without another word he was out the screen door and it banged behind him, the force of his exit too much for it to catch in the latch so it bounced several times before coming to rest. Charlie followed, calling to his dad to *hang on a minute*, and Alice allowed one single tear to roll down her face before picking up some washing and folding it as she stared into space. For once her mind was empty of everything she had to do. It was done, and now they all knew, they could start to move forward

'Dad, wait up.'

Charlie grabbed his father's arm and swung him around. 'You ok?'

'Yes all good, I actually am glad. It's time to get on with things and coming back here was becoming a chore.'

Charlie took a step back, he had never really understood his father at all, and for his own dad to say those words to him, was a low blow.

'Don't be unfair. Alice has done everything for us, our mother never cared and you weren't here, so I won't have you saying anything against her.'

Charlie rose to his full height and he could see his father realise his son was becoming a man and would soon out match him.

'Steady on, there are things you don't know. She was glad for the situation when we met and it suited me. Just seems it's now time to move on. I'm happy it's over, things had to change. I saw your mother the other day.'

Charlie took another step back.

'What other day? I don't understand, what did she want, is she something to do with this?'

The sneer on his dad's face frightened him.

'She's has everything to do with this. Alice served her purpose. Look, I've got to go Charlie, I'll be back for my stuff. I don't want to talk right now, I need to walk some things off.'

Jon turned to walk away and Charlie realised he had no luggage or backpack, nothing a man who was coming home might be carrying. Things weren't adding up in his head and he stared at his father's back as he rounded the fence.

Jon paused and called back to Charlie.

'Hey, have you seen anyone hanging around the shed?'

'No, why?'

'Been looking for a camera, have you seen it?'

Charlie shook his head.

'Well if you see it, can you put it aside for me? Don't turn it on, it needs to charge up first and you could damage the drive.'

Charlie nodded, raised his hand and watched as his father strode up the street with purpose, pulling his hoodie up and plunging his hands deep into its pockets.

Charlies head was reeling, from here Jon looked like a criminal and the clawing fingers of disgust he could feel in his stomach told Charlie he was. First thing after lunch he would go and see Harry and explain to him what happened. He would ask for the camera back. Hopefully Harry had put it aside somewhere and not looked at it. The chances were slim and Charlie knew any decision he made after retrieving it could change all their lives, far more than today's revelation.

Number 3 Bonbon Street

Harry and Moni

Harry saw him coming. It seemed strange to see him on his own. The boy's head was bent low and Harry had noticed Alice go past a few minutes earlier, a hand clutching the bar above the window as the car kangaroo hopped to the corner and he had heard her call blinker loudly as they rounded the end of the street without fully coming to a halt. Whichever one of them it was, he was glad they were coming, he assumed to apologise, Harry also knew he would have to fess up to the fact he no longer had the camera. The boy loped yet hesitated, seemed to do an about face then reconsidered and Harry saw his chest fill as he took a deep breath, then watched as he pursed his lips in a loud exhale. Yes this definitely was a child feeling guilty about something.

Alice's role in the saving of Claire, as Harry liked to think of it, had been enormous. She had not only recognised the problem and acted swiftly to get help, she had let Claire know she had an out. Alice had then secretly rallied everyone to help her so a smoke screen could be put up to divert Mark from knowing Claire's whereabouts. After Claire escaped, Alice had stayed away, only being with Claire secretively and when she confronted Mark. Alice then acted like she had moved on to some other cause so Mark would think Claire was miles away, not still hiding in his own street. Not for long though, they were moving her out tomorrow and he and Moni had been gathering a few things and setting up the little holiday home in readiness for her.

Harry stepped out into full view and Charlie stopped, one hand on the fence for support as he spoke.

'Um, hello Harry, I um, wanted to set you straight about the camera, um well, I was fooling around, I found it you see…in Dad's shed and I thought I'd take a few pictures of Jay, um when he came by, then you came and thought I was doing something else, but I wasn't I swear.'

Harry listened as the boy faltered as he explained, and even felt a bit sorry for him.

'See, it's Dad's camera apparently, and he wants it back, so I'm sorry for what happened, I really am, so Harry could I have it back now please.'

Charlie had straightened his shoulders and was now determined to have Harry return it.

'Well thankyou Charlie? Or is it Jay …Charlie, the thing is I no longer have it.'

Charlie's face dropped.

'What! Where is it, Dad's going to kill me… you didn't take it to the police did you?'

'The police! Why would I? No, Lisa has it. After you left me I dropped it, and when I went to pick it up Lisa heard me in the hedge and she thought I was spying on her. It's all a big mix up. I'm sorry Charlie it's the truth, I don't have it, although I'm happy to go with you now and ask her for it back and fully explain what happened.'

Harry could not quite work out the look on the boy's face. His shoulders had hunched back over and he almost looked like he would cry. Harry reached out and clamped a hand on his shoulder.

'It's alright son, we'll sort it out, can you go now or maybe later this afternoon, I'm not sure if Lisa is home at the moment.'

Charlie looked up and Harry could see the tears welling.

'I think my dad did something bad, and I don't know what to do. Some of the photos on there, they are bad, really bad and, and Harry, I need help.'

Harry reached over and unlatched the gate, guiding the boy into the garden. A movement caught his eye and he saw Maisie in the street, hesitating, watching them for a moment as Savannah danced around at her side waving to someone out of his view. Off for their walk he thought, yet even as he turned back to the boy, he could feel her eyes on them. Harry sat on the garden bench drawing Charlie down with him.

'So what's all this then? Tell me the truth now and we can sort it out. What do you think your dad has done, he's away anyway isn't he? And what's on this camera?'

Charlie was nearly sobbing now, glancing around in embarrassment at his tears as if hoping no one else would see them.

'It's ok Charlie, there's no one around, I'd take you inside normally, it's only, well, Claire is still here and so let's try to get this sorted before anyone else gets involved. Now what's on the camera?'

Charlie gulped loudly.

'I'm sorry Harry, I don't know who else to tell. Dad came back this morning, he and Alice are splitting up.'

As the boy paused, Harry could see he did not think it was a bad thing.

'I was worried you had seen the photos and I hope Lisa hasn't looked. It has photos of everyone on the street.' Charlie paused again. 'Well, not everyone, only the women.'

Harry looked shocked.

'What! Doing what, I don't understand.'

'I didn't study them, Harry, it looks like they didn't know they were being taken, there's one of Pat and she is, I don't like to say it, but she is naked, in her backyard.' Charlie took a deep breath, he had said it and the rest rolled free seeming to ooze out of his body as if he had no control now he had unleashed it.

'One was of Alice, it was inside the house but she was asleep, and some of Lisa, and Claire with the baby. Harry, there was one of Monique getting dressed. You couldn't see anything, not that I really looked. Harry, it made me feel sick. I think he is some kind of a stalker.'

Harry's anger was rising especially at the mention of his precious wife. Charlie continued.

'I flicked through them, some, not all because I knew something was wrong, and I didn't want to look. There are other women too, Harry, I think he stalks some of them and he might hurt them too. What should I do?'

The boy broke down in tears again and Harry sat stunned patting him on the leg in an absent fashion as he tried to take it all in. He had misjudged this boy and probably his brother too, Charlie was trying to do the right thing.

Harry's mind was reeling, what was happening in the world or was this pandemic making people more aware of what was going on around them. This was his street, his quiet little street where not much happened, how could it all be going on without him noticing. He snapped his mind back to the present.

'Right, well, ok. Look, let's get down to Lisa's and get the camera back, and go from there. Where is your Dad now?'

'I dunno, he left, he wants it back, he asked me for it, asked if I'd seen it. I found it in a box in the shed with some other stuff. I wish I'd never looked.'

'Come on now, what's done is done and who knows it might be a good thing. I'm glad you came to me and I want to sort this out. I don't want to judge until I see them for myself and, well, if it is bad like you say, the best thing is to have a chat with the police and get their opinion. You ready?'

Charlie nodded and Harry called out to Moni he was popping out for a bit to help Charlie. She came to the window and raised her hand looking at him quizzically before dropping it, allowing the curtain to fall back into place.

Charlie babbled the whole way, talking out the different scenarios playing out in his head. Harry listened, although the furrow across his brow showed his own thoughts were reeling. It was best to see the evidence first, maybe the boy overreacted or maybe they would not be as intrusive as he made them sound, Harry puzzled and somehow knew this can of worms would be a full one.

Number 9 BonBon Street

Lisa

Lisa heard Brodie speak and looked out as Harry and one of Alice's boys came through the gate. The branches missed Harry and the boy ducked to avoid them. Brodie was running late for a class as it was, so Lisa knew she would have to go out to speak with them.

They all looked up as she came out the door, drying her hands on her jeans as Brodie apologised and threw his gym bag in the car and reversed out.

'So, to what do I owe the pleasure?'

Lisa couldn't help the trace of sarcasm which was clearly making her feelings known. The boy frowned and held back. Harry was undeterred and stepped closer.

'Lisa, hello, we wanted to have a word with you, if we can. Would it be alright now, if you have time of course.'

Harry cleared his throat and didn't wait for her to reply.

'Young Charlie here came to me this morning because he thought I had his camera.'

'It's Dad's camera.'

'Yes it's Jon's camera apparently and he wants it back.'

Lisa looked horrified.

'Look Lisa, I know you think I was spying on you or something, when I had actually, only moments before, taken it off Charlie and he apparently had been hiding at the edge of your hedge waiting to spring out on his brother. He is a kid, a kid larking around, and he shouldn't have been there.'

Harry paused and getting no response he continued. 'I did mean to come to you sooner.' He waved his arm back towards the street. 'With everything going on we have all been distracted. I sincerely want to apologise, and say I'm sorry I frightened you, and could we have it back as Jon is asking for it.'

Harry stood with his head hung low, he felt like he was sure Charlie had, when he had approached him earlier. Harry felt guilty over the whole misunderstanding and hated to think Lisa did not feel she could trust him.

Lisa's arms were crossed firmly under her bust as she stood on the step above them. Harry could feel the anger and tension as it seemed to vibrate from her as she searched for words to express how she felt, and yet also maintain control.

Glancing at Charlie she said.

'Have you seen what's on it?'

Charlie's head shot up and the blood drained from his face, the boy started to cry and Lisa felt an urge to comfort him, but also revulsion as she remembered what she had seen.

'No I haven't myself. Charlie tells me it's not very nice, can we step inside and discuss this?'

'As if I would let you in after what I saw, can I trust you, either of you? I thought you were a good man Harry, and you have certainly proved it the last few days, to be honest, at the moment, I'm not quite sure who I can trust.'

Lisa was staring Charlie down, until his flustered reply brought her guard down.

'I think my dad is a bad man and I want to take it to the police, please Lisa, I need it back so I can decide what to do.' Charlie's plea made her recoil.

'It really is your dad's?

'Yes.' Charlie looked her straight in the eye as if willing her to believe him.

'Come in then.' Lisa glanced around as if suddenly she felt like someone was watching.

They settled in the kitchen and after offering drinks Lisa perched on a stool. Lisa put her elbows on the counter top, and with her hands in front of her face, she was rubbing one thumb against the other in an agitated way.

Harry again went over the story and they both sat staring at her expectantly.

'Well now, I have a confession. I did think you were spying on me Harry. A few times I've felt uneasy and by the time I've walked out, there is no one around. I have even walked down to the reserve a few times to check. Whenever I look up the street the only person I usually see Harry, is you, at your yard or poking about someone else's. You can come across as a bit of a sticky beak.'

Lisa paused for a breath and realised Harry was generally shocked by her statement. She held her hand up as he started to apologise and explain his actions.

'It's ok Harry, I am starting to see how I have mixed things up, you know what happened to my sister and I can over react sometimes to things which to someone else would seem ok.'

Charlie was staring at her and she took the deep breath she always had to have before she continued.

'My sister was murdered on her way to school Charlie, I won't go into details, but cameras, and men acting what I think is not normal, can upset me a lot, I'm suspicious of people sometimes for no reason at all.'

'I'm sorry,' he mumbled. 'Lisa, what Harry said is true, neither of us took those photos and some of them were really bad. I didn't look at them all. I think my Dad is sick and I want him to stop.'

'So Harry you haven't seen them?'

Harry swung his head from side to side.

'Well the ones I saw were of nearly every woman in this street and it was clear they were unaware of them being taken. At first I thought it was me over reacting, the more I saw, the more I knew they were not right. I haven't even told Brodie about them with the whole Claire thing, it seemed not so important for a bit. I went back to have another look and I took it over to show Pat.'

Their faces dropped as they realised more people were aware of its contents. Lisa continued.

'Pat had to know, there were some very revealing ones of her in her yard, and I felt she should be aware of them before I showed them to the authorities.' Lisa nodded at Charlie silently telling him she agreed with him. 'I felt the women in the photos should have a say. I was going to go and see your Mum too, and

Moni.' Lisa paused again as they absorbed everything she was saying.

'After Claire and all the happenings in our street recently, I felt like the women should have the power in this. I hope you understand why and it makes sense to you both.'

They nodded still not speaking.

'The thing is, Maisie was at Pat's and I don't know who she knows, it's someone with authority, so she took it and is getting back to me today with their thoughts on how to go forward. She was a bit vague but I think she has something to do with the police and she promised to be discreet.'

Lisa was surprised she had told them. Too late, it was out now and they both genuinely looked shocked. Charlie looked at Harry.

'So, should we go to Maisie's now?' He held his head in his hands. 'I wish I had never found it.'

Lisa almost felt numb, she wondered for a second if they were all overthinking this whole mess. A mess it was, so many people now involved, did any of them really know what it was all about? Maybe they should confront Jon, get it over with and find out his side of the story. It might be he was in the same position as all of them, maybe he too, had found the camera. Harry shuffling to his feet roused her from her thoughts.

'So what now? What do you think we should do Harry? Are we on edge because of Claire, and this crazy state of the world at the moment?'

Harry looked her in the eye, he looked tired and his face was drawn.

'We wait for Maisie. If I see Jon I'll tell him I confiscated it but I've misplaced it, hopefully it might buy us some time. I can't deny I have a bad feeling about this. I hope we have all made a mistake, and as you say, things have been tough for us all lately, but something about this worries me. Thanks Lisa, I know we gave you a fright but we are all in this together, we have your back, same as we do Claire's.'

Lisa watched them leave, the old man and the boy each lost in their own thoughts. A thousand questions pumped in her head which she hadn't asked, what else did Charlie find, where was it exactly hidden? Away as if it was not meant to be found, or casually left out in the open. The images also struggled to find a place in her brain and she pushed them aside, she would deal with this then try to let them go, she had enough memories without storing more.

Brodie would be back soon and she would tell him. She needed his support. Lisa hoped Maisie would be in contact soon, as it was always the waiting which was the worst part, an empty void before any decision could be made. Sighing, Lisa busied herself with mindless chores, her head in another space until Brodie's loud knocking made her realise she had unconsciously locked the door. Lisa grimaced. I will get to the bottom of this because no one is going to make me afraid in my own home ever again. Clicking the lock over, her husband's puzzled face appeared and she pushed herself into his arms feeling the need to be held by someone she both loved and trusted.

Number 7 BonBon Street

Jason

Jason couldn't stop smiling. The look on Savannah's little face when he turned up with the horse was unforgettable and it seemed her whole body was shaking in excitement. Maisie had made him coffee and they had watched delighted as Savannah found her pace and described to them all the scenery she was passing on her imaginary ride, even jumping over a gate and nearly falling off. Jason suddenly felt a deep desire for a child of his own, a longing he had not acknowledged before.

He felt comfortable with both Maisie and Savannah and was thankful they had chosen to move to his street. It was good to be making friends again and getting to know his other neighbours better felt good as well.

Jason felt different now he had decided not to hide his secret anymore and his talk with Maisie and her reaction to it, had boosted those feelings as well. For the first time he felt like himself, settled inside, he had even been thinking about his father and in a good way which surprised him even more. This morning when he had been at Pat's to pick up the horse he had contemplated telling her, then had thought about Savannah, if he was too long, she would have exploded with excitement. Should he randomly tell people? He felt so much release already by telling one, would that hold if he told more? The questions had rattled around in his brain and he knew he would like to tell Pat, she was open minded and kind hearted, he was confident she would take it well. Then there was Brodie, he would tackle him head on and Lisa would be supportive, he was sure. It was funny he hadn't even thought about dressing up today. Maybe after some time the councillor would be proved correct, and deep down Jason hoped he would be one of the ones who would be cured, then he could let go of the guilt and shame which ruled his life.

Wanting to clear his head Jason headed over to Alice's shed to scratch around and find the tools he would need to make

Savannah's surprise. He had often borrowed things from the shed, as Jon had from him, and he had also helped Alice out with a bit of maintenance from time to time, so he didn't feel bad about being there when they were out. Alice was probably on a driving lesson again and he had seen young Charlie having a chat with Harry which had surprised him, then again this whole thing with Claire seemed to have brought them all together in a strange way, one person's tragedy showed the strength of others.

The shed was open and Jason blinked several times as his eyes adjusted to the dimness inside, he would search at the back first and hoped Jon had some good pine pieces he could work with. The basic structure was the easy part then he wanted to try and carve in something fancy on the ends. A noise at the back made his stop.

'Alice, it's Jason, sorry I thought you were out.'
Jon's head poked around some boxes.

'Jason, hey mate how are you.'

'I didn't know you were back.'

'Came back to collect some things then I'll be gone again.' Jon paused. 'You might as well be the first to know, Alice and I are splitting up and I won't be back, well not to live here anyway.'

Jason was stunned.

'So sorry to hear it, look I'll get out of your way, I was going to borrow a few tools but no matter, it's about time I bought a few more of my own.'

'No problem, borrow what you like I'm only after a few things today, haven't seen a camera in here have you, when you've been rummaging around?'

Jason shook his head as Jon continued.

'I had it in a box with a few other bits I want, and now I can't find any of them. Probably the only things I want to keep anyway. I asked Charlie earlier then decided I'd double back for another look myself.'

Jason could feel the anger creeping back into Jon's voice. He knew what it was like to have a marriage fail and even though he and Kylie had been amicable, he too had felt a bit of anger at the time, it was part of the process.

'Look, mate do you want to come over for a cuppa have a chat, it's a tough time for you and I've been your friend as well as Alice's, I'm happy to lend an ear.'
Jason again felt a shift.

'Nah, thanks, but truth be known, if she hadn't said it, it was about time I did. Alice was a convenience, it's all she ever was. I needed someone to look after these kids as neither their mother nor I really wanted them. Oh, they're ok now, but they tie you down mate. If you want my advice, think about it if you ever want to get some sheila knocked up.'

Jason was shocked beyond belief and was struggling to keep his held back words from transmitting to his face. He had always liked Jon and his knockabout attitude, which he had obviously wrongly assumed came from him working out in remote areas mainly with other blokes, but now he felt he was seeing who Jon really was. Jason's stomach churned for Alice who, it appeared, had been deceived by Jon as well. Jason suddenly felt claustrophobic and started to step back away towards the shed door.

'Well I'll leave you to it. If you need a hand packing up your stuff or I'm even happy to help Alice if you want it sent somewhere.' Jason reached out his hand. 'It's been good to know you Jon, and all the best.'

Jon gripped his hand firmly and Jason backed out into the sunshine, he felt dirty somehow and even though he knew people often said things they didn't mean when they were upset, this he felt was different and part of him was annoyed he had judged Jon so wrongly. It was no wonder Alice always seemed stressed, you never knew what went on behind closed doors.

Back in his own space, Jason started making mental notes of everything he would need, at the same time as he dug deep in his own shed. Jason knew he was trying to keep his mind occupied as other thoughts came knocking.

Jason had liked Alice from the start and she had always been kind to him. He had admired the way she managed the boys and had thought her brave taking on the two of them, when so much of the burden of parenting had been on her shoulders. He had watched as Jon returned each time as the fun dad and at times himself felt like Alice was managing three children as Jon's silly antics showed he had never quite grown up. His growing friendship with Maisie was suddenly mixed in as he considered the two women. Suddenly there were two wonderful single women in the street, both of whom would need some time, and hopefully become close friends. This last crazy year had certainly shown him how much he needed them. His hands pulled up some lengths of old timber to discover a perfect piece for the job as thoughts of Alice's face cupped in his hands clouded his mind.

Number 6 BonBon Street

Claire

Claire was bent over in the car keeping as low as she could below the window. Harry and Moni were making animated chatter in the front, all of them nervous as they left the garage and the roller door closed behind them. Claire's heart was pumping wildly and she felt exposed even though the odds of her being seen were slim. Harry had been out and bought a baby seat for Sophie and one of those shade things for the side window. The baby was cooing loudly as the sun flicked through trees and the light played across the roof of the car.

'All good now.'

Harry called to the backseat and Claire straightened up blinking in the sunlight and adjusting her seatbelt across her lap. She let out a sigh.

'Do you think anyone saw us?'

'No we didn't see a soul.' Moni was quick to reassure her.

Claire didn't know how she would ever repay their kindness, and now with the baby seat and the groceries, she was trying to at least keep tab of how much money she would owe them. Harry told her not to worry, it didn't matter, but Claire was determined. One day, somehow, she would repay them, if not in money, then at least in kind.

The trip was not long and only made further by Harry taking tactical turns, to be safe, he had said.

The little house was beautiful, close to a few shops and a short walk from parks and cycle ways. Claire broke down as she entered, the generosity of, not only her neighbours, but of the people who owned this house, people she did not even know, overwhelmed her. Moni turned holding Sophie, and Harry dropped the bags he was carrying to comfort her.

You'll be right girl, he muttered as tears welled in his eyes also. Claire thought Harry had cried almost more than her. She wasn't sure if it was his age, but he'd had to use all of his emotions in the last few days and had done well to express them when needed, and yet also hold some in check. Although Moni was closer in age, Claire could not help to be drawn to Harry and his kind nature. She regretted now her thoughts of him as a busybody as she could see he hadn't a bad or suspicious bone in his body. He made her miss her dad and sometimes, although Harry would never know it, he made her cry more, his warm dad hugs making her feel she was loved and safe.

Moni bustled about settling Sophie on the floor in a patch of sun before unpacking the groceries they had bought. Claire could not believe Moni's generosity of spirit, she seemed to be everywhere yet never moving, her kindness seeped out and spread itself, settling upon you, reassuring you she was there if needed, yet never interfering. Claire's days with them, after the blur of her leaving Mark, had shown her their love for each other and also made her realise how Moni had made many a sacrifice by falling in love with an older man. If nature took its natural course Moni would lose her partner probably around the time others her age were retiring to spend time together, she would never quite fit into any one group. Love was a strange emotion she was realising, which had many facets to it. Some loved for a long time, some for a short time and a piece of it stayed with you no matter what.

Claire hoped one day she would be able to remember a good day with Mark, so she could tell Sophie a positive thing about her father, then again part of her wished he would disappear forever. As she felt stronger every day, Claire worried if maybe, in some dark way, she was like him, as ideas of poisoning him or wishes of something bad happening to him sneaked into her brain. She would never act them out though, she told herself, or deliberately hurt someone, and there lay the difference.

The sunshine filled the room and they again went over her thoughts and ideas for the days ahead. Mark had been non responsive and as yet Claire had not felt strong enough to talk with his family again. The solicitor had been wonderful keeping in touch and passing on messages from them, which all seemed positive, although she worried if she could trust them. *I trusted Mark, and look how it turned out*, she thought. Were his family trying to find out where she was, would they try to take Sophie? After all, Claire did not know if she had any means of support now. Harry had told her not to worry about the solicitor fee, as they were old friends and he would sort it, nor the groceries, it was all taken care of. Claire still was concerned and worried if Mark had found out how she had deceived him by having a secret account.

Sophie did the biggest yawn and they all smiled, Moni jumped up to wrap her tight and Claire was grateful. Even though Sophie was so tiny, the lift from the floor up made different muscles ache as they stretched beneath the still dark and angry looking bruises. At least it was a constant reminder of why she was here, and why she shouldn't go back.

'Do you think you will have children?'
The question blurted out before she had thought about it.
Moni looked at Harry.

'No, we won't. Harry has two grown children, who have children of their own. We don't get to see them anymore, Harry's children couldn't come to terms with their father remarrying. I think we both feel quite honoured to be spending this time with you and Sophie, and anyway, I always wanted to jump straight to grandmother status, all the fun and none of the responsibility.'

Although Harry reached over and took Moni's hand, Claire saw Moni's sad smile was hiding a lot of heartache.

'It was one of my main concerns before we were married, as Moni does love kids and she assured me they weren't on her radar.'

Harry's eyes never left his wife's face until she raised hers to look directly into his. Claire felt the bond between them, and although love was not a visible thing, Claire was sure she was looking at it right at this moment and it was greater than she had ever imagined. Claire wanted it too and was sad she had wasted her time on something less than what was in front of her now.

With the baby asleep they motioned it was time for them to go.

'Now I have this phone here for you, we won't be far and I've put Pat and Lisa's number on it, and ours too of course. I forgot about Alice, um, I know, I'll give her your number.' He took her hand. 'Day or night it's no trouble.'

Claire felt the tears again and she hugged him tight.

'Thank you, you saved my life, I can never forget it, any of it.'

Harry patted her arm and turned away, as both she and Moni knew he could not contain his tears. A quick hug to Moni with the promise they would be back tomorrow and they were gone.

On impulse Claire went to every window peering out looking for her silent enemy. He would not come in the shape of a man now, more as a ghostly figure that would change the course of her days as she looked over her shoulder, planned her exits, and learned to live again with a black shadow always in her thoughts as she tried to protect this little girl.

She was happy with the quiet, there was a lot to think about. She was never going back, no matter what happened, and if he tried to be in their life again she would disappear, as the risk for Sophie was too great. Mark had proved what kind of man he was too many times, and the look in his eyes the last time was something Claire would not forget. Claire could never let him near her daughter again, because even if he didn't hurt her, he would use Sophie as a bargaining tool.

Moni had told her to rest and take time to sort things out but the adrenaline and determination she had felt when she left was still with her and Claire wanted it to stay with her, to keep her moving forward. Losing her parents had been so hard and she had dealt with so many issues, emotions and worries about her future then, she could now see how she had fallen into the trap of leaning on Mark and his family for support as it, at the time, seemed to take some of the weight off her young shoulders. The trouble was she had relinquished some of her independence with it.

The help and support of these people, her new friends and neighbours was different. Maybe she was older and wiser, willing to take more notice. These people had shown her to be careful, think it out and not be eaten up by Mark and his actions. Sophie needed a mother who could trust people, and to encourage her to grow and love both men and women. All these thoughts then wound around back to the same conclusion, Mark had to make the right decision and stay away. One step at a time girl, don't react before there is something to react to.

Money was a concern as Mark had taken over control of the accounts. Her mother had whispered in her ear as she was growing up, *always save something for you.* Claire had also received some good advice from her parent's lawyer and even though she had fronted with the house deposit and the first lot of payments while they moved and settled in, she did have an account no one knew about, set up in a trust for her future, she hoped it was enough. Part of her wondered why she had never told Mark, it seemed her love was not always blind, more cautious and now she was grateful for her foresight.

The phone from Harry was really invaluable and she placed a call to her lawyer to see if she was aware of any news and to start taking a stand. Claire then called her bank and arranged an interview with the closest branch to ask for some private advice, as well as to see if she could repay Harry and Moni, and to possibly buy a small car or at least use the trust fund as collateral for a loan. Claire also needed to start collecting proof of her payments and to find out what Mark had been doing with the accounts since she last was allowed to look.

Claire realised how far she had sunk and how reliant on Mark she had become. Claire shook her head slowly, still shocked, now she was looking at it from a distance, at how much she had allowed him to take over. Little by little she had released her hold and slid without protest under his control. Claire wondered, if he had never physically harmed her, how far he would have gone psychologically, and would she have realised what he was doing. It all seemed so much clearer now.

No matter what stay strong she continued to repeat over and over. Don't think about the terrible things which could happen, make him small in your world, a nothing to you, Sophie, or our lives together. Let him rot in hell while you take back what is yours.

Sophie stirred and Claire changed her, trying to wake her a bit so hopefully she would sleep through the meetings later. The plan was set in her head and she felt confident even though she still pulled her cap low over her forehead before she wriggled the pram out the door and set off for the short walk to the bank. Sophie smiled up at her and Claire felt a rush of love for this tiny soul whose life was changing with each passing day even though she was too young to realise.

Number 4 BonBon Street

Maisie

As soon as Jason had left, Maisie's phone rang.

'I ran those photos and made a few calls, I think you have stumbled onto more than you know here girl.'

The deep voice of her boss immediately brought his image to mind and she could see him lying back in his chair slightly swaying from side to side as he spoke.

'Keep those cameras running twenty-four seven, we are sorting a team now, and Maisie, be careful, there are some not nice people living on your street. Send me a few stills from this morning if you can and keep a low profile until I get to the bottom of this.'

'Yes boss.' Maisie spoke with a hint of humour, although she knew the seriousness by his tone. 'I've been getting to know the neighbours and I told the girl who gave me the camera I would get back to her, what should I say?'

He hesitated.

'As little as possible, we don't want him to know we are onto him, see what you can find out without raising alarm.' He paused again and she could hear a shuffling of papers and knew by the change in his voice he was now sitting up straight and listening to someone else probably with one hand loosely over the speaker.

'Sorry, look I don't want to send an unknown into the street yet, this pandemic makes any movement stand out like a sore thumb. I think if you could come in, it would be best, we need to talk. I know this isn't what you signed up for on this case, you will understand when you see what hit my desk this morning. Go and placate the neighbours, how much you tell them is up to you. I'm confident you will know what to say, make sure you can trust them and get in here as soon as you can. Have you someone to mind Savannah?'

'Yes I'm sure someone will look after her. I'll sort stuff here and be with you as soon as I can, sounds serious.'

Disconnecting, Maisie was already thinking about whom she could trust, they all looked like decent people, on the outside. She would just have to trust her gut. Last night her boss had hinted to it being a much bigger case after Maisie had sent him the photos. It had made the hairs rise on the back of her neck. Talk about you never knew who lived in your street!

Maisie rechecked her equipment and sent the still shots of Jason and Jon outside the shed off to the big boys. It was this kind of game she wanted to get out of. Maisie realised how much she had changed, no adrenaline-rush pushed through her and there was only now a fear her life might be jeopardised by it all. Maybe she should confront Alice today or would it be getting too close to the situation? Probably would be, there was enough drama in BonBon Street for the moment. Maisie sighed and Savannah paused for a moment and looked at her with quizzical eyes.

'It's ok Maisie, things always work out.'

Maisie smiled at her far too wise little sister. As Savannah resumed her ride, Maisie thought the hardest thing today might be getting her off the horse.

'I've called my horse Snowy, because we rode over some mountains and all we could see was snow. It was so pretty Maisie, so very pretty.'

'Well, I think it's a very good name for such an adventurous pony, now how about we give him a rest and get some jobs done, he must be tired from climbing mountains.'

Savannah cocked her head to one side.

'Can my pony be a boy and a girl at the same time Maisie?'

'It can be anything you want it to be Miss Savannah, now hop down and cover the pony with this rug to keep it warm and we might pop down to Pat's house for a bit, what do you think?'

'Ooh, yes please, I love Mrs Pat. I can tell her what a good rider I am now.'

Since yesterday, this little one had blossomed, and all because kindness had crept in their door. Maisie was truly grateful, and hopeful, it would remain this way. With a deep breath she called Lisa and arranged to meet. Harry would have to wait, though she would like a quiet word with Charlie, or even Jason, to see if they dropped any unexpected clues.

Maisie ran a few ideas and conversations through her head. She did not want any of the men in the street to be aware of who she was, and what she was up to. If they knew it could blow the whole thing up, and they could lose track of him, though this time he would not be so hard to find, not now she had photos of him. They couldn't chance him finding out they were on his tail until they had all the irrefutable evidence in place. It may be her last job and Maisie did not want to blow it, she also knew it would change the life of at least one person in this street for the better. Good and bad always hand in hand it seemed lately, though this would be the extremes of both.

Alice waved as they ambled to Pat's. She will be glad when those boys get their licence Maisie thought, they were getting better, though it amused her to see the look of relief on Alice's face each time they returned. I've settled in so easily, once this was over it could prove to be the best thing to ever happen to us, it already is for Savannah.

Pat's smiling face greeted Savannah and she frowned as Mark stalked out of his house slamming the door and glaring at them before heading off down the path towards the reserve. Must need some air, Maisie thought, and her eyes followed him as he disappeared over the slope looking almost cartoonish as he disappeared bit by bit down the steep path. Pat raised her eyebrows and Maisie shrugged her shoulders, she had more on her plate today than to worry about some weasel.

Maisie asked Pat if she would mind Savannah for a few hours and both their faces lit up, especially when Pat pulled out a large crate of building blocks. Maisie knew Savannah would be lost in them for hours and probably only the horse would drag her home tonight.

Pat tried to ask a few questions, in a code like manner so as not to say too much in front of the child. Maisie reassured her it would be better to wait until she returned with some official information, it did look like they were on to something and she would let her and Lisa know what she could on her return. Savannah hardly raised her head as Maisie said goodbye and Pat walked her to the door.

'Don't worry she will be fine.'

'I know, thanks Pat.'

Maisie turned to go.

'Pat, I probably don't have to say this to you but, could you keep things to yourself, even with the people who do know about it. I find once people start talking the story changes no matter how much truth they speak. I'd rather hear what my boss has to say before we start looking sideways at someone. Harry may be innocent of all this, who knows, but I'd rather deal in facts and if word seeps out, the real culprit might disappear on us.'

'No trouble at all, I won't breathe a word Maisie. Now off you go. The sooner you get back, the sooner we'll know.'
Pat started to turn away.

'And don't worry.'

Maisie felt strange, she had quickly become used to having her sister in tow, walking away without her made her feel empty. I suppose this will be how it will feel when she goes to school. School may be a learning curve for both of us.

Lisa was waiting for her at the gate and hurried her inside anxious to hear any news or insights. Maisie glanced around, it was a comfortable home and even though the furniture looked sparse it was expensive and spread out in a modern uncluttered theme. No family photos hung on the walls and the kitchen was spacious and gleaming, not one item littered the bench and the splash back shone.

Lisa was looking at her expectantly and Maisie realised she was supposed to be answering a question of some kind, she shook her head and sat down on one of the fancy kitchen stools.

'Oh, um, tea please. Now I can't tell you too much and I must stress to you the importance of keeping things to ourselves. Have you told Brodie yet, about the camera?'

'No. Every time I've gone to, something has stopped me, and after talking to you, even though I trust him, I thought the less people who know the better, and it might save him some grief by not knowing.'

Maisie nodded, she had never known the deep trust love seemed to bring and wondered if it was a good or a bad thing. It didn't seem to have worked for Claire, then again Maisie did not know her full story as yet.

'Look, my boss was concerned and I have to go into the office to look at some things. He didn't want to talk about over the phone and seems concerned about several people in this street. Until we get to the bottom of it, you and I can't really trust anyone. I moved to BonBon Street for two reasons, one, I wanted to find a home for my sister, she has had a bit of a rough start to life. By sheer coincidence, my team needed some surveillance work done here, hence me getting the house and being a bit coy about myself, until the job was done.'

Lisa was staring at her and Maisie realised she had been rattling on as if Lisa knew what she did for a living and was totally following the conversation.

'Sorry Lisa, I've been working as an undercover cop. I was going to transfer out, then this surveillance job came up and my boss thought it would be a good way for me to settle into my life with Savannah and give me a permanent home. No one here was ever going to find out I was spying on them, and when the job was done, I would become a regular neighbour and my transfer would come through. Life was going to become more normal.' Maisie shrugged. 'It seems as though there is more to BonBon Street than meets the eye, and I fear what my boss has to tell me is a bigger case than when we started.'

'Wow, so who has done what, is it Harry or Jason, he is right across, you could see him easily from your place?'

'Until I go into head office, I know as much as you, something about the camera has triggered a connection to something else and whether I was watching the same person or what, we will have to wait and see. Thing is, I need you to please keep it to yourself or make sure you truly trust anyone you have to tell, I'll be back in a few hours and we can take it from there.'

Lisa nodded though Maisie could see a thousand questions running through her head.

'Pat is minding Savannah for me, so I might head off now. And Lisa also be aware, I might not be able to tell you a whole lot either when I get back. My boss did say if I trusted someone I could say things, and like you with Brodie, I don't want to burden you with too much or make you act unnaturally in any way if there is an operation going on. Please trust me Lisa, because when this is over I still want to live here and be friends.'

Lisa leapt off her stool and threw her arms around her. Maisie so denied of affection growing up was surprised and felt awkward, then softened into the embrace knowing this was a moment she was making another new friend.

Number 6 BonBon Street

Mark

Mark tried not to look as he stormed out across the street. The new bird was certainly getting friendly with the old girl next door and he wondered what her game was. He hadn't been out of the house much as alcohol had been his only companion, his head this morning told him to get out and breathe some fresh air.

His mother's endless messages were driving him insane, so what if he had pulled Claire into line a bit, it was none of their business. Even his father had called and told him to pull his head in, police were the last things they wanted on their doorstep again.

We pulled you out of enough trouble when you were young, you're a bloody fool. Claire was going to be the making of you, you've blown it again haven't you son.

Yeah well, thanks Dad for the support, it's not like you were a shining example to live up to.

Mark's head was still full of rage, he rubbed his temples in frustration, she had the whole street against him and at the moment, with this pandemic, it was the whole of their world. He had not really wanted to mix with any of them, now they all made themselves aware of his every movement and he could see friendships would never be made or rekindled after this.

Coming out of the tree line he saw a movement down towards the creek. Ahh, now there was someone he did want to see. Mark stopped for a moment. This had been the bonus of them moving up here, and to this street, it was so close, really what were the chances, he had thought at the time. They would be together like old times. A slow smile crept across his face, they could be together like he'd always wanted when they were kids.

Number 4 BonBon Street

Maisie

Maisie rifled through the paper work, things had certainly begun to add up. Like her, people all over the country gathered tiny pieces of information and one day something triggered enough to warrant all this information finally being linked further together.

'Well we certainly picked you a doozie of a street, didn't we?'

'You sure did! The connection to me alone was astounding, it seems all of these people are linked in ways they don't even know yet. I'm trying to get my head around it all. The minute when you think life can't get stranger than fiction, it does.'

Maisie's boss laughed.

'I think we have both been in this job long enough, to always expect the unexpected.'

'So what happens now?'

'Well, a lot of it could now hinge on you. Have you told Alice she's your sister?'

Maisie shook her head and filled him in a bit more about what had been going on.

'I've been trying to fit in and not let anyone know about my work. I did tell Lisa this morning.'

Maisie pointed to the rough map she had drawn of the street, indicating which house was Lisa's.

'After you filled me in a bit more last night I didn't know whether to approach Alice or not, so I erred on the side of caution.'

He nodded his head slowly.

'It's been decided to ramp this up before we lose him. I've also been torn about your situation and how I can keep you out of it. This damn pandemic makes things harder yet so much easier, all our clients have been in lockdown and easier to catch.' He chuckled as he said it.

'It's been quite a haul lately.'

Maisie almost laughed, he was a good man, an honest cop and a wonderful mentor, she had been lucky at times and meeting, and working for him had taught her a lot, not only about the job. He was the father figure she had never had.

'So how did these photos link in?'

'Come, we have a bit of a timeline on the whiteboard.'

They wandered out into the main office. Several colleagues acknowledged Maisie and one piped up.

'Good job Maisie, it's a bit of a can of worms we're sifting through.'

They had printed out some of the photos and the most graphic were placed in different sequences along the board. Maisie was relieved to see none were of Pat or Lisa.

'So, some of these date back a bit so let's start here. This is Sally Lisbon, fifteen years old murdered on her way to school in north western Victoria.

Maisie's boss paused waiting for her to see the connection. The girl's body lay twisted and bruised, her hands had been tied above her head and a photo was wedged in them clearly showing the same girl laughing at something in a school yard. Maisie thought she looked familiar and as yet couldn't quite put her finger on it, maybe it was a memory from a newspaper or television news when it had occurred. Her boss spoke up again.

'Sally was your neighbour Lisa's, sister.'

Maisie gasped and slapped her hand over her mouth, her eyes wide in disbelief.

'No,' she muttered as she looked again and slowly recognised the likeness. 'You mean … no, how could he move near her, what is he, a stalker of grieving families?' She shook her head trying to take it all in.

'Wait for it, it gets better. You obviously didn't go through all the photos because you would have picked it up. We ran facials on everyone on here, two of the others were missing persons, same sort of modus operandi, young girls, pretty, went missing before or after school but bodies never found. A couple of women in the middle here showed up, still alive but had prostitution raps and cocaine habits so long they now don't remember anything. Seems getting beaten up was a regular thing.'

He paused for a moment to make sure she was following.

'Timeline wise there are a few breaks, your young Claire shows up from time to time, we think it's her from your photos, as she is a bit younger. They are all normal happy snaps and she seems to know they were being taken.'

Maisie frowned.

'So Claire knew him when she was younger?'

'No, well maybe, we are fairly certain this camera belongs to Claire's husband Mark, and for some reason he hid it in Jon's shed. Some of the shots of your street seem to come from his direction, and, what does fit in is Mark's link back to Sally and the area where she lived. Mark was also the one who, he put up two fingers and wiggled them as speech marks, *found Sally*.

Maisie scratched her head.

'Then why would he move to BonBon Street, a whole state away from where he came from, in which also lives the sister of the body he discovered?'

'I did say it was complicated, so here is what we have worked out. Mark was a violent adolescent who skims under the surface of attracting the law. Sally goes missing and it frustrates him she can't be found, so he *finds her* and becomes the hero in his own mind. Nothing pinpoints to him, he's a sly bastard and I think he had planned this out fairly well and was good at covering his tracks. At the time he was a gangly kid, no record and upset enough he was not really considered as a suspect, although they did take his fingerprints and there is a recorded interview. He asked several times in the interview about the photo, at the time no one really picked up on it until we caught his reflection in one of these ones.' He paused for a moment to take a breath and point it out to Maisie.

'Now Jon you say, turned up yesterday and asked his kid for the camera?'

Maisie nodded, so he continued.

'Well he obviously knows about the camera and we traced him back and he is not from the same district as Sally, or Mark, all from Victoria all went to different schools etc. etc. I'm sure there will be a connection in here somewhere, we just haven't pinpointed it yet.' He scratched his head slowly as he chose his words and tried to solve the puzzle at the same time.

'So presuming he knows what's on the camera, and this other character has moved near him and has been sneaking in and out of his shed, we have to presume he was involved in some way or this Mark character has something over him to keep his mouth shut. Your surveillance did pick up Mark and Jon having a short conversation and on it Jon doesn't seem impressed by his companion. As I said last night, your easy insurance fraud job has spiralled into a full blown reopening of a murder case and possibly, hopefully, will find these other girls so their families can have some peace at last. He seems to have been almost brash about Sally, now we look back. So why didn't he brag about the other girls, do we have a copycat killer? I'm waiting on some more info from the Victorian boys but here's what we plan to do.'

Heads together, he mapped out the plan. The bonus, was the whole street was watching Mark and Maisie would soon know if he made any unusual movements. Maisie couldn't help think, if they put him away, it would give Claire a few clear years of freedom without worrying where he was and looking over her shoulder all the time.

Jon was going to be questioned, he had to be as the vital piece of evidence, had come from his shed. Warrants were being sought so both Mark and Jon's residences and outbuildings could be searched.

Maisie wasn't sure how Alice would react, when she found out it was Maisie who was partly responsible for her husband being questioned, and maybe charged, if he was guilty. It could break up their marriage or if she took his side and thought he was innocent, it would destroy Maisie's own dream of being part of her sister's life.

Time would have to be the teller of this tale, and if it was the sacrifice she had to make to get some criminal off the streets, then it was what she would do. Maisie's main aim was to help build a safer world for Savannah and the generations to come. No place better to start than in her own backyard.

Number 7 BonBon Street

Jason

Jason liked the feel of the smooth timber as he sanded and shaped it, he liked working with his hands. He had been out and bought the tools he needed along with the timber and paint. Meeting Jon had upset him and the thought of going back over there while he was still around had turned his stomach and prompted him to purchase the things he needed. He hadn't asked Harry, it was probably best to not get involved with anyone else, and who knows, if this turned out ok, he might make a few other things too. A man can never have too many tools.

A smile had played across his lips whenever he thought about Savannah and her happy laugh, it really was nice to have a child in the street, they showed no judgement of people and were accepting of who you were. Kindness was the key to their world.

He had seen Maisie come out of Lisa's and hurry to her own house. Her garage door slid open and he continued to watch as she drove away. Savvy must be with Lisa. He moved the sawhorses outside and started to bolt the frame together, he had decided to make some little cubbyholes on one side underneath and two drawers on the other side for storage, he had seen it on the Internet, the little cubes looked like horse stables in a row and he intended to buy some plastic farm animals to place in each one.

A movement caught his eye and Mark appeared up the laneway, a silly grin on his face. Jason turned away slightly, trying to concentrate on his task, here was another neighbour he wasn't interested in getting to know.

Jason heard his name. It was Mark.

'Oh, um, hi Mark, nice day for it.'

Mark stepped closer.

'I hope you're not involved in all this crap, few of these busybody's round here seem to think they know my business.' Mark was muttering yet also glancing up and down the street as he did.

'Claire and I had a few tiffs and she's gone to her mum's for a bit, has a touch of the baby blues, she should be back any day. Not that anyone around here will listen to my side.'

'Well, it's none of my business mate.' Jason grimaced as he said it, for Mark certainly was not his mate and never would be.

'I hope it all turns out for the baby, eh, she's the important one.' He turned back to his task and annoyingly Mark approached again.

'You've been in Jon's shed haven't you?'

Jason nodded and wondered how he knew.

'Haven't seen a camera have you, I lent it to Jon and now he can't find it.'

'No, can't say I have but I'll keep an eye out for you.'

'No worries, thanks mate.'

Mark turned away and Jason breathed a sigh of relief before Mark turned yet again.

'If you do, don't turn it on ok, wrecks the drive if you don't do it right.'

'No worries.'

Jason raised his hand and watched as Mark disappeared into his garage. He is a weirdo, Jason thought, and he shook his head, the sooner he's gone the better and why on earth would Jon have his camera? Jon wasn't there half the time and funny, now he thought about it, he had never seen Mark and Jon even have a conversation. Maybe the craziness of the world was having an extra go at each street and it happened to be their turn on BonBon Street at the moment. Best get this bed made so at least one child can have a comfy spot to dream her dreams, and he set to tightening the bolts which held it together.

Jason saw Alice return and hovered outside hoping she would say hello. He felt a bit guilty, wanting to strengthen their friendship by offering a kindly ear. Deep down he knew he was really smitten with her and even though it was only a few hours since Jon had told him of their separation, it had awakened in Jason the deep feelings he had for her, and he realised, had held on to for quite some time. Working methodically with the timber had given him time to think and sort his feelings. He knew it may all come to nothing, and he would have to take it slow, the thing was, whenever he closed his eyes it was Alice's face he dreamed of. Her kind, caring nature had warmed his heart and now all he had to do was tell her his secret. Her reaction would be all he needed to take the next step. Slowly at first, and hopefully after she had time to grieve the loss of her marriage, and of course make sure the boys were settled, then hopefully she would turn to find him waiting for her. It was a movie he played out in his head.

Maisie, he knew, would be a true friend. Even though Alice and Maisie were similar, in fact now he thought about it, they even looked a bit alike, they had the same slim build, rich brown hair and unusual eyes; somehow Jason knew Alice would be the one who held his heart. It was funny really, a worldwide pandemic and a frightened brave girl, who would ever have thought they would both come together to make him a better, and yes, a braver, person as well. Life was a funny game to play yet somehow at last, he was willing to jump in and see where it would take him. You had to be in it, to win it and Jason could now see how he had kept himself out of it. Now, no matter how it all turned out, at last he was at least willing to give living a go.

Number 6 BonBon Street

Claire

Claire was furious, their joint bank account was nearly drained and all of Mark's bills had been getting paid out of it. Quite a lot of withdrawals at the local liquor shop had been made and almost daily payments to, what the bank assistant believed, may be an online betting account. Yes the house was in her name, although there were notes of enquiries made by someone to try to change it. The bank took pride in its security of information though Claire found it was frustrating as well. When she had walked in, the assistant had blushed and turned away not knowing whether to comment on Claire's bruised face and arm. Claire was not flaunting it, she had wanted them to understand her situation without too much explanation.

A park bench beckoned and Claire was grateful to sit for a minute to collect her thoughts, the printed bank documents still clutched firmly in her hand. She could do this, she knew she could, there were early release clauses in her trust account and they had warned her to get advice as Mark may still have claim to some of it, they were married after all. She had left the rest alone except to arrange for a debit card for her small account, there was enough there to keep her going for a while. She was angry at him, not only for how he had hurt her, these new things were adding to the straws on the camels already broken back. How could he give no thought to Sophie's future or wellbeing, it seemed he really didn't care about his child or her welfare. Claire wondered what had happened to all the money he had been receiving from the government, probably gambled away with everything else. Claire took a deep breath, she had a house, she had a trust fund, she had a degree and she had this precious bundle of joy, more blessings than most and only one thing standing in her way. She hoped he would rot in hell, she only had to figure out a way to get him there, only then would she truly be free.

The dappled light through the trees was comforting and she unconsciously rocked the pram with one foot as she stared out across the park, lost in thought as different ideas of how to move forward tumbled around in her head.

'Hello Claire.'

Claire jumped, one hand grabbed the pram as if to flee as the other tried to gather the papers on her lap.

Claire's startled eyes looked up.

'Oh my god, it's you.' It was all she could say. Tears sprung to her eyes and one slowly rolled down her cheek, unchecked as she hung her head and quietly began to sob.

Harry rubbed her shoulder.

'It's alright love, sorry I startled you, I went to the house and when you weren't there I wandered down here, I wanted to check you were ok.'

Claire's shoulders still shook as she braved a smile.

'Sorry you gave me a fright, I'll have to be more careful, I shouldn't be sitting out here in the open.'

'Yes you should. You have as much right as anyone to walk around doing what you want to do, don't let him take life away from you.'

Harry sat down next to her.

'I forgot to give you the charger cord for the phone so I came back. I'm glad you felt brave enough to go for a walk, I'm proud of you.'

Claire did not know what she would have done without this kind man. She thought Harry was a true gentleman, an old fashioned one maybe, but a genuine one. He wanted to help everyone and jumped in where ever he saw a need, even if it meant unwittingly stepping on someone's toes. Claire smiled and took his hand.

'I'm so grateful for you Harry, and Moni, I'm so happy Sophie will have you in her life, it's one of the best gifts I can give her, some unofficial grandparents.'

Claire saw his eyes well up again and giving his hand a gentle shake suggested they go back to the house.

'We might get in a quiet cup of tea before missy here wakes up. For once I can make you one.'

They rose and ambled back towards the house enjoying the day and each other's company. Harry pushed the pram proudly and several woman glanced at them as they passed, watching a proud granddad spending time with his family.

The kettle on, Claire explained about her visit to the bank and her upcoming appointment with the solicitor.

'It seems there are some early release clauses on my parent's trust fund for me. I'm not really sure how much there is, the solicitor said it had been invested wisely and was substantially more than before, they are checking on it. My mother never liked Mark. She didn't know him well and didn't want to either. I used to sneak out to meet him, it was the only rebellious thing I ever did.' She looked at Harry.

'I was actually a bit of a goody two shoes and Mark, well, he was the tough guy at school, always had a crowd around him, he wasn't afraid of anyone. I liked being popular and I was, because of him.' Claire grimaced. 'It seems Mum's assessment was right, then suddenly they were gone and he was all I had to lean on. They say love is blind, I think I was downright foolish.'

Harry looked over his cup at her.

'Well it's not too late and as long as he leaves you alone you'll be fine, remember, you have a whole street to support you.'

'Do you think I'm foolish to stay, Harry? Shouldn't I be running as far as I can, he won't stop, I know it, there is evil in him and,' she frowned, 'almost a sadistic streak. He won't like thinking I have gotten the better of him.'

Claire reached out her hand.
'I want to fight him, I'm just scared he will come after not only me, but you and Moni and Alice, everyone who is helping me. I really believe now he is capable of hurting us all.'

Harry tried to soothe and calm her, a clear head was all she needed and Harry had great faith in the police and the justice system.

'Take your time Claire, you are safe for now so gather all the advice you need before you act. Mark might think he's a tough guy but he won't be able to fight his way out if you have all the facts and everything in place. Moni and I will support you in whatever you decide and I can tell you something you don't know.'

Harry paused.

'You getting away has brought our whole street together, we are so proud of you. All of us will do everything we can to protect you, you have my promise.'

Claire wondered where the tears came from, she thought she had cried enough for a lifetime yet they still appeared to trickle down her face, and fill her heart with both joy and sadness. How very lucky she was.

Number 8 BonBon Street

Pat

Pat was surprised at what a glorious afternoon she'd had. Savannah was such a joy to have around. Everything seemed new and exciting for her and she had let slip with a few things which made Pat realise this little one had already lived a lifetime no one, and especially not a child, should have to.

Pat and Keith had never been blessed with children, their nieces and nephews had always filled the gap. Pat's easy smile made children immediately warm to her and Keith had always had a gentle way of teaching them, whether it had been playing a game or working with tools in his shed, they had all enjoyed coming to visit when they could.

Savannah had been so excited with the blocks and they had built great towers before knocking them down in fits of laughter.

'Do you have blocks at your house?' Pat enquired innocently. Savannah shook her head.

'I have a bunny, not a real one, and some books and Maisie said if I'm good Santa might bring me a dolly, I'd like a baby one. Do you have a dolly Mrs Pat?'

Pat liked the way Savannah had picked a name for her, it took her another step away from her grief and made her sound whole somehow, not Keith's widow or Nurse Pat. Mrs Pat, had a nice ring to it.

'I do have a dolly. She is very old and I've had her a long time, from when I was a little girl like you. Do you want to see her?'

Savannah nodded. 'Ooh, yes please.'

Pat went to the spare room and delicately carried the doll in its satin gown back to the lounge room. She laid her down then showed Savannah how the doll's arms could move and her legs were soft down to the knees. The little girl touched the dress gently and stroked the ribbon which firmly tied the doll's bonnet on under its chin.

'Mrs Pat, she is beautiful, much too pretty to play with, does she sleep in your bed?'

'No she doesn't. My mother gave her to me so she is pretty special and it's why I am gentle with her. Look when you sit her up, her eyes open.'

Savannah stared at the bright blue eyes and long lashes.

'Oh my, she is almost real, isn't she. Maisie said we can get a baby one day, like baby Sophie. Do you think I could ask Santa for one too?'

Pat had to laugh.

'No I don't think Santa brings real babies, you will have to wait a bit longer for one of those.'

They had busied themselves most of the afternoon, Pat kept one eye out the window noting who was about. Jason was still working outside his shed, he had told her about his plans of a bed for Savannah, and it looked like he had made a start. Pat had paused at one stage when she saw Mark over there and even from here she could feel Jason's discomfort by the way he held his shoulders and didn't allow Mark to come any closer.

Pat sucked in her bottom lip, chewing on it slightly as she tried to imagine their conversation. She looked down to find Savannah standing beside her and her little hand slid into Pat's.

'He's a bad man Mrs Pat, he hurts people, like my daddies did. I don't want him to hurt Sophie's mummy anymore.'

Pat saw the grim look on her face and knelt down.

'Not for you to worry about. I'm sure Claire and Sophie are going to be fine.'

'Then why did she have bruises, like my mum got. It can't have been the baby.'

Pat stared back into her solemn eyes, Savannah's chin was out and her teeth were tightly clenched. Pat wasn't sure how to explain.

'I know he did Mrs Pat, because it's how I got this.' Savannah raised her light fringe and rubbed a finger along the scar on her forehead. Pat cupped her hands around Savvy's cheeks, fighting back her tears.

'He pushed me hard when I tried to stop him, he kept on hurting her. He wouldn't stop.'

Pat knew her face was showing her dismay.

'After the lights took her away Mrs Pat, Mummy never came back from the hospital, then Maisie came. I'm happy now, because Maisie said no one will ever hurt me again and Maisie doesn't lie.'

Pat was, probably for the first time in her life, speechless.

'Could I have a drink now Mrs Pat, I'm very, very thirsty.'

Pat went through the motions and every part of her was saddened when this beautiful child went straight back to playing as if that was how life was. What is wrong with people, she thought with a mixture of sadness and anger.

The afternoon disappeared and Pat let Savannah help her peel a few vegetables, by the time Maisie came back they would all be ready for a bite to eat. Pat was enjoying her company, it filled her day and made it seem life may return to the new normal everyone was talking.

Pat had given Savannah a bath, with bubbles, much to the child's delight and popped her back in her play clothes when the doorbell sounded and a tired looking Maisie stood on the other side of the door.

'Thanks so much Pat, I'm sorry I was so long, things are a bit complicated and I kept hoping you wouldn't mind.'

'No problem at all, she is a delightful child and has even helped me make the dinner so come in, I was about to serve hers up, it's ready so now we can eat together.'

Maisie made a sign of protest and as Pat would hear none of it, she ushered Maisie inside.

Savannah slipped off the chair where she had been waiting patiently and grabbed Maisie's hand.

'Look Maisie, we made a castle. And I had a bath with bubbles, Mrs Pat took a picture to show you, I even had them on my head!'

'Wow, what a lovely day you've had, I can't wait to see it. I hope you have been a good girl for Pat.'

'I've been the best girl ever,' Savannah replied, then cupped her hand to whisper. 'I really love Jason and the dogs, but I think Mrs Pat is my favourite.'

Pat felt a tear come to the corner of her eye and pretending she didn't hear the whisper ordered them to sit down as dinner was served.

They all were silent as they demolished the delicious meal. Maisie and Pat laughed out loud when Savannah sat back with a look of contentment on her face.

'And she can cook too Maisie, I like it here.'

'You look tired Maisie and even though I want to know where you were, there is always tomorrow, so why don't you head off home. No!' Pat raised her hand as Maisie indicated she would help clean up. 'I'll do this and tomorrow you can let me know what's what and we can go from there.'

Savannah yawned loudly and turned to hug Pat. 'Thank you for coming to play with me Savannah, it's been a lot of fun and I hope you come again soon.'

'Thanks Pat, you were a godsend today and hopefully, very soon, we can all live in this street feeling safe and happy.'

Pat raised her eyebrows, she understood the coded message the authorities were aware of what was going on, and for now, she would have to be content with that.

Pat closed the door and double checked the lock, she turned and looked back into her now empty house. The blocks were packed up as Maisie had insisted on it, yet the slight untidiness still held the warmth a child leaves in a room. Pat sighed, all she wanted now was Keith's arms around her, with no words needing to be spoken, just to be held by someone who understood her mood. In this moment she missed him like never before.

'Ah my love,' she muttered, 'some days are harder than others, but some moments are harder than days.'

Number 3 BonBon Street

Monique

Moni felt weary, the feeling of sleeping with one eye open had caught up with her. They had pulled it off, and Claire was safe for now. It still seemed surreal, although she had once read, hiding in plain sight, was actually a smart thing to do. Her friend who owned the house had checked in and was more than happy to be helping out, even though Moni knew it could not be a long term thing. Harry had forgotten to give Claire the phone charger, so she had sent him back with it, plus with a short list of supplies he could pick up at the grocery store on the way back.

Moni wandered into her dance studio however even it, could not enthuse her today. Maybe some fresh air is what I need. She changed her shoes and stepped out the door before this idea too, came to look like a chore. Her gardening hat hung on a hook inside the shed and Moni pulled it on roughly before glancing up and down the street. She turned to her left and was soon around the corner and striding confidently along the main thoroughfare. Moni had seen Jason buzzing in and out of his shed and wanting some totally alone time decided the longer walk around to the other side of the gully was what she needed. Even though she would have to jump the creek before returning back up through the pathway, the extra exercise would do her good and hopefully make her tired enough to sleep right through tonight.

Crossing a bridge Moni paused and leaned on the railing. The busier traffic behind her would never notice the tiny creek which wound its way around a bend before it broadened out at the base of the clearing behind their street. The reserve was a local secret, and, for the residents of BonBon Street, almost a private park all of their own. A rough bush path was almost unseen from the road and Moni pushed some low branches aside as she made her way, at a slower pace, stepping over the protruding tree roots and bruising the grass, as it tried to encroach its way across reclaiming the bare earth. It was cooler under the canopy of the trees and the smell of the eucalypts seemed to fill all her senses. Moni felt her shoulders relax and she took her time enjoying the quiet noises of the birds as they flitted above her annoyed yet wary at the disturbance. The path was almost a zigzag, gently winding down to the bottom of the gully and Moni could hear the creek now as it bubbled its way off to who knows where.

Moni paused for a moment, letting the strain of the last few days drain away. It would come back as they helped Claire in the following weeks, and Moni expected a quite stressful time as they waited to see which direction Mark would take. The sunlight filtered through the trees, seeming to chase the shadows back and forth along the grassy banks. Moni knelt and dipped her fingers in the cool creek enjoying the feeling as it pushed her fingers apart and bubbled up towards her palm as it met the resistance.

Baby Sophie will love it here when she is bigger Moni thought. Although children had never been in her plans, tending to Sophie and the baby's gurgling happy smiles had tugged at tiny hidden feelings which Moni was unaware she'd had before. She daydreamed for a while imagining a child in their house and the love they could both give to it. Was it the isolation they'd had to endure which had brought this on, the sense of loneliness the pandemic had brought with it, or was it Harry's age, the fear of when he was gone, she would have no one. Could this truly be something she wanted deep, deep down.

Harry, was the love of her life and even the tiniest thought of him still filled her body with a warm glow, yet maybe there was something missing. Crazy ideas ran through her head as she imagined his family's reaction if their father had another child, they would never reconcile she concluded.

A movement caught her attention, and she almost called out to reveal she was resting here in the shadows. The words seemed to catch in her throat, as at first she thought she wouldn't be heard from here over the noise of the bubbling creek between them. Moni stiffened as she realised it was a second movement which had stopped her.

Mark was not close enough to see his individual features, although somehow the movement of his hands and shoulders, and his increase in step, made her think he was agitated, or was he excited.

Excited she decided, as she watched him almost embrace the figure standing under the tree line. The other person stepped back and Moni saw them look around and she drew back into the shadows suddenly not sure of what she was watching here. Mark continued to step closer when two hands, like stop signs, held him back outside the other's personal space. Moni could see Mark was doing most of the talking but his words floated away and she could make no sense of them from here. A chill ran down her spine and for a moment she glanced back the way she had come wondering if she could slip back between the trees and retreat along the path.

Another movement as Mark stepped back into the sun and his laugh carried across the small flat clearly.

'No worries, man. It's cool, you remember though…'

She saw him pause and point his finger.

'… I know it was you.'

The breeze changed again and his parting words were swept away with it. Moni watched as Mark strode away confidently, shaking his arms loosely as if he was throwing away a stress he had been holding on to.

Moni still held back as her head debated and tried to analyse what had taken place. Perhaps Mark was trying to drum up support, trying to find a friend or ally in the street. Perhaps they knew each other from another time, there did seem, even from this distance, to be a familiarity between the two of them. Moni wasn't one to pry and it was this quality in her which kept her sitting there silent and still. She watched as the figure ran their hands through their hair and rotated their shoulders as if trying to relieve the tension there. They took a step towards the creek, then reconsidering, much to her relief, turned and made their way slowly up the rise towards BonBon Street.

The light breeze turned again and Moni caught the tendrils of hair as they blew across her face and she tucked them back behind her ear. Taking a deep breath, she decided to try not to let what she had seen make her judgemental of anyone, after all, she did not hear what was said. It was really was none of her business, then again she might take more notice of things, and people around her from now on, and maybe keep some of the information about Claire a bit closer to home.

Moni watched as the figure disappeared from sight and rising up, dusted the stray leaves and a few spots of the moist soil from her clothing. Without really thinking it through she turned and made her way back up the pathway. The birds no longer protested, but rather stayed quiet as if they too did not want to give her presence away. She was half way home before Moni acknowledged to herself she didn't want anyone to know where she had been, or for now, who she had seen.

Number 9 BonBon Street

Lisa and Brodie

Lisa felt like a cat on a hot tin roof. She had started and stopped so many tasks today she was driving herself mad. She thought Maisie would have gotten back to her last night and even though part of her understood Maisie had to be careful with whatever information she had, Lisa felt wound up inside wanting to get to the bottom of the whole camera thing so she would know who in this street she could trust and who she couldn't.

Her sister Sally was playing heavily on her mind, as if she was tapping at her brain wanting Lisa to put some pieces together. Last night's fitful sleep had made her mind feel heavy and confused and the jigsaw pieces wouldn't connect.

Maybe a girl chat was in order. She wouldn't let out any secrets, though maybe a cuppa with Alice might reveal what she knew about the camera which had been stored in her husband's shed.

The hedge caught her hair at the gate and as she paused to detangle and pat it back into shape, she saw Mark walk out of Jason's yard and she stood quietly watching as he strode over to his open garage, reversed the car out and drove away. It was not only what he had done to Claire, and Lisa had to admit, she didn't really know Mark at all, there was just something about him which frightened her and made her feel dirty or grubby at least. It was as if he could dissolve any safety barrier she could put up and she would be defenceless against him.

Part of her was ashamed. For all her talk about women's safety, she had not even taken the time to introduce herself to Claire or notice, as Alice had done, the bruises on her body. Yes, she could make the excuse, Claire and Mark had moved in as the first lockdown had happened, however if she expected other women to be watching out for her, maybe it was about time she took a more active interest in those around her. Maybe this was the message Sally was trying to tell her, to get out and mix and stop moping about. Sally was gone, her parents were gone. The person who had destroyed her family was out there somewhere and he should not stop her from living.

Lisa looked up at the hedge and the wayward branches which had caught her hair, and Brodie's clothes, every time they walked out the gate. *I might get a ladder now and cut it back, make a symbolic gesture to open up my life again and to stop hiding in the past.*

Lisa turned back and finding the ladder in the shed, she grabbed some gloves and secateurs and set about opening up, not only the entrance to her home, but as she saw it, also the entrance to her future. *I have a good man, and hopefully, fingers crossed, a new precious life growing inside of me. Oh please,* she prayed silently and a warm glow spread through her as if to confirm it.

Brodie was surprised to find the gate open. He was also two steps in before he unconsciously ran his hand over his head and realised, for once, there was nothing tangled in it, or his clothes. Lisa was coming out of the shed and she laughed at the look of surprise on his face.

'So what's this then, no more combing the leaves out of my hair every time I come in or out. Let me see.' Brodie put on a stern face as if he was thinking hard. 'It should save me at least ten minutes twice a day. Now what will I do with all the extra time I'll have on my hands?' Lisa laughed and tapped her finger on her chin.

'Mm, let me think about this for a moment, I'm sure all those chores I ask about will now be done in no time. If only I had thought of this before.'

Brodie put his hands to his head and groaned dramatically.

'I was headed off up to Alice's, then Mark was out talking to Jason and I suddenly decided to cut it back. What do you think really? It is better isn't it?'

They both stood back and surveyed her handy work.

'Well as long as Pat doesn't move her house three metres to the left, I'll still be able to run out here naked to amuse my wife.'

Lisa showed a shocked face then giggled.

'Well, I didn't know it was going to be a regular event,' she teased as he pulled her into his arms from behind, wrapping them around her and folding his hands across her belly. She covered them with her own.

'I felt like I wanted to open our lives up to the future,' she whispered. 'I've been hiding too long and I've really only now realised how much I had been winding an invisible blanket around me to protect myself from the world.'

Brodie rocked her gently.

'I get it, it's great. Sally and your Mum and Dad would be here if they could my love, and maybe it is time they let you go.'

Lisa nodded as a single tear rolled down her cheek and she turned in his arms to face him.

'I'm so lucky to have you, to have someone who understands. You've been so patient, and you are right, Sal would want me to move on, she would be happy for us. I finally feel as if I'm moving on from the grief and I want to make memories for the future, good and happy ones.'

Brodie cupped her face.

'I've loved you since the first moment I saw you, you don't have to thank me, I am excited for what lies ahead. Let's make Sally and your parents proud.'

Lisa held him tightly. Brodie was her world, the most thoughtful, kindest man she had ever known. Yes, it is time. It's time for me, Brodie and our family. Sometimes, she might struggle or have a setback but she knew Brodie would be with her and would always have her back.

'Come on then woman, how about a cuppa, or do you want me to walk you up to Alice for some girl time?'

'Let's go for a walk down to the creek. We can have a coffee after we get back. I've felt restless all day and it would be nice to get out.' Lisa said reaching out to take his hand.

'I do have something to tell you. Although I was going to wait for Maisie to come back, at least when she does get here, you will be up to speed.'

Brodie stooped and looked at her quizzically.

'I'm not following but ok, a walk, followed by coffee and an afternoon off is exactly what I need. So come on tell me this mysterious tale.'

Lisa swallowed loudly. It was a shame to dampen his mood though she really needed to let him know what else was going on in their street before the cops came in guns blazing. Well probably, in reality, they would sneak in, and it would all be over before anyone realised. Lisa did want him to be wary of Jon as she didn't want her Brodie associating with him any more than was necessary until they found out exactly what was going on.

Closing the gate firmly they set off around the corner, heads together as Lisa began to tell her husband about finding the camera in the hedge and evidence it may contain about violence against women plus Maisie's secret mission for moving into their street. Lisa knew he might be cross she had become so involved in it all before she told him, at the end of the day, she was glad the sequence of events had occurred and justice might be served for a family somewhere who had suffered or were still suffering.

Number 5 BonBon Street

Alice and Jonathan

Alice felt a bit flat. The energy she'd had, leading up to her talk with Jon, had seeped away. She knew she had hurt him, his short, curt responses to her had hurt her feelings too. Hopefully he would think through their discussion and choose his words more carefully next time.

It was what they both wanted, and Alice decided it was more because she had been the one to end it, which had hurt him more than the suggestion of the breakup. Jon had always been a bit moody, a man's man sort of a bloke, and it was his strong confidence and assertiveness Alice had been attracted to.

In foster homes from a young age, Alice had built up a fear of men, their physical strength was something she had witnessed often and as she was moved from town to town, then state to state, there had never been one home, one person or one family, where Alice had felt comfortable or safe. Jon had come into her life not long after the last foster home door had shut behind her and she nervously was trying to find her feet in the world where daily rules no longer applied. At a pub one night she had been attracted to his smile which crinkled his face around his eyes and made them seem to shine brighter.

Looking back Alice could acknowledge now, how vulnerable and insecure she had been. How easily she had clutched onto the first real person to show her some attention, for herself, and not for some financial benefit they would receive every fortnight, or some lewd sexual behaviour they felt they were owed for having her in their home. It was because she had fought back and won, or run away, she had been moved on and regarded as a troublemaker in most social worker's notepads.

Jon had loved her, he had said so many times, in the beginning. Now it was clear the feelings and circumstances which had brought them together no longer applied. Alice was happy to have had the boys and watch them grow. It had helped her to grow as well. Jon had given her the solid and stable life she had longed for. In the end, for the many minuses, there were far more pluses, and by being forthright and upfront with Jon, it showed Alice how much she had matured, no longer a scared kid hiding her fears below the surface.

Hearing the thread of Claire's story as it trickled down the street, Alice came to realise the first part of her own life had been turmoil, whereas these last years had been solid and secure. She really did have to thank Jon for this, stability was what she had craved the most. Her thoughts turned to her mother and she wondered if maybe, her life too, had taken a turn for the better.

Alice could vaguely remember her. The memories of the day she had been taken were blurred with shadows and the emotion of a child, neglected and not wanting to stay, yet desperately afraid the unknown alternative may be worse. Claire could never go back to see her parents, for Alice, the opportunity was there and tiny debates scuttled in her head as to whether it would be a good idea or not to start the process of finding out where her mother was now. One firm image she did have was the silhouette of her mother, as she was carried away. One hand resting on her raised stomach and the other cupping it underneath as she rained abuse on the social worker, even though, as Alice now realised, she made no attempt to drag her daughter back into her arms. Feeling quite stupid Alice thought it may not only be her mother whom she might find.

Jon felt like a cad. He was sorry for the way he had spoken to Alice, and about her. It wasn't the suggestion of the separation, and inevitably a divorce, as actually the reason for his return was to suggest the same agenda. It was the guilt, seeing the boys made him feel guilty. Most would think it was due to his absence with the job, the truth was, he, too, had never wanted them. It had been fun watching them grow at times, although now they were nearly adults they could go off and make their own lives. Jon hardly thought he would be missed. When his wife, Sharon, had left him, it was the guilt which made him stay. They had tried. Young, pregnant, and in an age when violent protests were being staged outside of family planning clinics, they had been coerced into going full term with adoption at the end. Being twins had ended their plans.

How can you give up two? This had been the constant cry and so they had plunged unwillingly into parenthood, trying to be who others expected them to be, each day a struggle. It was probably a touch of undiagnosed depression, and she hadn't been uncaring in all those years, only distant, and when opportunity knocked his wife had grabbed it with both hands and never looked back. No thread of motherhood ever plagued her with guilt, and his salary was never enough to keep her in the life she craved.

Jon had stayed, met Alice, and life had seemed to snowball along at its own pace as he slotted himself into a lifestyle which had suited him, and held back the critics, as the boys were being cared for by their substitute mother.

Jon knew he had used her, he couldn't lie, Alice had been willing and at the end of the day he had given her the things she had most craved, stability and a readymade family. He would give her the house and the boys would be looked after. They were more like young mates, as he too had never really felt the strong bond of parenthood he heard others express.

Telling Charlie he had seen his mother was probably a mistake, bad timing, although he knew they would find out eventually. Jon's chance meeting with her had reignited old flames, and the sullen, confused woman who had left him was now strong, independent and happy like the girl he had first fallen in love with in his teens. Sharon was the love of his life and their decision to reunite was what had also prompted his return this time. When he had spoken to her of the boys, she had become distant and looked at him as if he was talking about strangers.

'I don't care Jon, I never did. I played the role society expected of me and it didn't fit. They were always going to be better off without me. I truly don't care if I never see them again, Alice is their mother now and she is welcome to them.'

Jon had been a bit shocked at first yet it had always been her devil-may-care attitude and her selfishness which had attracted him. He loved how she built up a wall of indifference for him to break down, and it turned him on as they played the game, each of them vying to be in control, which always lead to an explosion of fiery passion. His family had never liked her, calling her snobby and rude. For Jon she was an addiction which had crawled under his skin when they first met and he now felt, no, he knew, he could no longer live without.

Jon rounded the corner. The one thing he had promised Alice was to help the boys get their licence by doing a few turns around the streets in the car, so they could get their hours up. Sharon would be cross if he was too long, yet one tiny thing in the back of his head was urging him to do the right thing and at least support Alice in this.

He could see from here the car was not in the drive and as he faulted, he saw Mark cross the street heading for the reserve.

Now there was a waste of good air. Jon had never liked Marks attitude. Even on the first day they met, Jon had known Mark was someone to be wary of. Mark had approached him the other day, almost the minute he had arrived back, wanting to know if he, Jon, had seen his camera. Mark had stashed it in Jon's shed, not asking permission of anyone, he said he had slipped over one night and put it there as, *nod, nod, wink, wink* he had a few shots on there he didn't want his wife finding. Jon, about to walk in on his wife and kids and tell them it was all over had told him to *f off* and stay out of his shed. Although Mark had sulked away, Jon knew he would be back. He had almost forgotten about it until he was leaving and at the last minute, had asked Charlie. The idea about wrecking the drive had popped in his head. After all, who would know what the sicko had on there, best to warn the kid away, though he hoped he had found it, as Jon certainly didn't want Mark loitering around. Although he'd had a look the other day maybe he should give the shed a quick search now and lock it up for once.

Number 4 BonBon Street

Maisie

The paperwork always seemed to take forever. Double checking each *i* was dotted and every *t* was crossed, every page stamped or signed correctly so no one could come back at them. Things were moving behind closed doors and Maisie was glad to not know the full extent of the whole investigation. Her initial insurance watch had been pushed aside and from what she could make out the company itself was looking to be the likely culprit, and Jon an innocent victim. Once they questioned him about his association with Mark, and their past together, the next set of detectives would move in on the original case she had been employed to do. Jon's life would be turned upside down for a while as he waded through the procedures, if he was innocent it would be frustrating and slow, if he wasn't it would move swiftly as the conclusions were reached.

Maisie knew she had to fulfil her promise to Lisa and tell her what she could about the situation. Her boss had a big discussion with her about what would and could be said. At the moment the links to Lisa's sister were circumstantial and they certainly didn't want a member of the public taking things into their own hands and jeopardising the case.

Alice was also playing on her mind and Maisie had a strong urge to tell her of their relationship before everything went down. If she forged a bond now, maybe it would hold strong through whatever happened. She had to make her decision as time was ticking, and she didn't want to be in their house when things started to happen.

Savvy was playing with some water outside. A bucket of water and a paint brush had kept her occupied all morning as she painted the walls and bushes with her imaginary colours. Again it had been Pat who had given her the idea and Maisie realised how much she didn't know about simple childhood joys.

Maisie glanced out the window again. Alice had returned and she could see one of the boys exiting the car. Alice seemed to be resting for a moment needing a brief reprieve before the next lad hopped in. Jon appeared as if he had been watching from afar, waiting for their return. Alice still sat in the car as he approached and Maisie watched on wanting to protect her sister if there looked like a shred of trouble. A movement at her side made her realise Savannah too, was watching, her little eyes taking in people's actions and assessing them warily as no child should have to do.

'She looks like Mummy.'

Maisie froze as she digested the words, out of the mouths of babes as they say.

'Well, Savvy.' Maisie knelt down so she could look at Savannah straight on. 'I have a bit of a secret to tell you.'

Savannah's eyes opened wide.

'Is it a puppy?'

'No.' Maisie laughed. 'This might be better than a pet.'

Savannah stood quietly and Maisie could see her trying to figure out what could be better than a puppy at this moment in her life.

'It's a secret for now, see Alice over there.'

They both turned to gaze across the street.

'I found out when our mummy was younger, before she had me, she had another baby.'

Savannah's mouth formed an *O*.

'That baby is Alice.' Maisie raised her hand and pointed. 'So it means Alice is our sister, our older sister.'

Maisie could see from Savvy's puzzled face she was quietly calculating how this could be.

'So Mummy had Alice, then she had me and a long time later, she had you. So, the same as we are sisters, Alice is too.' Maisie could see how Savannah digested this information and a smile played across her lips.

'Maisie, does this mean we are going to be a real family?'

'Maybe, I hope so. Now you know how I said it was a secret?'

Savannah nodded.

'Well, it's because Alice doesn't know yet. She doesn't know we are her sisters. Do you think she will be excited?'

Savannah nodded wildly.

'I was thinking we might go and tell her now, it will be a bit of a shock for her, won't it, to find out she has a cute little sister like you.'

Savannah clutched her arm.

'Do you think she will like me Maisie? She won't hurt me will she, if she doesn't like me?'

Maisie picked her up and held her tight.

'No I think she will be very kind lady. I've been watching her with my machines and she seems very nice. Will we go now?'

Maisie could see Jon getting in the car with the other twin, so it seemed it was his turn to be the driving instructor. Alice was standing at the gate watching as they exited the drive and turned towards the entrance to BonBon Street. Now or never she thought and putting Savvy down opened the door. Maisie felt the adrenaline start to rise as it fought with her fear.

They were hardly to the gate when she called to Alice and looking both ways they made their way across the street towards her.

'Hello you two, come in, goodness we have hardly caught up since the book club meet, with everything, well, I have tried to keep a low profile and now Jon is back.'

Alice had stopped and realised they were both staring at her. Maisie saw Lisa come to her gate and glance up the street towards them. Maisie waved and again called out, this time to Lisa.

'I'll be down shortly.'

Lisa waved and still stood. Maisie could almost feel from here, her anxiety to know what was going on.

'How are you Savannah?' Alice said and Savannah pulled back behind Maisie suddenly shy in front of her.

'Alice, I have wanted to talk with you about something and, well, I've not known where to begin.'

Alice stared at her and even in this moment Maisie couldn't believe Alice was not seeing her own unique coloured eyes staring back at her from their two faces.

Alice crossed her arms in a defensive way and Maisie stepped forward, in the end blurting it out in a rush.

'It's nothing bad, well I hope not, it's, the thing is I'm your sister, and Savannah is too.'

There. It was done. Savannah peeked around her leg waiting for Alice's reaction, and Maisie realised Alice had reached out for the fence post to steady herself as the news hit her like an invisible force.

Alice glanced between the two of them as the penny dropped.

'I remember you. No, not you as such, as they took me away, I realised her tummy was big and recently when the memory returned to me, I put it together.'

Alice knelt down, a shocked look still on her face. She put her arms out to Savannah and said to her.

'I'm so very happy to meet you.'

As the little girl stepped into her sister's arms, Maisie realised tears were streaming down her face and the anxiety she had felt, disappear, to be replaced by a sudden joy. She had been correct and Alice was the good person Maisie believed her to be.

Savannah stepped back looking into Alice's face as if noting the similarities there.

'Mummy went to the hospital and never came back so Maisie came and now we are a family. Will you be our family too?'

Alice was nodding and she rose to her feet, taking Maisie into her embrace and they rocked each other trying to fill the empty gap which had been hiding within them both, and mourning their wayward mother who had not given any of them much of a life. At least now, she had given them each other.

Wiping her eyes, Maisie looked around.

'Sorry to spring it on you, I couldn't wait any longer.'

'Why didn't you tell me sooner? I know I'm crying but wow, I'm excited, we have so much to talk about.'

'I had to protect Savvy, and I don't want to offend you, but I had to make sure you were not like our mother and telling you was a safe thing to do. I want her to have a better life than I did, and I'm presuming you had, in our mother's care.'

Maisie could not stop the tears and looking down she realised they were all holding hands as if playing ring-a-ring a-rosy, and her legs felt like jelly, so they might all fall down. The thought of the silly children's game and them all joined together brought a smile to her lips and releasing her hand she wiped her eyes with the back of it.

'Come in.'

Alice was urging, then the questions kept spilling out and neither of them could move away as they exchanged snippets of their lives with each other.

Maisie felt Savannah pull her shirt as she saw her tug on Alice's hand. Alice again knelt to look her sister in the face.

'Alice, does this mean the big boys at your house are my brothers? I'd like that because now I only have sisters.'

Alice and Maisie laughed.

'No, Savvy, Charlie, and Jay are not your brothers and it's a bit hard to explain, if they are anything to you they would be your nephews.'

Savannah looked puzzled and Alice placed both her hands on Savvy's waist as she waited for the little girl's reaction to the news she was, or could call herself, the boy's auntie. Savannah's face was priceless and they both had to laugh.

'Does it mean I can boss them and make them play with me?'

Alice laughed again.

'Well, we will have to ask them won't we? I'm sure they are going to be very excited to have you in our family.'

Overwhelmed, Alice burst into tears again and Maisie too, knelt with her sisters as they all hugged not wanting to lose hold of each other again.

'Is everything okay?'

Lisa's voice broke them apart and Maisie realised how odd it must look, the three of them huddled together on the ground at Alice's gate.

'Yes, sorry Lisa, I was coming to see you, um, I, I had to talk to Alice.'

Maisie stood and reached out her hand to Alice. Lisa gasped as she looked back at three identical pairs of eyes, their colour heightened by the tears and glowing with the happiness they were all feeling.

'Oh my,' she exclaimed. 'Did you know you all have the same eyes? It's amazing. I don't think I've ever seen anything like it before. They are so unusual, what a coincidence.'

Alice and Maisie clutched hands.

'We are sisters. All of us, me, Alice and Savannah.' Again tears rolled down her cheeks. 'I've known for a while. I had to tell Alice as she didn't know, and now, now we can all be together.'

Lisa looked shocked and stood as if frozen as she digested their news.

'How incredible, when did you find out? Wow, it's fantastic.'

Savannah stopped them as Maisie and Alice both went to speak at once.

'I need to go to the toilet Maisie.'

They all looked at her and Alice was first to grab her hand.

'Here, come with me Savannah, you can use mine.' Alice swung Savvy up in her arms and they hurried down the driveway and disappeared around the back.

'Lisa, I'm sorry, I was coming to you when I saw the opportunity to speak with Alice.'

Maisie found herself still wiping away the odd tear from her eye. 'I can see you are anxious still there's not a lot I can say at the moment.'

'It's ok Maisie, this is such a huge day for you, and I want to hear all about this too. If you can tell me, did the photos lead to anything, or anyone?'

'Look, they did, and if you can wait a bit longer one of the detectives is going to come and talk with you.'

Maisie faltered hoping she was not giving Lisa a clue as yet. Even though Maisie knew it would be hard when she found out, it would only be extra worry and emotion for Lisa until the outcome was confirmed. Maisie reached out to Lisa.

'Before Alice comes back, the photos have led to another case, nothing to do with the one I was working on. I can tell you it was a major piece of a puzzle and my colleagues have been working around the clock to get everything together to enable them to make an arrest.'

Maisie rubbed Lisa's arm.

'You did well Lisa, everything is about to happen and after it does we can talk more openly.'

Maisie glanced across the street as she heard a door open and saw Mark staring at them from his doorway. He seemed to stumble and his unsteadiness told her he had been drinking. Lisa was talking and Maisie tuned in again to what she was saying.

'… have been worried and I want to help. Is it Jonathon? The camera is his after all.' Lisa had lowered her voice as she watched out for Alice's return.

'Please don't ask me questions Lisa. I hope Jon isn't involved, try to be patient and let the facts tell the story. It won't be long now and we can't have anything jeopardising the case so, if you could keep this conversation to yourself, for now. I promise it should all be revealed by the end of today.'

Maisie was surprised as Lisa hugged her.

'I don't want to think the women in some of those photos may have been hurt, or are being hurt. I miss my sister so much I never want anyone else to feel like this.'

Maisie held her as Lisa's tears flowed. It was going to get more emotional for Lisa, and maybe, hopefully at last she would be able to grieve for her sister without the long shadow of the killer's freedom overshadowing her grief. Hopefully they would all get to see justice being done.

Mark had stumbled his way to his front gate and was trying to undo the latch, Maisie suddenly felt a need of urgency and slipping her phone from her pocket she glanced at the part message exposed on her screen.

Leaving now, try not to be involved…

Lisa still held her and Maisie knew she had to move her on, and hopefully persuade her to go home. Glancing again at the message she realised it had been sent more than ten minutes ago.

'Look Lisa, I do have some work to do and I have to talk to Alice again, for now I want you to go home. Is Brodie there?'

Lisa nodded.

'Good. I want you to go home now and as soon as everything is done I'll come over. I promise. You have to go now Lisa, the less people in the street the better.'

'What! So he's here, there's a maniac in our street still. I thought you meant it was another case, somewhere else. What is really going on Maisie?'

Lisa was indignant now, hands on hips her voice slightly raised and demanding more information. Maisie realised the slip up she had made. The sound of a car slowing for the corner behind her increased her anxiety.

'You have to go Lisa, I'll explain later, please, go now.'

Lisa turned and Maisie took in her raised tense shoulders. She would rather hurt Lisa's feelings for a short time, than have her exposed to what might be overheard as the arrest took place. At least their subject was out in the open so there would be no need to knock down doors today.

Mark was at the gutter and stumbled down over it steadying himself with his arms outstretched. He was ranting and Maisie tensed, so much for not getting too involved she thought.

'So you, you're involved in this too, are ya. You and that bitch help my Claire get away… I won't forget it you know, she's a liar you know. I never touched her.'

He was stumbling, sometimes half falling, reaching down with one arm to the surface of the road to steady him, before trying to again pull himself upright. Maisie glanced down the drive, Alice was obviously giving her some time with Lisa or Savannah had distracted her to get a treat of some kind now she was her new sister. Either way Maisie was glad they were inside and away from, not only Mark but also the situation which was about to go down.

Maisie remained at the gate turning her head slightly to see the progress of the car out of the corner of her eye. It had rounded the corner and was kangaroo hopping its way towards her, Jon and the boy. Seems the gangs all here, was one of her last thoughts as she noted her boss's car and another unmarked police car turn slowly into BonBon Street not far behind them.

Mark was past the white lines which intermittently marked the centre of the street. He was still cursing and oblivious to the traffic coming towards him. Maisie stepped forward, with the backup so close she could stop him herself and it would all be over in a matter of minutes.

A sharp engine noise filled her ears and a bright sun reflection flashed across her vision blinding her momentarily from the unfolding scene. As if in slow motion she saw the car as it struck, heard a squeal as tyres gripped, and felt, rather than heard the scream as it escaped her lips.

Number 9 BonBon Street

Brodie and Lisa

Lisa had told him about the camera on their walk, and Brodie had held her tight knowing how much the images were weighing down her soul. Her fear of cameras was irrational, it was not like the camera had murdered her sister or anyone using one was a likely murderer either, he also knew she could not dismiss the association of Sally, and the photos found at the scene, from her head.

The walk had done them both good. Lisa had caught him up on everything happening in BonBon Street, though he could still not understand Maisie's role in it all even though Lisa had been quite thorough in her detailed retelling. Brodie had let her talk as he tried to determine if Maisie was an insurance investigator or some kind of undercover cop, it didn't seem to add up. He wished Lisa had shown him and he would have dealt with it himself, now there seemed so many others involved he would sit back, support his wife and see what unfolded. He was now up to date on Claire and her whereabouts which he actually noted on his phone in case it was ever needed and had been as surprised as Lisa had been, when he heard Pat's little secret. You never knew about people really once they closed their doors. Maybe they would be interested in a fitness class at the nudist club? It could be a whole untapped market, Brodie mused to himself.

Brodie realised Lisa had gone quiet, and he watched her beautiful face as she in turn stared at the bubbling creek, its soothing sound releasing some of their tension and hopefully carrying it far away over the rocks and down through the trees. It was good to talk.

'I have a bit of secret news too.'

Lisa turned to him and suddenly felt nervous.

'Do you now, so what little secrets have you been hiding?'

Lisa bit her bottom lip and although his forehead creased as he found the words to reply she tried to keep it light hearted.

'Is it a surprise for me? An early birthday gift perhaps?'

'No, but if this all comes together, you may get the best birthday present of your life.'

Lisa could see he was excited and his face was animated as he started to tell her his news.

'The tv station approached me. After my interview, they apparently had a huge response and now…wait for it, they want me to do a regular segment.'

Lisa's mouthed dropped open in surprise. Brodie continued.

'I was going to wait until it was a bit more finalised, now they want me to go in next week for meetings and …'

The smile seemed to cover his whole face and his eyes looked like they were alight with flames. Lisa clutched his arms and could feel them shaking with his excitement.

'…there was even some talk it could lead on to a show of some kind, maybe with me as the host, or in some kind of health format with others.'

He clutched her upper arms.

'This is it Lis, this could take the business to the next level, imagine the opportunities it might create. I'm so excited.' His face dropped for a moment. 'I hope I don't stuff it up, this could set us up for life and if a baby comes we can give it the best life and education. I've been trying to think of a slogan, you know like some newsreaders do. *Arise with exercise* or *strengthen your thighs with exercise*.'

He stopped as he realised Lisa was laughing.

'Oh Brodie, I'm so proud of you, you're amazing, my gorgeous husband is going to be famous. One thing though, I suggest you leave the wording to the writers so you can concentrate on the fitness classes.'

Brodie again drew her into his arms.

'It's all coming together Lisa,' he whispered in her ear. 'It finally seems like the world has done a big shift and it's our turn. Our time is now and all the stars are aligning to make our dreams come true. I love you so much.'

Lisa felt the tears form and felt she couldn't hug him hard enough to show him how much she cared, it was true, the stars were aligning and it was like a huge cloud had been lifted off their lives and the sun finally was blessing them with her rays.

As Brodie held her tight and she listened to his heart beating in his chest, she knew it was time to tell him her final secret and at least if anything happened, they would be in it together from the start. Although it was still early days and yet to be confirmed, Lisa could not keep it to herself. She raised her hands to her husband's cheeks and tilted her head back so she could watch his reaction as she told him.

'I think I'm pregnant.'

Neither of them later, remembered what was said, they both knew the surge of joy which exploded inside of them, and seemed to shoot out of every pore, could not be contained.

Words tumbled out of both their mouths as they dreamed of the days ahead and they turned to make their way home. A doctor's visit would soon confirm they would become a family in the New Year and Brodie's interview, they were positive, would go well. As they reached the top of the rise and Lisa trailed her fingers through the leaves of their hedge enjoying the smell which permeated the air at her touch, every sense seemed to be heightened as if the happiness they were feeling was enhancing everything around them.

Brodie glanced up the street, he could visualise their children playing here, riding their bikes and calling out to neighbours who would all smile and wave back. For a moment he thought life could not get any better, only this one thing seemed to mar their street and the sooner Maisie and her friends sorted out whatever was happening, the better. Brodie was still surprised Jon may have something to do with it, it would again prove you could never really know someone if they didn't want you to. The sooner Mark left the street, the safer all the women would feel, and if Claire moved back their little one would have a playmate close by. Brodie shook his head and squeezing Lisa's hand guided her in through their gate, he felt so proud of them both, with all they had been through they had pulled together and were coming out the other side happy, content and looking towards the future.

As he watched Lisa walk down the path to their door he recalled the first time he had set eyes on her, they had been young and carefree and for some time he had been watching her from afar.

The first time she had turned and smiled, then laughed at something he'd said, he had become obsessed with her. It had only been an instant, and even at their young age, he had been determined to make her his forever.

As she turned and held the door for him he saw the same smile, and knew he had made all his dreams come true, she was his now and forever.

Number 5 BonBon Street

Jay

Jay was enjoying the one on one with his Dad. In a way he was glad his parents were splitting up. Alice deserved better, she had always been there for them both. For Jay, she was more of a mother than his real one, who he now barely remembered, or ever gave a thought to. Charlie had been the one to resent Alice, often blaming her for what, in hindsight was clearly her coping with their father's absence and their mother's disinterest. Seeing Alice step up and help someone in need, had brought them all closer and Jay could see how Charlie had softened towards her and let some of his inner guard down. The jovial clown image had always helped Charlie cover his true feelings, and Jay was actually proud of the closer family they had become. The separation, to Jay, was a relief, as he felt easier now to express his feelings with Alice about his parents and the paths they had chosen.

Today as his dad chatted easily between instructions of where to turn or when to ease off the accelerator, Jay was enjoying being spoken to as an adult. His dad had always played the fun dad, playing ball with them and fooling around as if they were all the same age before disappearing for weeks on end. Jay realised now how much Charlie was like him and was happy as his father now talked seriously and he could see the man underneath the clown mask. Jay also felt he was driving better, Alice never spoke much and sometimes when he had glanced at her white face he'd realised how much she had sacrificed for two boys who weren't even her own.

People often spoke of Charlie and him as if they were one. They were close, there was no doubt, and enjoyed the same things, though they were also different. Jay was quiet to the point where those, who didn't know him, thought he was sly or sneaky, all he really did was try not to draw attention to himself. Enough people stared because of their likeness so he shied away from them staring for any other reason. Charlie's outgoing personality covered them both, although the older they were getting, Jay could see he was starting to display more of himself to the world and have some degree of separation from his look-alike brother.

They pulled up at a park and decided to stretch their legs before heading back. Leaning back on the car, watching as people walked their dogs and children chased the birds, Jay decided the time was right to question his Dad about something which had been weighing on his mind.

'Dad, can I ask you something?'

'Anything, I know it's a tough time for you and I haven't always been there for you both, I promise I will try harder. Now you are bigger maybe you can come and stay with me more, if you want to of course.'

'Sure, no problem, it's about something else. A while ago I was in the shed and I found a camera.'

'You didn't turn it on did you? Mark, from across the road told me he put it there and when I asked him why he was in our shed he made some crack. I think he's a bit of a lowlife. Do you have it?'

'No, I left it there. Dad, I did look, um, I haven't told anyone else, they, the photos, they weren't nice. Alice is in some, she was sleeping. I think he's been in our house without us knowing.'

'What, what do you mean, he said they were photos he didn't want his wife to see, not, Alice. My god, how bad were they, did your brother see?'

'The ones of Alice were of her sleeping, some in bed and I saw one where she was asleep at the table. Dad, there were some of Pat across the road and um, she had no clothes on and some of other girls were like it too. I didn't know what to do, so I've done nothing, I didn't even tell Charlie. Dad, I'm scared and I've been watching out so he doesn't come back, can you help? I don't want him to hurt anyone else, hurting Claire is bad enough. He won't hurt Alice will he?'

Jay was nearly crying now, the weight of sharing the problem releasing his pent up emotion. Jon hugged his boy.

'You did the right thing by telling me, now what is this about Claire, what did he do to her? Come on, hop in the car and fill me in. Seems I've missed out on some of the gossip on BonBon Street. I will say, the sooner Mark exits our street the better for all of us, he and his camera can take a long hike to nowhere for all I care.'

They talked for quite a while. Jay in the driver's seat felt his father was at last listening and learning about the youngest of his sons, they may only have been born a few minutes apart, but Charlie never let him forget he was the first one. A little part of Jay wished they'd had this conversation a long time ago, on the other hand he probably wouldn't have been as responsive to it as he was now. He watched his father closely as he spoke of his misspent youth, his mates, their mother and some of the events and feelings leading up to her leaving. Jay realised he was feeling drawn to his father in a new way with his honesty, though he was also seeing a cold streak, an almost hidden callousness or resentment behind some of the things he spoke of. Both were silent for a time as they stared out at the world going by, each of them more understanding of each other yet for Jay, there was also a feeling of separation as he realised his father's opinions and moral code were different to his own. Alice's face flashed into his head and he felt the deep love of the mother she had been to him, fill his soul. His father had been honest and would always be part of his life and Jay knew he would always be grateful to him, grateful for finding a woman like Alice to raise them. Jay also thought it had probably been better his father had chosen the life he had, away from his children and not having a huge influence over the life they led.

As they reversed out, Jon reached over and patted Jay on the shoulder.

'Good talk son, I'm glad we can go on, as mates as well, you're an adult now, look at you, driving the car and all. It's like I said, I had to find my own way in life and what happened in the past is gone and we can all move on from here. It's time for you to make your own mistakes and learn from them.'

I'll never make mistakes as bad as you, Jay thought, nor treat people like a chore or an inconvenience. Jay drove confidently back towards BonBon Street. He felt like he had grown up in the last hour or so, and recognised deep down he loved his dad, though at the end of the day he did not agree with him on many subjects, especially his treatment of Alice. Even so he shouldn't feel bad, it was ok to not share someone else's opinion and to have your own morals to live by. Alice had given him good grounding and he felt confident to step out into the world as a strong and independent man, in spite of his birth parents.

Number 6 BonBon Street

Mark

Mark was drunk, he knew he was drunk. The days had been a blur of drinking, sleeping and in sobering moments, trying to find his wife before things went out of his control. The place was a mess too and he needed someone to tidy it up. He had been stupid to hit Claire but this being locked in all the time had limited his usual activities. Being here, away from everything which was familiar to him, sucked as well. No one here praised him or patted him on the back. He needed to be the top dog, he fed on the attention. Claire had taken it away, it was gone as more and more people heard what he had done to her. The bitch had told not only his family and neighbours, but some of his mates as well, their self-righteous wives convincing them he was not a person they wanted to be associated with in the future. The grog wasn't helping he knew, he wasn't stupid. It made him feel good, even if only for a while.

He saw her out the window. She was talking to the one from next door, his neighbour, he couldn't recall her name, he wasn't even sure they had been introduced. Her house was locked up tighter than a drum, and he had noticed the slightest glow at night in her front windows and something made him more cautious and he had been careful to give it a wide berth on his nightly adventures, he was sure she was up to something. He had been clumsy, it happened when he didn't feel in control. Claire thinking she had out smarted him had thrown him, he had to admit it. Once she was back he was sure his world would start coming together again. Hiding the camera across the road now proved to be a mistake, and he was annoyed at himself and with Jon, who he was sure was lying to him. Thoughts raged in his head and the inner demon which fed his urges and desires was getting hungry to be fed. The conflicts between them and the need for all this to be sorted out and things to get back to normal, his normal, were being both soothed and muddled by the alcohol he consumed.

They were still talking, the bitch Alice and the other one with the child. He blamed her the most, he knew she was the ring leader. It was her who had fed ideas to Claire without his knowledge, sneaky is what she was, and he had been watching her closely ever since. She was smart, acting like she didn't know where Claire was, he knew she was fake, trying to lay low so he wouldn't know it was her who had helped Claire get away. Thought she was too smart for him, he would show her, in fact he might go over there now and tell her what for, yes tell her off in front of her little friend there. Let's see what you have to say now, eh, bet she backs right off he told his inner self. Maybe she's the one with the camera, maybe it's why she's being so smug, probably thinks she has something over him. Well he'd show her, yep he'd go now, see what the bitch has to say for herself.

Mark steadied himself at the door, then again as he reached the gate. They were still there and he was determined now, now she was in the open and her lads were out. They were very protective and after a small encounter with one of them, Mark had backed off from sneaking into the house at number five too often.

He had made it to the curb, she had noticed him and he could no longer see the child, he wondered what her game was, after his little chat Alice would back off, see Claire was a liar and, if he took the right approach, she might help him get his wife back from her little hideout. Yes. It's what he would do, explain not complain, his eyes lit up for an instant as he caught himself rhyming and adjusted his thoughts which seemed clear and concise to him yet to anyone else would not have made an ounce of sense.

He stumbled on the curb, she was watching him, and he saw her eyes shift as he made it to the centre line. Alice began to move when he realised it wasn't her. He could have sworn it was, they had all switched around just to confuse him. It was the other one, did she live here too? And Sally, what was she doing here, it was a school day. He saw the other one take her arm and push her to the side, stepping in front as if to shield Sally from him, no it wasn't Sally, too old, it was the other one, Lisa, he had watched her, she had been lucky, Sally had tried to interfere, she knew, she was going to give it all away. He would tell her, explain how her sister had called out her name. He was focused on her now and saw her mouth open, so much like her sister that day. His mind raged as the car hit and noise filled his head, the world went silent as his body was flung high in the air and he seemed to float in a void for a moment. The roar hit again as he slammed to the ground and it seemed he could hear every bone as it shattered within.

The pain was so bad and he felt himself rise away from it, he could still hear the screams, other noises were gone. He could see with one eye as feet ran towards him and voices called out loudly. Someone took his hand and his last effort was to try and form words to speak to the one person he knew, was trying to help him.

'Mate …' he muttered softly, and they whispered back a reply. He spoke again, although he would never know if it was heard, as his eyes closed and the endorphins tried to block the pain.

Number 5 BonBon Street

Jay

Jay wasn't sure what had happened. They had turned the corner and
Mark was staggering across the road. Even from a distance they
could see he was focused on their house and the people in front of it.
The car had kangaroo hopped around the corner and suddenly it
seemed he was gripping the wheel and his foot was flat to the floor
trying to make it home before Mark got to them. His dad had pulled
the wheel, he had felt it, he felt tears in his eyes and the thud was a
sound he would never forget as Mark's body hit the bonnet then
seemed to fly out of their way. They stopped in what seemed like
forever, his foot jammed on the brake still holding it hard, even
though they were no longer moving.

They were nearly at Lisa's, the hedge looming in front of
them, his hands still gripping the wheel, his knuckles white, as
people started to scream and he saw blue flashing lights in the
mirror. His dad's face was white and he was not moving, frozen
with his seatbelt firmly in place.

'Dad, Dad, are you alright, I'm so sorry, I'm so sorry.'

Alice was at the window, the heel of her hand pounding,
demanding.

'I'll say it was me.'

Jay was shocked as his father's eyes turned towards him and
knew in his heart it was true.

Alice had the door open, her voice was raised, her hands
touching him, checking to see he was ok.

'I'm alright, I'm so sorry, my foot slipped, I don't know, is
he ok … he's not dead is he?'

The shock made him feel like a robot and everything seemed
to be in slow motion. More sirens could be heard and Alice made
them both get out and sit on the grass. Jay felt weak, drained and his
mind kept running over the events of the last few minutes. He had
thought about hitting him for a second, he would not let him hurt
Alice, he knew it was wrong. His dad had grabbed the wheel, it was

as if he was aiming for Mark and as Jay tried to stop him, they had hit. He had killed someone, he was sure he had, it was the rest of it he didn't understand.

People were running and shouting, he could see Brodie and Lisa, the little girl from across the road was standing in their drive as if lost and not knowing which way to turn. BonBon Street seemed to be full of vehicles, some with flashing lights, all parked higgledy, piggledy across it. Jay could see a man in a suit and paramedics working on Mark, another carrying a bag was approaching them as he heard a shout and felt his brother's arms around him.

Number 3 BonBon Street

Harry and Moni

It was a scene Harry had never encountered before, seeing it was in his own street, added to his horror. He had been sweeping the shed when it happened, close at the door watching the dust fly out only to settle and wait to be walked in again. The squeal of the tyres trying to grip the tar, made him move faster than he had in a very long time.

A shout to Moni to call for help, and he was out the gate taking it all in as the tragedy unfolded. It was Alice's car, and Maisie was there. Lisa was screaming and no one made any attempt to make her stop. Brodie was running from the other direction, as he was. Two other cars were stopping and Harry briefly wondered who they were and what they were doing in his street. Maisie seemed to be everywhere and Harry tried to assess where he could help the most. He grabbed Lisa by the arms and she almost fell into them as if she had been waiting for the support. Brodie reached them.

'You ok Honey, not hurt.' Lisa shook her head. Brodie rubbed his hand on her back and looked directly at Harry.

'Look after her mate. I know some first aid so I'll try to help.'

Harry nodded and held her firmly, easing her down onto the grass as he wasn't sure how long he could support her weight. An ambulance rounded the corner and Harry wondered how they could have gotten here so quick. He saw Maisie was still in the mix then watched as she and Brodie stood and moved away from the body. Lisa sobbed and watched, as he did, as the paramedics moved in to begin their work. Brodie came back and held his wife. Alice had run down to the car and Harry could see it was the other boy, not Charlie who exited the driver's seat. Silly boy he thought and such a shame at this young age, to have this happen to him. Charlie ran past brushing his arm and apologising for doing so in his rush to get to his twin. Now he knew him better, Harry could see how different the two boys were, yet they had always seemed to be so alike.

Harry looked around again, taking in the scene. He would let the paramedics do their work and stay out of the way. Brodie was still consoling his wife and Alice was with Jon and the two boys. He turned and saw Savannah, standing as if frozen, only her eyes moving as she took it all in.

'Hello sweetheart.' Harry knelt on one knee in front of Savannah, partly hoping he could block some of the scene from her sight.

'Mummy's busy right now so why don't we sit over here and I'll wait with you until she's finished.'

Savannah looked straight at him as she took his hand. Pushing on his knee with his other hand, Harry managed to pull himself upright and the little girl giggled as he staggered slightly trying to regain his balance.

'You're funny,' she said as he led her over to a low retaining wall on the edge of the drive and sat down. Their backs were to the accident scene and he tried to engage her so she wouldn't turn around to look. It did occur to him she seemed calm, considering the circumstances and not intrigued at all by the flashing lights and emergency vehicles. Something told him she had seen it all before.

'When my wife Moni comes, we will see how long mummy will be and I might get Moni to take you to our house for a bit. Would it be ok, if we ask mummy first of course?'

Savannah nodded and with a tiny grin corrected him.

'Maisie's not my mummy, she's my sister. And guess what.' She glanced around to check no one was near and put her finger to her lips.

'I got a new sister today, she's over there. Her name is Alice and she's very nice.'

Harry watched as she smiled and drew her shoulders in as if giving herself a hug.

'And do you know what else, those big boys are going to be my Aunty.'

Harry didn't really follow, although as Savannah seemed pleased with herself, he was happy to keep her safe and occupied. He glanced over to see how things were progressing and saw the men shake their heads. He knew what it meant and as shocking as it all was, it seemed like a relief as well.

Moni came into view, she had spotted him then had held back not wanting to get in the way. Harry waved and she edged along the fence until she reached him.

'It's Mark.' Harry spoke softly, conscious of the child. Moni placed her hands over her heart.

'It's conflicting, isn't it?'

Harry knew what she meant, sad a life is lost, someone's son taken from his family, yet they could see a release for Claire and Sophie to live a full life without fear, now, maybe two lives had been saved. Sophie only had to know her father passed away, she need never have to know more, until she was old enough to fully understand.

Harry felt a bit guilty with his thoughts, a man lay dead and a boy would never forgive himself because of it, yet he could not dismiss the pluses. He had grown to love Claire and the baby as if they were family. Harry bent his head down to Savannah.

'What say you go along with Moni and have some ice cream eh, and I'll tell your mum, I mean, sister where you are and she can come when she is finished talking with all these people.'

Savannah looked at him with her big eyes and he could see how unusual they were, and their likeness to Alice now he was piecing the child's story together. She nodded and went willingly to Moni and took her hand.

'Mummy went away in one of those to the hospital. She never came back.'

Harry heard Savannah say it as they turned to leave, and Moni glanced at him and raised her shoulders in question. Harry saw Moni squeeze the child's hand and hoped his wife would have an answer to satisfy the child.

'Well, you are so lucky to have Maisie then, aren't you? Now I hope you like strawberry ice cream because I think it's the only flavour I have today, would it be alright with you Savannah, strawberry?'

Harry saw the child nod and skip a step as her little mind looked ahead towards the treat, leaving the carnage around her exactly where it belonged.

Harry surveyed the scene again. Mark's body was now inside the ambulance, he had worked out the unknown men in the other cars were police and must have been close by on some other investigation as they were here before he was out his door.

The second lot of paramedics were helping the boy, and a man in a suit was speaking to Jon. Another police vehicle arrived, the local ones who had assisted Claire and served Mark the notice. Brodie and Lisa still held each other close, and Harry took the opportunity to catch Maisie's attention as she stepped back for a moment to survey the scene.

'Maisie.'

Harry raised his arm to attract her attention and she made her way towards him.

'Harry, Mark didn't make it, I guess you can see.' Maisie shook her head.

'I will need Claire's address. My boss,' she nodded towards the man in the suit, 'said he would go and I told him I would prefer to be the one to tell her.'

'Yes, I think it would be good too. It's kind of you. Can I go with you, would it be allowed? I think Moni would like to be there as well, then we can stay on with her, I don't think she has anyone else.'

Maisie almost looked glad.

'Yes, thanks all fine, it's not an easy thing to do and it will be a great comfort to Claire to have the support, I'm sure.' She twisted her head around. 'Have you seen Savannah?'

'Yes, sorry she's at my house with Moni. I thought it best to get her away, although she saw most of it I think. It didn't seem to faze her, all the lights and sirens.'

'My little sister has had a big life for a little girl Harry, thanks for looking after her.'

'What happens now?' Harry noticed she was still keeping an eye on everything and everyone as she spoke.

'It's this way Harry, my boss was actually coming here on another matter, it was to do with Mark and also I have been on another case, concerning someone from BonBon Street, don't worry, it was more a surveillance job, although it did uncover some extra evidence, which caught us up in a bit of a web of intrigue. We were, in laymen's terms, going to swoop in today and pick up everyone in our line of sight, and hopefully fill in all the gaps.'

Harry glanced around the accident scene, most of the residents of BonBon Street were in sight, except for Pat. He wondered who else had spiked police interest. Brodie and Lisa were speaking to the local police. The boy was being assisted into an ambulance and he could see Charlie fidgeting at the door of it not knowing what to do. Alice was now speaking with Maisie's boss and he saw her rub Jon's arm.

'Once the forensic team are finished we will get this all cleaned up and because we have so many witnesses, plus with police being on scene as well, this will all be wrapped up fairly swiftly.'

'What about the boy?' Harry nodded his head towards Alice and her family at the end of the street.

'Look I can't quite say to be honest, he's a learner and his instructor grabbed the wheel. The case will probably be they tried to avoid, plus Mark was intoxicated, it will be something Jay has to live with. Once the process is complete I would think he will go forward without a record. Could you do me a favour Harry, could you ask Moni if she would mind staying and looking after Savannah. Claire may want to come back here anyway, otherwise I will arrange for her to be taken there as soon as I get back. I'd ask Pat but I don't think she is there.'

Maisie's name was called.

'I'll come and get you soon.'

Maisie hurried away and he could almost see her invisible cloak of professionalism go on.

Harry moved back towards the house, he would let the professionals wind it up and the last thing they would need is people in their way. The love seemed to hit him as he stepped through the gate. His selfless Moni was inside, again caring for someone and he looked to the heavens to thank whoever for the day their paths crossed and he saw her beautiful smile for the first time.

Number 6 BonBon Street

Pat

Pat turned the corner and couldn't believe her eyes. She pulled into Maisie's driveway and hurried out onto the street. One ambulance was already pulling away and the other one seemed to be about to move on as well. Pat scoured those standing in the street trying to account for all her neighbours. Alice's car was down near Lisa's hedge and stopped at a funny angle, the police seemed to have stopped anywhere and there were a few other cars she didn't recognise crisscrossed along the tar.

Pat felt shocked and panicked, and saw Brodie skirting around towards her.

'Pat, it was Mark.'

'What! What did he do, oh my god, is it Claire?'

'No, she is safe.'

Brodie reached her and put out his arm to comfort her.

'Mark was hit, he's dead. He died here at the scene. Alice's boy was driving and Mark was drunk, he came out on the road and …'

Pat covered her face with her hands, a life was gone and she knew how the tragedy would tear a family apart. Deep inside, Pat felt for once it could not have happened to a nicer bloke, this old Australian saying meaning the opposite, somehow seemed appropriate, although she would keep these thoughts to herself.

Claire would be free, as would Sophie. Pat often wondered about things and if they were meant to be. Was it written in a big invisible book somewhere? Somewhere karma was stored and expelled at the strangest times. Brodie's arm was a comfort and he explained the police were already on their way to BonBon Street to question Mark about another matter and witnessed the whole thing. The boy would probably not be charged and Jon was being questioned about the camera and his relationship with Mark. Brodie did not have the full story and Maisie had suggested her colleagues would like to speak to Lisa later. They were leaving it until after Claire had been told.

'Where's Claire now?' Pat knew it would be hard for Claire, it was enough to lose someone without all these extra emotions going on.

'At the safe house, Maisie and Harry have gone to tell her. Savannah is with Moni so I think they might bring her back here for a while.'

'Is everyone else ok Brodie, which one of the boys was it?'

'It was Jay. Jon was in the car with him. He's physically fine, in shock of course. Jon is too and seemed a bit stunned when they started to talk with him about the other stuff and Mark. I couldn't hear what they were saying. He seemed annoyed by whatever it was. I don't think Mark was his favourite person either.'

Brodie paused for a breath and although Pat did not want to appear to be gossiping here at an accident scene, she did want to know all her friends and neighbours were now safe and well.

'Jason is fine and it happened right in front of Lisa. Luckily she wasn't hurt, she is shocked and of course upset. It's a good thing really, to have that creep gone from our street.'

Pat had thought it, yet it still shocked her to hear it spoken out aloud. She thought Brodie should not be so vocal because apart from anything else, there was the too soon factor. Pat moved slightly away as she suddenly felt uncomfortable. She wasn't sure what to do, go to her house or wait here.

'I might head over to Moni then, I'm quite friendly with little Savannah, so I'll see if Moni wants a hand. Thanks Brodie, let me know if I can do anything to help.'

Pat crossed the street and only turned back as she closed the gate. Brodie was still standing in the same spot, one hand was rubbing his chin and he appeared to be deep in thought. Shock affected everyone differently, and coming out of it, as the body juices regulated themselves, was the time to be still and let everything fall into place, Pat would probably see a lot of it in the days to come as the residents of BonBon Street came to terms with what had happened here today.

Six weeks later...

Lockdown was on again. The residents of BonBon Street were again confined to their own area as the health authorities scrambled to contain another outbreak of the dreadful virus. They were all happy enough and it had become a regular thing for them to sit in their driveways in the afternoon sun and call out any news to each other or check up on someone's welfare. Public gatherings had been allowed up to twenty people before, now it was back down to five again so they were all playing it safe.

Maisie loved this little street. Mark was gone and there were still a few things to sort out, but he would never harm Claire again.

Pat had suggested some counselling and Claire agreed it might help as well. She wanted to be a good parent to Sophie and if doing so required some help, then she should take it. Pat had reassured her seeking help did not make someone a bad parent, it made them a better one, and Claire could understand what she meant.

At one stage Claire had loved Mark. He had killed those feelings with every downward movement of his hand and callous word from his lips. Claire did not want to distrust all men, nor let her daughter take on those feelings as well. Because she had been fooled by one bad one, it did not mean all men were the same, you only had to look at the men in this street to see the balance weighed down on the side of good. They had all rallied around her with support of one kind or another. This street, in the end had saved her life, as had everyone in it.

Claire told Maisie she felt no ill will towards Jay, it was an accident and she was glad there had been no repercussions for him which would scar his life on paper, although she knew he would be scarred on the inside. Alice had said he was still struggling with some issues and Maisie had made sure they had help available from organisations associated with the department.

Jon had moved out and had also been cleared in the insurance fraud case. It had passed out of Maisie's hands now as the company itself was taken to task over their fraudulent activities by people higher up than her. He had denied any knowledge of the photos and Maisie's surveillance cameras had identified Mark sneaking in and out of their shed so it did seem, after all, he had hidden it there without Jon's knowledge.

Savannah was glowing in her new role as aunt to the boys and she had certainly lightened their moods many times as she bossed them into playing games with her. Maisie thought Savannah had the whole street wrapped around her little finger, from Jason with his dogs to Pat, who adored her.

Harry and Moni had been amazing. From the first time she saw him and decided he would be the sticky beak of the street, to now, was a world away from the kind gentle man she had come to know. Maisie had watched him with Claire. When they had told her about Mark, Harry's kindness, patience and foresight into what she should do next had touched Maisie's heart and wiped away any negative thoughts she had ever felt about him.

Moni too quietly checked on everyone and often unseen, filled in gaps no one else knew were there. Meals were delivered to homes, baby things collected and washed, even lawns were mowed by a husband, who would rather be talking, and was getting used to receiving dark looks from across the way until the job was complete. They were truly the caretakers of the street and everyone in it. Funny enough, now, no one minded at all. Maisie had come to this street looking for a family and had, it seemed, found a much bigger one.

Jason had come out to everyone. He had been nervous as they had all gathered and talked several times. The events in BonBon Street had bonded them all together, so one night he blurted it out. Maisie had squeezed his hand as she saw tears form when no one seemed fazed by his announcement, and Brodie had stepped forward clearing his throat.

'Well, um, Jason, um mate, I was about to ask you all to a party for Lisa's birthday, now I think it should be a cross dressing party and maybe you can help me with my outfit.'

Jason had stared at him, poised, as if expecting it to be a joke. As Brodie moved towards him, his hand outstretched, the tears did fall as Jason had taken it and realised Brodie was offering him his full support. Maisie felt her own tears as the two men embraced.

Pat had also come clean. They would all keep her secret and with so many knowing about the photos she had wanted to clear the air about her lack of attire in her own yard. Charlie had made them all laugh.

'Well I'll make sure I knock really loudly and call out if I come over then Pat.'

They had all laughed, probably Pat most of all.

'I'll have you *textiles*, know it's very liberating and you are all welcome to join me at my club any time. We have a sewing group and a games room, it really is lots of fun.'

'What's a textile?' Moni looked puzzled.

'All you lot.' Pat replied. 'You're all wearing clothes, textiles get it, oh dear it's a nudist joke.'

Maisie had seen a look pass between Moni and Harry, but had been laughing so much, she did not think about its meaning.

Lisa had been the one hardest hit. The investigation had the evidence Mark had been at the scene of her sister's murder and his role in it would eventually be concluded at a coroner's inquest. It was also now proven he was involved, or had been at the murders of two other girls and probably a few more which were yet to be determined. Some scrunched up scraps of paper Alice had retrieved from her pocket and put aside for no reason at all except she had been distracted on the day by her conversation with Jon, had been the connection they needed. They were mud maps of shallow graves, faded and torn yet still decipherable with enough clues to find two bodies so far. The police had scoured the box and the shed looking for more or the notebook from which they had been torn. Moths and mice had left their mark on them and everyone hoped they would be able to piece together the rest.

BonBon Street was noted on one, but they assumed it was just to mark it as one of his starting points. He was clever enough to put the cross on the vacant land at the end of the street, away from his own home if there was ever an investigation. Mark had tried to be clever and cover his tracks, yet it had somehow been a part of his game, to leave clues as well, as if hoping to be found out. Whatever the reason or no matter how much evidence they uncovered, they would never really know the answer to how deluded he actually was.

Even if he had lived, they doubted he would have confessed. The evidence on the camera was still only an assumption he was the one who had taken the photos, he could have, with good lawyers, argued a strong case about supposed ownership and content, being two different things, or demanded proof it had actually been him who committed the murders. It was something no one would ever know, although some families may get some peace now he was gone.

Lisa firmly believed it was Mark who killed Sally. Charlie, Jon, Alice and Jay had all been interviewed. The ring Charlie had seen was identified as belonging to another missing girl; they were yet to find her body. Charlie also fished out the daisy necklace from the pocket of a pair of jeans on his bedroom floor. On seeing it, Lisa had burst into tears turning the charm over to reveal the engraved *S* for them all to see. Daisies were Sally's favourite flower she had told them, and her sister had worn this chain every day. The department had promised to return it to her, when their investigations were complete, a tiny possession of her sister's to hold on to.

Why Mark had moved to this street or tried to implicate Jon or someone from house number five, was not known and Jon still felt a cloud was hanging over him with no due cause. At the end of the day, Jon's shed may just have been a convenient and accessible place, close by but far enough away for Mark to think they would not connect it to him. Claire said Mark had been the one to choose the house as she had not travelled in the last stages of her pregnancy, only seeing it for the first time when they moved in. Whatever was Mark's motive for choosing BonBon Street would never be known. Claire was just grateful it had been the one to save her life.

As they all settled back into their new normal, the news of Lisa's pregnancy gave them all hope for the future. Another playmate for both Sophie and Savannah meant the joy of children's voices would ring out around BonBon Street for years to come. Maisie could not be more thankful she had taken a chance and moved here to find her sister.

BonBon Street

The summer solstice had passed and restrictions became almost non-existent. The year looked bright and though people still carried masks as a precaution, the shops were open and people were back at work. Fingers crossed it would stay this way as vaccinations began to be issued to protect them all from the dreadful virus. They certainly were the lucky country, with many others around the world still in hard lock down, Australians had been able to be out and about enjoying their sunshine and outdoor life.

Pat's camper was packed and they were all as excited as her about the big adventure. Pat would be heading north, taking it slow and had promised to give them updates about her travels. Alice was going to fly to Darwin in a few months to meet her and spend a few weeks seeing the sights in the Northern Territory. Maisie thought her sister would burst from the anticipation before then, and she was excited for her to be getting out and doing the things she had always dreamed of.

Jon, and everyone in the street, promised to keep an eye on the boys. He had moved back in with their mother, and as yet, Charlie and Jay had no interest in going there. Jason had promised to feed them a few nights a week and Maisie could see the affection going between him and her big sister, even Savannah had teased her one day about it. Maisie was happy for them and also proud of the way Jason encouraged Alice to chase her dreams.

Maisie was going to keep an eye on Pat's place while she was away, it suited them both. The owner of Maisie's house had decided to sell and Maisie had jumped at the chance to, not only own her own home, but to know she, and Savannah, could now live permanently near Alice and the other wonderful people of BonBon Street. While they did some renovations Pat said they could use her house if things were too messy, or noisy with the tradesmen Maisie had hired. It had also given Pat the opportunity to ask Harry for her keys back and he was able to confess he had misplaced them in his shed and been ashamed to tell her.

Savannah was excited to sleep in the new bed Jason had made for her. The detail on it showed the trouble he had gone to and it brought a tear to Maisie's eye and warmed her heart to think of how lucky they were. Maisie was excited for whatever the future may hold.

Maisie and Claire had become close too, and Savannah loved the way Sophie tottered around behind her. Sophie's cute dribbling smile showed off her new teeth, she didn't seem to miss her father at all.

Harry and Moni had surprised them all, taking the lease on Pat's cabin while she was away. Moni had confided to Pat how relaxed and accepted she felt at the club. Her initial fears had been replaced with an unexpected contentment, as both she and Harry had been welcomed, for who they were, and not judged in any way, shape or form, either by their physical appearance or their age differences. Moni said it was the one place they had found where they were both content, and it had opened up a whole new world for them to share together.

Pat backed out of the driveway, the tears had been shed and replaced by happy smiles as they all gathered to wave her off and wish her well.

'See you in Darwin,' Alice called and they all stood until she rounded the corner, her hand waving out the window as she disappeared out of sight.

The group dispersed, each of them a little sad to see her go, yet happy for Pat and her big adventure. It had been a big year, for the world and also for the residents of BonBon Street.

'Are you coming?' Lisa stretched her hand out toward Brodie.

'Yeah, I'll be there in a minute.'

Brodie heard doors closing, and conversations disappearing behind them. He wandered to the centre of the road. The image of Mark's body flashed in his head and Mark's last word, *Mate*. Brodie had held his hand in those last moments.

'They'll blame you,' Brodie had muttered back almost willing him to die before Maisie came back with a first aid kit.

'Nah mate, I left one close.' Mark's voice had faded away as the last breaths left his body. Brodie's forehead had been creased in puzzlement as someone from behind grabbed his shoulder and urged him to move back away from the scene.

If Mark was dead a lot of blame would be pushed his way and Brodie's past would be completely clear. A case solved with no loose ends.

They had been mates, of a sort, though Brodie was glad he was gone. From the beginning Mark had been a pest, wanting to take photos and souvenirs, it wasted their time and made the chances of them being caught more likely. It hadn't been keepsakes Brodie was after.

When Mark had moved here and hidden the camera in Jon's shed, it had been irritating, although as it had panned out, no one suspected Brodie had any part in it. The pandemic had kept he and Mark far enough apart for anyone to notice. Brodie had tried to tell him he didn't do rough stuff anymore, well, not much once he had his Lisa. He had used those other girls, the wannabe lookalikes …the ones before he owned her. The ones after, were just a habit, an urge he couldn't resist. None of them had been as perfect as his girl, none of them.

He had been wondering how he would get Mark out of his life once and for all. Until Mark moved into BonBon Street, Brodie had been good, well mostly, the exercise, the flattery and adoration of some of his clients and the boost to his ego by the television deal, had seemed to be enough, most of the time. It had crossed his mind to get rid of Mark and lead the blame back to Claire, it could have worked. This had worked out so much better. Mark had set himself up all on his own, it was almost perfect.

Brodie had always been obsessed with Lisa. From the moment he saw her for the first time, he knew he wanted to be with her for the rest of his life, she calmed his inner demons and soothed his soul. She really was an angel here on earth, he was convinced of it.

When Sally stumbled upon what he and Mark were up to on their secret late nights out, she had come to warn him off her sister. Brodie hadn't known then, Mark was already stalking her and taking photos, pinning Sally as their next victim.

It had just happened, he had meant to warn her off, tell her she was mistaken. Sally wouldn't listen and made threats. Nothing and no one was going to stop him from living his dream life with Lisa and in the end he had made sure of it. Sally had gone down fighting.

Mark's death now meant Brodie could move on. He would never have to look over his shoulder again as each photo unravelled Mark's involvement, and the scribbled maps ensured the noose tightened more around his already deceased neck.

Lisa was still waiting at the gate.

'I'm coming now, my love.'

Brodie waved for her to go in and to himself he said quietly.

'I'm just laying some ghosts to rest.'

Lisa turned away, but not before flashing him a smile, and rubbing a hand over her growing belly as her sister's restored chain gleamed at him from around her neck. Ahh, he loved her so much, and now, thanks to Mark, Brodie could almost guarantee, Lisa would never know it was her own husband who had murdered her sister.

Life was good.

The Development...

       The utility pulled around the corner and the driver noted the locked gate ahead. Nice little street he thought as he pulled up in front of it and rattled in the console for the keys. He stretched a little as he got out, it was early and the boss wanted him to look over a few things before the heavier machinery arrived. Unlocking, then pushing back the gate, he returned to his vehicle already visualising a tarred road and the eight new houses which hopefully would be sold off the plan before the month was out. Funny name, BonBon Street, but then again, it's only a name. I wouldn't mind living here myself he thought as he drove through the gate.

       A bright patch of daisies caught his eye. They were on a slightly raised patch of ground, an almost perfect rectangle he calculated, and close to the hedge which surrounded the last house. It almost looked like they had been planted there, then again, maybe they buried their dog on the vacant site, or they could just be self-seeded, possibly blown across from inside the hedged garden. Whichever the scenario, they would soon be crushed back into the earth when the machinery arrived to start digging the footings. He stopped his vehicle and checked his phone, they weren't far away. I'd best get to work, he thought, and turned his mind to the job at hand.